HER EVIL STEPBROTHER

had virtually imprisoned Lady Margaret Barbara Heather St. Vincent in a shabby, out-of-the-way country estate, hoping to keep her secure from the attentions of any marriageable lords. For if Heather failed to wed before her twenty-first birthday, her entire fortune would be settled on her stepbrother. And, until the day Heather's childhood friend Geoffrey Curwen, Viscount Morpeth, was stranded on her doorstep by a broken coach wheel, it seemed as though the dastardly scheme was bound to succeed.

Geoff, although not ready to marry Heather himself, was perfectly agreeable to whisking her off to town and introducing her to the most eligible nobles in London society. And Heather soon had countless admirers dangling after her. But she had long since set her cap for Geoff himself—the one man in Regency England who seemed immune to her charms—and she swore she'd sacrifice all her wealth rather than settle for anyone else!

THE RELUCTANT SUITOR

SIGNET Regency Romances You'll Enjoy

- [ ] **AMELIA** by Megan Daniel. (#E9487—$1.75)*
- [ ] **THE DETERMINED BACHELOR** by Judith Harkness. (#J9609—$1.95)
- [ ] **THE MONTAGUE SCANDAL** by Judith Harkness. (#E8922—$1.75)*
- [ ] **THE ADMIRAL'S DAUGHTER** by Judith Harkness. (#E9161—$1.75)*
- [ ] **A LONDON SEASON** by Joan Wolf. (#J9570—$1.95)
- [ ] **A KIND OF HONOR** by Joan Wolf. (#E9296—$1.75)*
- [ ] **THE COUNTERFEIT MARRIAGE** by Joan Wolf. (#E9064—$1.75)*
- [ ] **THE GOLDEN SONG BIRD** by Sheila Walsh. (#E8155—$1.75)†
- [ ] **LORD GILMORE'S BRIDE** by Sheila Walsh. (#E8600—$1.75)*
- [ ] **THE SERGEANT MAJOR'S DAUGHTER** by Sheila Walsh. (#E8220—$1.75)
- [ ] **THE INCOMPARABLE MISS BRADY** by Sheila Walsh. (#E9245—$1.75)*
- [ ] **MADALENA** by Sheila Walsh. (#E9332—$1.75)
- [ ] **LORD DEVERILL'S HEIR** by Catherine Coulter. (#E9200—$1.75)*
- [ ] **THE REBEL BRIDE** by Catherine Coulter. (#J9630—$1.95)
- [ ] **THE AUTUMN COUNTESS** by Catherine Coulter. (#E8463—$1.75)*
- [ ] **LORD HARRY'S FOLLY** by Catherine Coulter. (#E9531—$1.75)*

* Price slightly higher in Canada
† Not available in Canada

Buy them at your local bookstore or use this convenient coupon for ordering.

THE NEW AMERICAN LIBRARY, INC.,
P.O. Box 999, Bergenfield, New Jersey 07621

Please send me the SIGNET BOOKS I have checked above. I am enclosing
$_____ (please add 50¢ to this order to cover postage and handling).
Send check or money order—no cash or C.O.D.'s. Prices and numbers are
subject to change without notice.

_____

_____

_____ State_____ Zip Code_____
Allow 4-6 weeks for delivery.
offer is subject to withdrawal without notice.

The Reluctant Suitor

by
Megan Daniel

A SIGNET BOOK
NEW AMERICAN LIBRARY
TIMES MIRROR

For Roy—for every reason

NAL BOOKS ARE AVAILABLE AT QUANTITY DISCOUNTS
WHEN USED TO PROMOTE PRODUCTS OR SERVICES. FOR
INFORMATION PLEASE WRITE TO PREMIUM MARKETING
DIVISION, THE NEW AMERICAN LIBRARY, INC., 1633
BROADWAY, NEW YORK, NEW YORK 10019.

Copyright © 1981 by Megan Daniel

All rights reserved

SIGNET TRADEMARK REG. U.S. PAT. OFF. AND FOREIGN COUNTRIES
REGISTERED TRADEMARK—MARCA REGISTRADA
HECHO EN CHICAGO, U.S.A.

SIGNET, SIGNET CLASSICS, MENTOR, PLUME, MERIDIAN AND NAL
BOOKS are published by The New American Library, Inc.,
1633 Broadway, New York, New York 10019

First Printing, March, 1981

1 2 3 4 5 6 7 8 9

PRINTED IN THE UNITED STATES OF AMERICA

PUBLISHER'S NOTE

This novel is a work of fiction. Names, characters, places, and incidents are either the product of the author's imagination or are used fictitiously, and any resemblance to actual persons, living or dead, events, or locales is entirely coincidental.

Chapter One

"Hell and the devil confound it!" exclaimed the Right Honourable Geoffrey Curwen, Viscount Morpeth, throwing his hat to the ground in disgust by way of punctuation. Hands on hips, he glared balefully at the broken shaft of the very smart curricle from which he had just been none too gently tossed. The Belcher handkerchief knotted around his throat quivered with indignation at this ignominious treatment from a vehicle that had cost him an outrageous sum only last month, and was not, of course, paid for as yet. Unfortunately, very few of the luxuries that the Viscount enjoyed were paid for, as he was always sadly out of pocket. On top of all else, he had made the ridiculously long trip to Wadebridge in Cornwall only to lose five hundred pounds on a disappointing prize fight. This had been followed by a visit to a great drafty pile belonging to his friend St. Cleer. If he'd had the least idea what a devilish uncomfortable place Cornwall was, he'd never have come. If his friend would insist on inheriting such a barn of a place, why could it not at least be a little nearer civilization? Why, this neighborhood was nearly as bad as his own place in Northumberland, and that was practically in Scotland, for God's sake!

He had finally been heading back to London in the devil's own glum mood. To make matters even worse, he had followed St. Cleer's advice and taken a supposed shortcut to the London road that led him across a corner of Bodmin Moor. He was now chilled to the bone from the ceaseless wind of the moor and more than ever depressed by the unrelieved landscape of rocks, heather, stones, furze bushes, and granite. And now, just when he was finally clear of that deuced moor and could see a tree or two again, one of his blasted horses had shied at a rabbit and dumped him unceremoniously into a ditch, ruining his new leathers into the bargain. Now how the devil was he to get home?

He tried vainly to brush off his buckskins, and stared down at his sadly scuffed Hessians. On his return to London, if he ever got there, his valet would be scandalized. But then that would not be a new condition for the long-suffering gentleman's gentleman. He had long since given up hope that the young Viscount, his master, could be brought to a proper realization of the sartorial elegance to be expected from one of his rank. Geoffrey Curwen was much more interested in his comfort, though his clothes were, of course, of the very best quality, from the best London tailors, and they did set well on his solid shoulders and strong, well-muscled arms.

A powerfully built young man of medium height, or perhaps a bit less, with a springy walk and an air of good nature, he was also possessed of a round boyish face with a ready grin and a wide brow, over which a shock of soft, sandy hair had a tendency to fall endearingly. Now he gave a shrug of his shoulders, and carried his compact and athletic self to his horses. These were being gently soothed by his excellent groom.

"Well, Chale?" he asked. "Bad, is it?" Some of his anger and frustration turned to real concern for his horses, a set of beautifully matched bays that were his pride and joy and for which he owed a considerable sum. He ran a practiced hand over a slightly swollen forelock with a frown.

"No permanent damage as I can see, me lord. A little strain and a scrape on Tric here, but I fancy one o' my fomentations and some spermacetti ointment'll heal him up nice an' smooth, pretty as ever he was. Trac seems to have come off scot-free, jest like he always does, me lord."

"Humph! Couldn't have seen that curst rabbit, you know!" muttered the Viscount with a small show of indignation.

"Aye, I do knows it, me lord, and who should I be to say otherwise, who knows well that yer lordship drives to an inch." The cheery, red-faced groom seemed to wink.

The young Viscount was not to be taken in by the soothing words of a groom who had known him all his life, for they were belied by a strong tone of sarcasm. Fond of his young master as he was, Chale had to admit that the gentleman was more than a bit ham-handed with the driving reins. A bruising rider, he tried to apply the admirable hunter's maxim, "Get over the ground if it kills you," to his driving horses as well.

Still and all, his friends generally admitted it to be his single fault where sporting pursuits were concerned, and blamed it on his natural impetuosity.

Reassured on the score of his horses, he turned his attention to the problem of where to go from here, and how to get there. He was in the middle of Cornwall, in the middle of nowhere.

"Beggin' yer pardon, me lord, but I'm thinkin' as how you won't go any farther this day in this here curricle."

"I ain't such a flat I can't see that! Daresay you've got a notion what I should do?" His frustration came out in a tone uncharacteristically sharp from one who was almost universally liked for his good nature.

"Why, yes, me lord, in course I do!" The Viscount was forced to grin at the rejoinder. "You might be rememberin' a lodgegate we passed a mile or so back. Bound to be someone there who'd give a night's bed to a real viscount, I'm thinkin'. I can lead the horses slowlike on to Polyphant. Can't be more'n five miles, I daresay, accordin' to Lord St. Cleer's directions."

"Oh, the devil take St. Cleer and his blasted shortcuts!" Lord Morpeth looked around in disgust and came to a reluctant decision.

"Be dark in a couple of hours. Might not even be an inn at Polyphant. Curst bore, but there's no getting out of it. Take Tric and Trac on ahead. I'll beg a bed at that place back there. And see you're here first thing in the morning for me. I'll ride back in a gig if I have to!" He made a grimace of distaste at thought of the depths to which he was willing to sink to get himself speedily out of Cornwall. And without further ado, he struck off down the road.

Though the merciless winds and the barren rocks of the moor were little more than a pair of miles to the south, and the air was brisk, here at least were trees, and green hedges, the first he'd seen for miles. Spring had definitely come to this corner of the world. He walked past clusters of primroses, peeking prettily from the hedges, their creamy petals winking in slanting shafts of sunlight. Pink rhododendrons nodded, birds called to each other, and the air was full of the sweet, heady, new scent of spring.

But Viscount Morpeth noticed none of this glory. He was still in a foul temper as he called out loudly at a sad-looking gatehouse. No answer came. The windows, on closer inspection, showed the unmistakably lonely look of a house long empty, gazing out blindly onto a quiet landscape. The big rusty gates weren't locked, as the Viscount discovered with a kick that swung them open with a creak.

Ahead of him lay a row of lovely old elms, their venerable branches just swelling into leaf. They stretched and curved off into the distance, and into their slight shade he plunged.

His poor temper was exacerbated yet further when, rounding the curve at last, he found nothing but more lane. On and on it went. Twenty minutes later he was still walking, and he'd still seen nothing but yew trees and firs and what he loudly stigmatized as "these blasted elms!"

Grinding his teeth in despair, he was about to give up and turn back when a new sound reached his ear. It was a light laugh, clear and unmistakable, the laugh of a young girl. Then came another, louder and lower. They didn't sound very far off, so he pushed on.

Over a little rise and around another bend he walked, with renewed purpose now that the end of his trek seemed within hearing at least, if not sight. Quite suddenly a small but nicely proportioned manor house came into view. Before it lay a prettily laid-out Italian garden, now in a sad state of repair, its fountains choked with weeds, an ornate sundial lying on its side on the tall grass, and the rose bushes being squeezed to death by the undergrowth.

And here was the source of the laughter. His face dropped in comic disappointment as he saw that the sound came from nothing more interesting than a pair of servant-girls, playing at battledore and shuttlecock on the overgrown lawn, hitting the feathered birdie over a low ornamental hedge. But at least they were a sign of habitation. He saw that one of the girls, she of the louder and more raucous laugh, was of ample proportions, with pink country cheeks and a big smile. The other was a tiny slip of a girl, looking to be about sixteen, pale and skinny and entirely unprepossessing.

As the Viscount neared the house, they stopped their game to stare, open-mouthed, at the approaching stranger. They were off to one side of the garden, and the Viscount, after a quick appreciative glance at the larger of the two, would have strode on past them to the house. But he was stopped abruptly by a screech of delight seeming to escape from the littler servant-girl.

"Geoff! Oh, Geoff! It really is you! It is! It is!" She picked up her cumbersome fustian skirts and petticoats, revealing a much worn pair of heavy shoes, and ran toward him. He stopped dead in his tracks at the sound of his name coming from this unknown child. He was further taken aback by two arms being violently thrown about his neck, causing him to be ruthlessly hugged.

"Oh, Geoff! How very good it is to see you! It has been so long!"

Viscount Morpeth reached behind his neck to peel off the two roughened, and probably grubby, hands and stared down into a piquant oval face and two of the biggest, most expressive violet eyes he had ever seen. Recognition dawned, and he held the girl at arms's length. "Heather? That you, Heather?"

"Of course it's me, silly. Who did you expect to find on my grandfather's estate?"

"But where exactly am I? Curricle broke down, you know. Had to walk . . . didn't know . . ." He trailed off in confusion. This day had been too much for a mind that, while kind and good and full of a great deal of common sense, had never been appreciably exercised.

"Well, you are at Heathside, in Cornwall," she stated with the air of a midget schoolmistress. "I am the Lady Margaret Barbara Heather St. Vincent, as you very well know, for you have known me for most of your life—though it's true that you haven't seen me for five years, at least, or is it six?—and this is Ellen, my dearest friend," she finished, indicating the strapping wench at her side, who was, in fact, the servant she appeared to be.

Ellen made a small curtsy, not in the least bashful or

awed by the Viscount, but frankly appraising him in her direct country way.

"And now you must come inside with me, Geoff. Mrs. Bing will give you a cup of tea. Oh, Geoff, I am *so* glad you've come to visit me, for we never have visitors you know. And luckily Cousin Honoria is away now so you may stay."

She had grabbed his hand and was pulling him up the short stairway to the great oak door of the house. As she pushed it open, he noticed that no servants came into the flagged entrance hall to greet them. The young girl headed immediately for the kitchen. Before Geoff could protest, he found himself standing in that high-ceilinged, cozy room, full of the delicious smell of chickens roasting on a spit before a huge open fire, and being frankly studied by a large, open-faced housekeeper, her brown eyes neither suspicious nor trusting, but obviously curious.

"Bing! This is Geoff, my very oldest friend in the whole world! The Honourable Geoffrey Curwen, I should say. His father is Viscount Morpeth, and he used to live next to Grandpapa's estate in Kent, and I have known him forever."

The Viscount coughed lightly and bowed to the housekeeper. She returned a small curtsy. "Not quite true, though. M'father died two years ago. I'm, uh, I'm Viscount Morpeth now." The housekeeper's curtsy, mid-stride as it was, deepened ever so slightly, and a spark of interest came into the frank and not unkind brown eyes.

"Oh, I'm sorry, Geoff. I didn't know. We never hear anything of the world here."

"Doesn't surprise me a bit," he muttered.

"How I've missed you, Geoff, and Kent and all the fun we used to have. The way you used to let me tag at your heels! You were very good to me. You were my friend." The words held a wistful note, and the girl turned a pleading face to Mrs. Bing. "He may stay, mayn't he, Bing? Please say he may. Please?"

The woman did not answer at once, but continued to study the young Viscount as though weighing him in some way. She had long been worried by the situation here at Heathside, but had not been able to come up with a satisfactory solution. Perhaps this young nobleman, if he were a true friend to her Young Miss, would be able to help. He had a good honest face. Mrs. Bing believed in faces.

As the round-faced woman gazed at him in thought, the Viscount was struck by the incongruity of what he had so far seen at Heathside. Heather said this was her grandfather's estate. She was the daughter of an earl and came from a family of large fortune. What, then, was she doing dressed like a servant, living in a shabby, rundown estate in this odd corner of the world? And why should she have to beg her housekeeper for permission to have a guest in the house?

Before he could make any sense of the situation, Mrs. Bing spoke in a broad West Country drawl. "And what would ye be doin' in this part of Cornwall, my lord? We get few travelers hereabouts."

"Shouldn't wonder, ma'am. Curricle turned over in a ditch. Rabbit, you see. Nowhere to go. I didn't know Heather lived there. Lucky that. Just coming from St. Cleer." He gave her a grin whose boyish charm had often gotten him his way and added, "Daresay it was my own fault, that flip. In a hurry to get to Launceston. I'd just crossed the moor, you see."

Mrs. Bing now gave him a genuine smile. "Ah. So ye'r not a Cornishman, sir?"

"No, by God!" he exclaimed, struck with the full horror of the thought.

"I thought not." Mrs. Bing smiled. Then she seemed to come to a decision. "Ye'll want to tidy up a bit, no doubt, after your accident. Ellen, do ye go up to the West bedchamber and see it's made comfortable for his lordship. And mind ye take up some nice hot water as well."

"Oh, thank you, Bing! Thank you!" cried Heather, throwing her arms around the lady's neck.

"Now, Lady Margaret," she admonished, using Heather's proper name and title. "What'll his lordship be thinkin'? An' I'll wager yer hands are in need of a washin' as well. Now go ye upstairs to tidy up, and mind ye put on a clean apron. I'm sure his lordship must be anxious fer his dinner, and it'll be ready in less than an hour." She shooed both girls from the room, leaving herself alone in the big old kitchen with the young man who was now more confused than ever.

"Well now, yer lordship. Would ye mind to sit down awhile till yer room be ready? I'm not one to be open with strangers, as ye might guess, but ye look a proper friend to my Young Miss—and well does she need one, that's sure—so I'm goin' to open my budget with ye."

The Viscount was taken aback both by the lady's words and by her suprisingly confiding manner, and was not at all certain he wanted to know what was in her budget. But she didn't look the sort of woman who, having once made up her mind to a course of action, would be easily dissuaded, and he was intrigued by what he had seen of the "family" at Heathside. So he did as he was bid and sat himself down in a surprisingly comfortable chair before the fire.

"Are you Heather . . . uh, Lady Margaret's, guardian, Mrs. Bing?" he ventured to ask when she did not speak. "Are you mistress here?"

"Humph!" she snorted. "Oh, there be a mistress, all right. Properly speakin', it's Lady Margaret's brother, the Earl of Stonington, as is her guardian, and much he'd care if the little lamb were to die tomorrow. In fact, it's rare pleased he'd be if she did!" Overcome for a moment by an emotion that was not at all natural to her kind bosom, she had to busy herself with the roasting chickens and get her anger under control.

Then she seated herself opposite the Viscount and began her story.

"There by Lady Margaret's cousin, Honoria Stapleton, who the Earl has seen fit to send to take care of his sister. His half-sister, he'd remind ye, an' there be part of the problem sir. It's ashamed of her he is, because her mother were a merchant's daughter. My lamb's blood ain't blue enough fer his fine lordship, but her money's good enough, that's sure!" She gave a bitter little laugh. "An' so he brought this cousin, Miss Stapleton as I said, to keep watch on her. More like a gaoler than a guardian is what she be! Just now she be off to her sister's in Bath or ye'd not have stepped past the front door, me lord. It's God has sent ye to us, I'm sure, and I pray ye can help my lamb, fer someone must, and her time do be runnin' out."

Thoroughly intrigued by the housekeeper's doleful tone, the Viscount sat quietly in his chair and listened as Heather's story unfolded.

Chapter Two

At that very moment, Miss Honoria Stapleton was sipping a fragrant cup of tea and stretching her old toes to the fire. How she was looking forward to the day, now only weeks off, when she could at last leave her tiresome duty behind and retire here to Bath, to live in comfort with her sister and remain free from financial worries for the rest of her life.

Miss Stapleton was a woman hard on sixty years with more than a bit of the pinched, dried-up spinster about her. Her parchment-colored skin stretched tightly across high cheekbones and a beaky nose and pulled itself so severely away from a slash of mouth that the thin, bloodless lips seemed not to be there at all. The deeply sunk, dark eyes could flash with anger, and even, occasionally, with intelligence, but their more usual outlook was one of iron will and determination.

Just now, however, the nearly black eyes held an unaccustomed spark of animation and what looked like hope, as she savored the tea and munched on a macaroon. She sat ramrod straight as she always did, though she had allowed her iron self-discipline to grow a bit lax of late. She hated everything about Heathside, that lonely hole in Cornwall where she had been immured for six years now, and where she knew herself to be so thoroughly disliked. There was no one there to talk to, nothing to do. Nothing but wait. She had taken to sleeping a good deal too much and eating a few too many of Mrs. Bing's scones. She realized, in fact, that she was becoming quite indolent. But all that would soon end. Her Cornish exile was nearly over.

She turned eyes which missed very little in this world toward the elegant shops in Milsom Street, just below the windows of her sister's modest but comfortable lodgings in

Bath. The windows glittered with all manner of things that Miss Stapleton had never been able to buy. It seemed that she had spent the whole of her adult life gazing at luxury through leaded glass windows. In a very short time now, she would be able to walk proudly into any of those shops and point a knarled finger at nearly anything she chose. The shopkeepers would fawn and scrape, anxious to keep the custom of such a valued patron as Miss Stapleton.

Her distant cousin, the Earl of Stonington, had promised her a very comfortable annuity to begin on the day that his sister came of age, *provided* that she was still unmarried on that day. For the moment Lady Margaret Heather St. Vincent turned twenty-one, her fortune, one of the largest in England, would go to her half-brother and guardian, Beauregard St. Vincent, Sixth Earl of Stonington. This would, however, come to pass only if his sister was still unmarried.

Honoria Stapleton's job for the last few years had been to make absolutely certain that Lady Margaret remained unmarried until then.

And a rather trying job it had proved. At first the task had been a simple one, though Miss Stapleton could find no joy in the rundown house in an obscure corner of England to which she had been sent with her charge. But the girl was a biddable child, and rather plain and awkward in the bargain.

But as the child grew into a woman, her cousin was dismayed to see the duckling turning into quite a lovely swan. She had the rich ebony hair of her mother, blue-black lights glistening in the richness of the soft waves that fell past her shoulders. Her huge, wide eyes were the color of violets and sapphires skillfully blended into a limpid shade all their own. It seemed singularly unfair to Miss Stapleton that the girl, whose mother was, after all, a nobody, the daughter of a merchant, should have been given both beauty and a fabulous fortune, while she, Honoria Stapleton, great-granddaughter to a duke, had neither and had consequently dwindled into a sour old maid. And why shouldn't this dab of a girl end the same, she thought with the bitterness that comes with a wasted life.

Honoria had taken what steps she could to keep the young beauty from shining forth by the simple expedient of severely limiting her firmament. She was still more than a little afraid of the child's loveliness, though whom she feared might see her and snatch her away in such a remote place was a mystery.

The brilliant hair could be, and was, always hidden under an enveloping cap, which also shaded the smooth, white brow. The long-fingered and delicate hands were kept roughened and red from the farm chores and housework in which the girl had, perforce, to share. But the patrician bones of her father, the Earl, were still far too evident in the fine straight nose and the elegant line of the jaw. The porcelain complexion, though coarsened from exposure to the winds of the moor, still glowed with a sheen difficult to disguise.

In her simple fustian gown, heavy shoes, and oversized cap, she still looked remarkably like a very pretty child playing dress-up. Her cousin was quick to recognize this fact, and so was at great pains to keep the girl well hidden from any eyes that might pose a threat to the rosy future that now lay just beyond Honoria's grasp.

"More tea, dear?" asked Miss Stapleton's sister, as she lifted the pretty little flowered pot. "It is still quite warm."

The widowed Mrs. Wardwell was a decided contrast to her sister. She had, quite young, married the man she loved. And though they had not been blessed with children, they had been happy. On her husband's death some years ago, Mrs. Wardwell had retired contentedly to Bath where she contrived to live quite comfortably on her small jointure, gossiping with friends, visiting the Pump Room, and generally filling her life with the quiet amusements of the once-fashionable spa. Her contentment was manifest in her easy smile, and in her bulk, spreading out in a quantity of chins and sausagy fingers, whose main occupation was carrying delightful cream buns to her little bow-mouth.

"No thank you, Henrietta," replied Honoria with a trace of a smile. This widowed sister was practically the only person in the world that ever saw Miss Stapleton's face crack into anything resembling a smile, for she was the only person, other than herself, that Honoria cared for. "I fear, sister, that I must begin my preparations for returning to Heathside."

THE RELUCTANT SUITOR 13

"But, Honoria! You've been here only a fortnight, and you always remain with me for at least a month."

"I know, Henrietta. But I cannot be easy in my mind knowing that Lady Margaret is not being properly seen to. You know it is only a little over a month now that I must wait for my reward for this tedious chaperonage of her. It would be foolish beyond permission in me to allow anything to jeopardize the arrangements at this late date."

"I suppose you are right, dear. You know I have never perfectly understood why you must be with Lady Margaret until she comes of age. I mean, why the Earl has promised you all that money."

"I have explained it to you several times, Henrietta," she answered with the long-suffering air of one admonishing a particularly recalcitrant child. "Lady Margaret's grandfather left his entire fortune to her, his only grandchild. But he made the bequest conditional on her marriage and only if that event took place before she should come of age. If she did not, the fortune would go to the Earl, her father, who in any case was the trustee. When he died a year later, the trust devolved on his son, the present Earl, Lady Margaret's half-brother. He, of course, realizes the impropriety of such a fortune going to a little nobody of a girl with a merchant for a grandfather, and he intends—quite rightly in my view—to see that the money comes under the control of the nobility. He himself will inherit the entire fortune when his half-sister reaches twenty-one, unmarried."

"Well, dear, I'm afraid I don't understand at all why her grandfather should have left his money in such a very odd way."

"You might be glad that he did! When I am free to move here to Bath and share housekeeping with you, Henrietta, you'll find yourself benefiting to no small degree from the Earl's largesse!"

"Yes, of course, dear. It will be very cozy. Do have some more tea. And another biscuit?"

"So ye see, sir," Mrs. Bing concluded. "Unless my Young Miss can find a way to leave here and find herself a husband in the next few weeks, I don't know what's to become of her, poor child."

"It don't make sense!" said Geoffrey, his face twisted into a frown as he struggled to understand this absurd situation. "I remember the old man, her grandfather. Seemed devilish fond of Heather. Why would he serve her such a back-handed turn?"

"Well, I don't think he meant to, sir. And properly speakin', it was Lady Margaret's father, the Earl that was, ye know, that was meant to have the care of her. He were a fine gentleman, and he really loved my poor lamb's mother, even though she had no handle to her name. And such a pity it was that she died when my lamb were but a babe. Her grandfather were that afeared of the fortune hunters bound to swarm around the poor lass. He were sure the Earl'd be able to keep off any nasty ones till she come of age. Fer he'd have had to agree to any marriage, ye see, the child bein' under age. And so the old man figured she'd be safe enough from 'em till then."

Mrs. Bing let out a hearty sigh at the unfortunate way fate had of mucking up the best-laid plans. "The old gent didn't have much feelin' fer the good sense of females, I reckon. He feared what might happen to the child when she'd no one to say no to her, so to speak, if she'd not found a proper husband, one her father approved of, by the time the money was to be rightly hers." An edge of bitterness crept into her voice, and she almost snarled. "The old fool shoulda knowed that my young lady has a deal more sense'n that. For all she's an innocent lamb, she's a good head on her shoulders. An' so I woulda told him meself if I'd had the chance." She seemed to be speaking to herself, reciting the ills of her young mistress as she had been doing for years. "But no. Her grandpapa left it all for her papa to settle. Her future, I mean. An' I'm sure all woulda been well, me lord, but her papa went an' got hisself killed that self-same year. That put the poor orphan at the mercy of that scalawag half-brother of hers." She shot him a glance of some alarm, a bit taken aback by the strength of her own emotion. "Beggin' yer pardon, me lord, but a scalawag he is, fer all he's an earl!"

"Stonington's a curst rum touch! Wouldn't trust him to care for a dog, much less a girl. He wouldn't care that she's his sister, long as he could find a way to get her money." The Viscount was truly shocked by the story Mrs.

THE RELUCTANT SUITOR

Bing had told him, not least by the fact that such a man as the Earl of Stonington had such power over his friend.

"I see ye know him, sir. I heard tell he were a nasty little boy, and now he's grown up into a Nasty Man, for all his fine title and his nose so high in the air that he's ashamed of his own sister."

"Ashamed? But damme, why the deuce should anyone be ashamed of Heather?"

"An' well might ye ask, me lord. He never did forgive his father fer marryin' trade. Holds the name of St. Vincent very high, ye know, though he's no credit to it, to be sure. A trifle too high, if ye ask me. I 'spose he expected his poor papa to stay a widower all his life!" she said with an audible humph! in her voice. "Just because my Lady Margaret's grandpapa were a trader is no call fer Bo St. Vincent to think his father'd sullied his name when he married the old man's pretty daughter. He was always happy enough to spend the old gent's silver, right enough!" She puttered about a bit at the old oak worktable in the center of the room to cover her agitation. Then with a flourish of a big butcher knife in Geoffrey's direction for emphasis, she said, "And he *has* found a way to get her money, me lord. He's the trustee, an' I'm a Duchess if he han't been goin' through my Young Miss's money like water. And why shouldn't he, he'd ask ye. In another month or so it'll all be his anyway, all legal like. He just don't feel like waitin'!" Geoff was shrinking back into his chair as the knife helped Mrs. Bing make her points. With great relief, he saw it replaced on the table with a clatter of disgust. "Oh, I shudder to think what's to become of her, me lord, when her birthday do come. For then she'll be no earthly good to him at all. Ye've got to help me find a way to stop him, me lord. Can ye, do ye think?"

"Think on it. Have to do something." The pair lapsed into deep thought, staring into the fire while the rich aroma of roasting chickens wafted around them.

Mrs. Bing's ruminations seemed only to bring her attention back to the problem of those chickens and what on earth else she was to serve the Viscount for his supper. There were some nice apples in the larder. She'd have to see what she could do with them. And she'd have Elly lay a fire in the front sitting room. She couldn't ask a viscount to eat in the kitchen!

"Well, be ye off now to tidy up fer dinner, me lord, fer it'll not be long in the makin'. An' here's Elly to show ye up. Be ye back in half an hour, mind, or 'twill be burnt black."

With that the lady bustled back to her chickens and her larder, as though they'd been calmly discussing the weather this past half hour. The Viscount, bemused by being thus ordered and mother-henned by a mere housekeeper, turned obediently to follow Ellen up the stairs.

"This way, yer lordship, sir," she was saying. "Yer washin' water's set out nice an' hot."

Almost immediately he found himself in a large, sparsely furnished bedcamber, chilly and a bit musty from long disuse, with late shafts of pale sunlight coming through windows grey with the dust of ages. But the linens were clean and fresh, and the water was hot, and Ellen had brought some daisies from the garden to set on the washstand.

In a very short time the Viscount had made all the improvements in his appearance that were possible in his limited circumstances, with neither his valet nor even a traveling case. He'd managed to remove the worst of the mud from his hands and his Hessians, had run dampened fingers through his sandy hair, and had reknotted his Belcher handkerchief around his neck.

Having finished this meagre toilette, he shrugged at his still far from pristine image in the badly spotted mirror and sank into a wing chair in front of the cold grate. He then tried to make some sort of sense of the odd situation which Mrs. Bing had just described.

Heather had looked so fresh and innocent there on the lawn, with a badminton racquet in her hand and a laugh in her eyes, that it had come as a shock to realize that she was nearly twenty-one. It was true that she'd been about fifteen when he'd last seen her some six years ago. And since he knew she was but three years younger than himself, he should have realized at once that she was not the sixteen-year-old she looked. In fact, in society's eyes she was dangerously near to being on the shelf in terms of her marriageability.

THE RELUCTANT SUITOR

He remembered with a crooked grin how she had been used to dog his steps whenever he was at his father's estate in Kent, where she lived with her grandfather on a neighboring estate. The Viscount had done a good deal of his own growing up there, particularly before he'd been sent off to Eton, since no one in his family was particularly fond of the drafty, ugly baronial manor of Morpeth near the Scottish border.

He and Heather used to ride together through the meadows and fish together in the stream and have wonderful make-believe fantasies about knights-errant saving damsels in distress. The bright little girl was a monkey, a well-plucked 'un, and always ready for a lark.

But now it seemed that she had become in truth the damsel in distress that she used to love to play-act. Geoffrey Curwen, however, had great difficulty seeing himself in the role of knight-errant, however dashing the image may seem. Dashing, yes. But damned uncomfortable, too, he was sure. The Viscount didn't like being made uncomfortable.

Funny how little he had thought of Heather in the years after her grandfather had died and she had simply disappeared from the neighborhood. No one seemed to know where she had gone, but everyone supposed that she must be with relatives who would love and care for her. How wrong they had been, he thought now, a feeling of guilt at his lack of worry over the girl bringing a deep frown into the blue-grey eyes.

Well, he didn't see what he could do about the situation now. Especially as Heather's birthday was so near. But he would think on it. It'd be a devilish shame if no one were to come to her aid. He'd better see what he could do. He sometimes had quite superior ideas when he really concentrated on it. Surprised himself, even. Yes, he'd think on it.

With a sigh that didn't quite come off as world-weary as he would have liked, he mentally put on his shining armor, picked up his lance, and plunged into the fray. He descended the stairs.

Chapter Three

As the Viscount reached the great hall, his nostrils were assailed by the cooking odors in his dinner, and he realized with a pang that he was devilish sharp-set. He was standing with one foot on the bottom step, trying to decide which way to turn, and almost decided on following his nose to the lovely smell, when Heather tripped into the room, calling to him in a chirruping voice.

"Oh, Geoff, there you are. Bing says we may eat in the front sitting room. Just the two of us. Isn't that famous?" She laughingly took his hand and pulled him across the hall into a rather shabby but spotless parlor. "Usually when Cousin Honoria is away I eat in the kitchen with Bing and Ellen, because it is so much cozier. And when she *is* here, I have to sit in the drafty old dining room freezing usually, and trying to make silly conversation. I am very good at making silly conversation, of course, but this will be so much more fun, don't you think? And we are to have a fire as well!" She was nearly overcome by the luxury in which she was being allowed to share because of the Viscount's presence.

Usually the only fires allowed outside the big homey kitchen were in Miss Stapleton's bedchamber and in whatever room she chose to sit that day. The comfort-loving old woman, like most people, had no difficulty at all in convincing herself of what she preferred to believe, which was that her cousin, a healthy young girl, had no need of a fire in her room and was, in fact, the better for the lack of one. She, however, an old lady, would surely die of the Cornish damp if her rooms were not kept constantly heated.

The fact that Miss Stapleton had hardly ever had an ill day in her life was not allowed to cloud her judgment on this point. And so Heather, on all but the warmest days, was wont to spend many of her waking hours down in the kitchen, cheerfully mending linens before the big open hearth, chattering to Bing and Ellen, and forgetting for awhile her sad future prospects.

She now tripped merrily over to the crackling fire that fended off the early spring chill creeping into the room, and spread her fingers to its warmth. Geoffrey looked around the once-elegant and now sadly decrepit parlor.

It was a well-proportioned room, papered in what had once been a gay floral print, but was now reduced to varying shades of grey with only touches of color here and there where prints and paintings had once hung. The soft green curtains were of fine silk damask, now patchy, the bottom edges having been turned several times to cover their fraying. The elegant furnishings, threadbare as they were, were still quite comfortable, and a small burlwood table had been pulled up cozily to the fire and laid with china for two.

To Heather's immense satisfaction, the Viscount formally offered his arm and led her to one of the chairs. He held it for her and saw her comfortably seated before disposing himself in the opposite chair. To him such good manners were natural, no longer even thought of but something he did without considering. But for Heather, it had been many years since she had been treated with such civility, and she basked in it.

No sooner had they settled themselves, than Ellen appeared with a laden tray and began to serve them. She gave Heather a suspiciously conspiratorial look as she placed the simple but tastily prepared meal before them. Then with a proper curtsy to each in turn, she quit the room.

"She the only servant, but for the Bing woman?" asked Geoff when Ellen had gone. He had never in his life been served by a maid-of-all-work, and the possibility that there were no other servants in this big house appalled him.

"Oh, no," said Heather. "There is also Jurby. He doesn't live in anymore, though. He has a very snug little cottage in North Hill with his sister, and he is the loveliest old man. He's really a coachman, you know, but there is only old Betsy, the mare, now, and she's well past her prime,

I'm afraid. Of course, Jurby is a bit past his prime as well, so I expect that's all right. He brings the coals and makes such repairs as we can afford and such. And he does still drive the whiskey now and then when Cousin Honoria goes visiting or takes the air. She doesn't like to be seen in such an old-fashioned carriage, I think, so she doesn't go out very often."

"Should think not!" cried Geoff in disgust at the very idea of driving out in a whiskey.

"Well, yes, it is rather shabby, and Cousin Honoria is very proud," she said, ladling out a savory-smelling brown soup thick with beans and barley. "And then there's Jem. He's the son of one of the farmers, and he sleeps in the stables. He doesn't do much of anything, really, but Bing likes to have a male on the grounds."

"Quite right, too."

"Yes, I suppose. But Jem is only eight years old, and I shouldn't think he'd be much good if a burglar came and tried to murder us all in our beds, would you?"

After pondering the question a short moment, he responded. "Shouldn't think so. Much better get a dog." He bit into a roasted chicken leg with relish.

"Oh, I've begged Cousin Honoria forever to allow it, but she swears she won't have one anywhere on the estate, much less in the house."

"Sounds a curst old witch to me, your Cousin Horrifica."

Heather laughed enchantingly, and Geoff beamed, pleased by his small successful foray into the realm of the wits.

"Well I don't think she is evil, precisely. I daresay she has not had a very nice life here either. But I admit she can be unpleasant at times, and just a bit selfish," Heather concluded. "Things are always much more pleasant when she goes to visit her sister, and she comes back much happier as well."

"Sounds like she deserves Cornwall," he muttered.

"But Cornwall can be very beautiful, Geoff." She lifted the cover from a small side dish. "Oh, look! Apple dumplings! Bing must have taken a fancy to you. She *never* makes dumplings for Cousin Honoria." Heather helped herself to a generous portion of the delicacy and dove in with zest, continuing her narrative between swallows.

"I have quite grown to love the moor. Its wildness can be very beautiful. I like to walk across the downs to Dozmary pool. The heather is so pretty," she finished innocently.

Geoff grinned at her. "Yes, she is."

Heather, to whom the idea of fishing for compliments was totally foreign, blushed rosily. She covered her confusion by taking a second helping of stewed cucumbers. "Of course it's not like Kent. Sometimes I do long for the wide green meadows where we used to have such fun. Is it still the same?"

"Couldn't say," he answered. An uncharacteristically black look replaced the grin. "M'father sold off the estate before he died. Haven't been around there since."

"I'm sorry to hear that. We had such good times there. And so many friends," she added wistfully. "Why did he sell it?"

"Had to! Sold nearly everything that wasn't entailed. Didn't know it at the time. Never told me he was in Dun Territory. Found out quick enough when he died, though. Never saw so many collectors in my life! Been on short rations ever since."

This was not exactly true. Oh, it was certainly true that the young Viscount was rather deeply in debt, or as he would have put it himself "badly dipped and punting on tick." And it was also true that a large load of that debt had been inherited from his father, whose untimely demise had been a sad shock in every way to his son.

The old Viscount had been a dotingly fond husband and father, and he simply could not bear to deny anything to his wife and only child. Consequently, both of those beloved ones had gone through life with no more idea of the value of a pound than a child has, perhaps less. To pay for the extravagancies they had never learned to do without, he had gone deeply into debt, selling off many assets and heavily mortgaging those that he couldn't sell because they were entailed onto his son.

In consequence, Geoffrey Curwen, after inheriting a staggering load of debt, continued regularly to add to it, trusting to chance to help him somehow come about.

It must be said in Geoffrey's defense that he had, of late, begun to pay rather more attention than previously to his sad affairs. His man of business had been at great pains to explain his situation in very clear terms. The Viscount had so far advanced to the point of making firm resolutions to limit the number of hunters he would run next season to only six, and his new pairs of boots to two in number. And he would not give Chale, who had not been paid in months but stayed on out of a genuine fondness for the Viscount, the rise in salary he had more or less promised him last year.

"Oh, dear," said Heather. "Do you mean your father left you with a lot of debts? How unfortunate."

"Unfortunate? I should think so! Devilish uncomfortable is what it is. Afraid to walk down Bond Street anymore. Never know when one of the curst shopkeepers'll pop out a window and stick another blasted bill in my hand! Daresay I shall have to stay off the Haymarket as well before long. Owe Fribourg nearly a century for snuff and cheroots." He lapsed into an uncomfortable awareness of the drawer in his study overflowing with bills. He comforted himself with a mutton chop.

"How odious it is that we should both be made to suffer just because someone else left things so inconveniently. Here I sit with two hundred and fifty thousand pounds that will never do me any good at all, while you are left with nothing but bills. It doesn't seem very fair to me that we must . . . Geoff, why are you looking at me so?"

"Two hundred and fifty thousand pounds!" he sputtered. His attention snapped back to Heather like a piece of stretched India rubber suddenly released, snuff bills, mortgage payments, and all fluttering off to the blackness that was the back of his mind.

"Yes. It's in the Funds, I believe, or some such thing. Grandpapa seemed to think that the safest way. Of course, I also own this poor dilapidated estate, and the one in Kent. You know how much nicer it is. I do hope it is being properly taken care of."

By this time the Honourable Geoffrey Curwen's sparkling blue-grey eyes were nearly popping from his head, and his mouth was hanging open. Heather looked at him and began to giggle.

THE RELUCTANT SUITOR

"Why, Geoff, you look for all the world like a new puppy after a hard run. Whatever have I said to make you look so?"

He seemed to find his voice at last, though when he spoke it came out as a sort of gasp. "Two hundred and fifty thousand pounds! I knew the old man'd cut up warm, but mean to say! Quarter of a million! In the Funds!"

"It is rather a lot, isn't it? And if you only knew how little we run this house on! I don't know what is happening to all that money. Bo never talks to me of business matters as Grandpapa used to do. In fact, Bo never talks to me at all. He hasn't even been to see me in over two years." She sounded puzzled as well as hurt by her brother's neglect.

Geoff looked around him again at the shabby room and the remains of their simple meal. He crossed to a French window, two of its panes badly cracked, and looked out onto the tangled and overgrown garden. Then he looked back at the girl in the big cap, gazing quietly into the fire. She'd turned into a pretty little thing, this romping playmate of his childhood. A bit skinny, but still . . . Two hundred and fifty thousand pounds, he thought, jolted by the immensity of her fortune. It could well make her the richest woman in England.

Though the young Viscount's social consciousness was still in the infancy of its development, the full injustice of Heather's situation hit him hard. He strode over to where she sat by the fire and blurted out, "You ought to get away from here, Heather. Not a fit situation for you. Father an earl. Dash it all, you're Quality! Shouldn't be living like a servant. It ain't right."

"Well, I admit it is sometimes not very comfortable. In truth, I have often thought of running away. I don't see much future for myself here. And in any case, Bo may not allow me to stay after I come of age, for then Heathside will be his. And of course, I quite understand that no one is likely to want to marry me when I am a pauper, as I certainly shall be quite soon. I'm afraid it makes me feel horridly low sometimes."

She gazed sadly into the fire again, but she plucked up her spirits almost at once in her usual way. "I might try for a position as housekeeper. I do think I should make an excellent one, for I have learned to run Heathside with the *strictest* economy."

"You run it? What of this screwed-up old cousin of yours?"

"Oh, Cousin Honoria hates to be put about by such things. And in truth, I do not think she would be very good at it. While I am *very* good at it, you know. I can dress a joint of beef or mend a sheet very well. And I know all about tending the garden, because Bo says we may not have a gardener." She mused a moment and added, "I do sometimes wonder that Bo cannot send us a little more money for the running of Heathside, but I expect it has to do with the way the trust is tied up. Grandpapa was a bit odd about such things."

"Deuced odd! And what does old sour-face do all day then?"

"Sour-face!" giggled Heather. "You have hit her off perfectly, though how you could know I don't understand." She proceeded to tick off her cousin's varied activities. "She is very fond of writing long letters to her acquaintances in London and to her sister in Bath, where she plans to go and live as soon as I am of age and she can leave Heathside. She delights in reading novels and society journals of every description, memorizing all of the scandal and hoping, no doubt, to one day put it to good use. She talks to the vicar when he comes to call. And she eats. I don't know how she has kept from becoming quite stout. She insists that Bing always make her fresh scones with clotted cream and thick strawberry jam, though it seems we can ill afford it. But since she is the only one allowed to eat them I suppose it is not so very much." Heather had not been able to keep the slightest note of irony from her voice. Geoff's face wore a gathering frown. "Well anyway, you can see that I should make a very good housekeeper. But Ellen says it will not do, and I expect she knows more about such things than I do. She says I am far too young for a housekeeper."

"Quite right, too," exclaimed Geoff.

Heather had dreamed up any number of plots for her escape over the last few years, some of which she now recounted to the Viscount. They ranged from opening a milliner's shop to dressing up as a boy and signing on somewhere as a stable hand to becoming a ballet girl. But all her plans had suffered in common from a sad impracticability, a fact which Heather was far too commonsensical not to acknowledge. And so she had remained at Heathside.

She looked earnestly at Geoff. "Perhaps I could find a position as a chambermaid. Do you not think . . . ?"

"No!" ejaculated the Viscount with unwonted vehemence. "A chambermaid! No one'd hire you for one thing. You're Quality. Daresay you wouldn't like it anyway. Devilish bore, I should think. Your friend's right. Wouldn't do at all."

"I daresay you are right. For with no one to give me a character, I shouldn't think anyone would want me." An unusual degree of seriousness crept over the pretty face, tinged with a flush of fear. Her voice dropped a bit. "But, Geoff, what *am* I to do? I know Cousin Honoria plans to leave Heathside soon. She talks of nothing else, and I believe my brother has promised her rather a large annuity on my birthday. She dislikes me excessively, you know, though I have never understood why."

"Have to marry, that's all," he stated with an admirable grasp of the obvious.

"Well, I do think old Mr. Twitchit, from Polyphant, would marry me, for he looks at me so very particularly when he comes to call on my cousin. And whenever he thinks she is not looking he tries to hold my hand," she added with a little shudder that she was unable to subdue. "But, but . . . oh, Geoff, he is *old*, and *fat*, and he . . . he . . . smells of garlic! I do not think I could bear it!"

To the Viscount's immense chagrin, Heather covered her face with her hands and broke down into shuddering sobs, little crystal teardrops running out from between her long fingers and dropping unheeded onto her coarse white apron. He gingerly placed an arm about her and patted her shoulder. "Here, Heather. No need for that. Mean to say, no cause. Make your eyes all red. You won't have to marry any fat old Twitchit. No one can make you. Daresay no one'll try. C'mon then. Give us a smile."

She lifted her head from his shoulder where she had allowed it to droop comfortably and gave him a watery smile. After one final hiccough, she managed to speak.

"I'm sorry, Geoff. Really I am. But I have been so very lonely and unhappy here. And when I try to think what will become of me, I am so very afraid. What am I to do without a shilling to my name and no one to care what happens to me?"

"Fustian! No one to care? Mrs. Bing! She'll care. And your friend Ellen. And, and . . ." Here he seemed to be momentarily stumped. "Well, anyone would, if they knew. Dash it all, Heather! Only one thing for you to do. Find some nice fellow to marry you. Be happy. That's the ticket."

Heather, to whom the idea was not exactly a novel one, looked at him in her intent, considering way. Then her face lightened like the sun. "Geoff! I have the most wonderful idea! You could marry me!"

"Me? Devil a bit! Don't want to get married!" He considered briefly. "Well, daresay I shall someday. Got to keep up the name and all. But not now. Not yet. No, dash it all. Deuced fond of you, Heather. You know that. Do anything for you. I ain't ready, that's all." He began to squirm a bit uncomfortably.

"But don't you see, Geoff? It's the perfect solution." Heather had taken off her heavy shoes and had her dainty feet tucked up cozily beneath her. She perched on the very edge of her chair in her enthusiasm. To the Viscount's alarmed eyes, she was beginning to look as though she were about to pounce. "If we were married at once, you would have my fortune to pay off all those horrid debts you told me about. And I would be free to leave Heathside and Cousin Honoria. We could go to live in London," she went on, warming to her topic, as the Viscount froze a bit. "And I could have lots of pretty dresses and go to parties and eat whatever I liked." She paused and dropped her voice again, her animation quite gone. "And I wouldn't have to be lonely anymore."

Geoffrey, who all his life had taken for granted the things that Heather most wanted, was struck by the meagreness of her wishes, and it was brought home to him just how unhappy his little friend's life had been since leaving Kent. When he spoke his voice was warmer and kinder, but still quite firm.

"It won't do, Heather. Nothing personal, understand.

Do almost anything for you, you know I would. Ain't ready to be leg-shackled, that's all. Besides," he continued, drawing out his biggest card, "everyone'd call me a fortune hunter. Damme if they wouldn't be right, too. Wouldn't like that at all. Friends sniggering and such. No. Won't do at all. Better think of another way."

"Is it because you don't love me, Geoff? I know that you don't, but I would try to be a good wife." She was attempting to sound very sophisticated and pulled herself up quite straight. "It would only be a *mariage de convenance*. I have read of such things, and I know that gentlemen often have, well, outside interests. I would try very hard not to interfere in your life. And you must admit that my fortune would make you much more comfortable," she finished on a practical note.

"Deuced comfortable," he muttered with feeling, but he remained resolute. "No, Heather. Good notion for you, not for me. Better find someone else."

"But I don't know anyone else," she pointed out reasonably.

"Have to find someone," he answered with the growing feeling of an animal upon whom the cage door is about to swing closed. "Have to think. Give me a minute. Bound to have a notion." He sat down on a chair and put his head into his hands as he gathered all his powers of thought. Heather watched him intently, certain that her lifelong hero would find a way to help her.

Suddenly his head popped up and he smiled. "Hah!"

"What is it, Geoff?"

"Got a notion! Knew I would do, too, if only I had a moment to think on it. Ask m'mother!"

"Lady Morpeth?"

He looked at her blankly. "Only mother I've got!"

A memory came to Heather of a beautiful golden-haired lady with a tinkling laugh, clear green eyes, and a very kind smile. She had always seemed like some sort of fairy princess to Heather.

"Very knowing one, m'mother. Always has an answer." His brows lowered a moment as a new idea came to him, and he let out a soft "Hmmmm. Not always the right answer, come to think of it. Hardly ever is, if it comes to that. Wonder why it never struck me before. Oh, well, nothing else for it. This matter'll be right in her direction. Knows everything about the ton, that's certain. None better." A nod of decision caused a lone shock of sandy hair to fall over one eyebrow but was ruthlessly flung back by a sturdy and impatient hand. "Yes. She's the one we want. Ask m'mother."

"But, Geoff. What are we to ask her?"

"Why, to invite you to stay with her, of course. Launch you into the ton. Fire you into the Marriage Mart. Find you a husband. That's what you want to set things to rights, Heather. A husband! She'll find you one."

"Oh," she answered softly, not sure how she felt about this idea. She realized that here was the one possible chance to remove her from Heathside. Could it be taken? Should it?

"Geoff, do you think she might?"

"Why not? Easiest thing in the world. You've turned into a devilish pretty girl, Heather. Anyone'd be happy to marry you."

"Anyone but you," she reminded him.

"Well, it's just that I ain't ready, you see," he defended himself. "But she'll find you one. Pack your bags. Carry you off to m'mother tomorrow. Only thing for it. Daresay you'll be glad to leave this place. Never saw such a gloomy hole in all my life!"

"But do you think, Geoff, that she mayn't like the idea? She hasn't seen me for years and years, and she is so pretty and fashionable. I can't simply barge in on her without so much as a by-your-leave." Much as she might want to, she could have added. "It won't do in any case, you know. They'll never let me go."

"Hold on. Have to think some more." And he lapsed into a deep study again. "Got it!" he said at length. "Won't tell 'em. Won't know where you've gone!" he stated proudly as the very crux of a brilliant plan. "Well, maybe Mrs. Bing. But she won't peach on you. Practically begged me to take you away."

"She did? Bing?"

"Promised her I'd try to help. And so I will. We'll leave first thing in the morning, and you'll . . . Oh." The hand that had been excitedly shoving back the sandy hair fell into his lap as a very sobering thought occurred.

"What is it, Geoff?"

"Haven't got a carriage," he stated bluntly. "Curricle's broken up."

"Couldn't it be fixed in Launceston? And then we could go?" She had allowed herself to be convinced about his plan, and had grasped at it like a buoy to keep her from going under. She couldn't bear the thought that it might float out of her reach again.

"Wouldn't do anyway. Take us three days to get to London in a curricle. Ruin your reputation for sure. Then I'd *have* to marry you! No, by God! Won't work that way. Have to find another way."

Heather tried not to be too hurt by the vehemence of his reluctance to marry her and became her usual practical self again. "Couldn't we go on the Mail?"

Geoff shifted uncomfortably in his chair. "Thing is, haven't got the blunt. Pity, but there it is. Not even sure how I'll pay for getting that damned curricle fixed." Reflecting for a moment on the ignominies of poverty, he found himself mentally counting the pitifully few coins that remained in his purse. "Might get myself to town on the Stage, but can't pay for two, and that's flat. Give me a minute."

This day was proving a very sore trial for Viscount Morpeth. He was not at all used to having such extraordinary mental demands made on him and seemed to have grown a trifle rusty from lack of practice. It took him several minutes this time to come up with something usable. But at last he looked up sharply and peered at Heather.

"When does old scrab-face come back from Bath?"

A tiny ray of hope dawned in Heather's violet eyes. "Not for another fortnight, most likely. She never stays less than a month. Why do you ask?"

He clapped his hands in triumph. "Simple! Tomorrow I'll take the Stage to town. Get me there in a pig's whisker, you know. See m'mother. She'll invite you. Get another roll of soft." He noticed the confusion on her face. "Blunt." Confusion still reined. "Money!" At her pleased "Oh!" he continued. "Come back and fetch you in a proper chaise, with an abigail, all right and tight. You'll be safe in London before old Cousin Annoy-us even knows you're gone."

"But won't they just come and fetch me? Surely they will find out easily enough where I've gone."

"Fustian! Why should they? You'll be safe as houses with m'mother. Fine woman. Take good care of you."

"Geoff, do you really think she might invite me to come? Really?"

"Course she will. Why not? She always liked you. Daresay she'll like to have you with her. Like it of all things. Deuced glad I thought of it." Any further thoughts he might have had on the matter were ruthlessly cut off by a quite ferocious hug from Heather, who proved surprisingly strong for all her diminutive size.

"Oh, thank you, Geoff, thank you! You are the most wonderful friend!"

For the second time that day the Viscount peeled the girl off his sadly crushed Belcher handkerchief, this time with something more of tenderness in his touch for this vulnerable friend of his childhood.

"Damme if you won't take the ton by the ears when m'mother finishes with you," he said, looking at her with new eyes and trying to imagine her in a ballroom, in a pretty, fashionable gown, glowing in the candlelight. "Devilish taking little thing, that's what you are, Heather. Not just in the common style. Shouldn't be surprised if you're riveted before the Season's fair started." The tiniest frown crossed his light eyes. He couldn't imagine Heather married and was not at all sure he found such a picture satisfactory. With that face and her fortune, there would certainly be no lack of offers. They'd swarm around her like flies to the honeypot.

And what other choice did the poor thing have, with that moulder of a brother treating her so shabby? Too bad, though, that there had to be such a confounded hurry about the thing. If she could have just waited a few years . . .

Chapter Four

To the Viscount's pleased surprise, Chale returned the next morning driving neither a gig nor a farm cart but Geoffrey's own newly repaired curricle. He'd had to pledge his gold watch to get the work done, but he trusted his master to see it returned eventually. The curricle was being pulled by two neatish skewbalds, hired from the same stable in Launceston where the repairs had been made. Tric and Trac would be in no condition to travel for some days yet, but the skewbalds were rather better than anything Geoff would have hoped to find in these parts.

He and Heather observed the approach of the equipage from the sitting room where they had been downing a good country breakfast of porridge, bacon, and fresh farm eggs. Geoff was washing it down with a mug of home-brewed, Heather with a glass of milk, the budget at Heathside running neither to morning coffee nor to chocolate for any of the inmates save Honoria Stapleton.

At sight of Chale coming round the bend of the elm-lined lane Heather jumped from her chair and bounded to the window.

"Who can that be, Geoff? We never have visitors, you know, except for the vicar or Mr. Twitchit (and here she could not suppress a little shudder) and now we have had two in as many days. And such a fine carriage!"

"You like it?" he asked, his voice full of pride. "Only had it a month. Deuced expensive, too."

She swung to face him with an excited smile. "It's yours? Really? Oh, will you take me for a drive in it? I've never been in anything half so fine."

"Why not?"

With a clap of her hands, she ran toward the door. "I'll fetch my cloak." She paused in the doorway. Her face was shining. "I'm so glad that you came, Geoff. And especially when Cousin Honoria was away. I don't really think she would have let you stay. And she certainly would not have let me go driving with you. I'm so very glad you are here." And then she disappeared.

She was back in a wink. Before Geoff rightly knew where he was, she had pulled him out into the morning sunshine. Chale pulled the curricle to an elegant halt just before the porch.

"Mornin', me lord," he hailed with his characteristic lopsided grin. He jumped nimbly down from the curricle and went to the horses' heads. He was favoring Heather with an appreciative stare. He had an eye for a pretty girl and wasn't above flirting with a chance-met serving-wench. Geoffrey coughed him back to attention.

"The Lady Margaret St. Vincent," he said by way of introduction. The groom's gleam quickly turned to brief amazement, and almost as quickly to the obeisance expected of a servant. He saluted her with a light touch of his forelock.

"Taking her for a drive," explained Geoff as he examined the splotchy horses with a keen and not unsatisfied eye.

"The luck was with me as ye can see, me lord. Had to go as far as Launceston, but I found me a good man there. That shaft's solid now, I'll swear. And these here monkeys move along right well, for all they're farm bred." He patted the muzzle of one of them familiarly.

Heather moved to the horses as well. She stroked their brown and white noses and murmured to them softly. They seemed to understand, for their big heads nodded in appreciation and they snorted a friendly response. Chale watched this performance closely, and the young lady went up a notch in his esteem.

"They're beautiful, are they not? I have so missed horses since coming to Heathside. May we go now, Geoff?" The beautiful eyes were shining with excitement, and Geoff was taken aback again by how big and expressive they were. They seemed to have little flecks of yellow in them when she was excited, like irises in spring. The long, dark lashes swept prettily up almost to her eyebrows.

THE RELUCTANT SUITOR 33

"Oh, sorry, what?" he asked, pulling himself from their violet depths with an effort.

"Our drive! C'mon."

"Oh, right! Good notion, that." She was pulling him toward the curricle with a happy laugh.

"They'll pull you along right fine, me lord, so you needn't worry fer the young lady. I'll be here waitin' to drive you to Launceston whenever you want."

"Launceston?" asked Geoff uncomprehendingly.

"I thought as how yer lordship was wishful of leavin' Cornwall and headin' back to London. You can't drive Tric and Trac, but I reckon you can hire these here brutes fer the first stage or two. I can bring the bays home by easy stages, me lord," he explained patiently.

"Oh, right. Exactly so."

"But, Geoff. Won't it take a very long time to drive yourself all the way to London? You promised you'd hurry."

"Oh, right. Exactly so," he repeated. "Oughtn't to take the time to drive myself. Quite right." He looked to Chale, on whom he had long since learned to rely for the answers to all sorts of vexing questions. "Thing is, I'm in a bit of a hurry, Chale. Can I get the London Stage at Launceston?"

"No, sir," the groom answered flatly. Geoffrey's face fell, but Heather's was looking even grimmer. The groom only looked curious. "But you can get the local coach to Exeter, me lord. From there you can catch the *Telegraph* right to the Gloucester Coffee House in Piccadilly."

"Done," said Geoff, relieved to have the question settled. "You can bring the curricle back yourself, Chale, when the bays are ready to travel." He turned to Heather. "C'mon then. One turn around the park, and I'm off."

"I wish you didn't have to go so soon, Geoff," she said as he handed her up into the carriage.

"You want to leave here before old platter-face gets back, don't you? Have to go to m'mother. Get you to London. You'll be safe with her. Can't stay here, and that's flat. I'll arrange it all."

He gave the horses the office to start, and they moved forward with a little lurch. Heather, letting the sunshine seep into her soul, filling her with light, gave herself up to the enjoyment of the drive.

The Viscount was a bit nervous driving unfamiliar cattle and didn't say much until Heather turned to him with a grin as he wheeled around a bend toward the dilapidated old gatehouse.

"How well you drive, Geoff." He flashed her a smile that could melt the sun.

"Well, been doing it forever, of course."

"I should love to be able to drive. Is it difficult?"

"Ain't easy, of course. But I expect you could learn. I'll teach you."

"Oh, Geoff, would you? I'm sure I couldn't want a better teacher."

All the animadversions of his friends, and even his groom, on his driving skill flew away as he basked in this obviously superior opinion of his abilities. "Course I will," he promised rashly.

They chattered gaily for awhile, but soon it was time to turn back. Heather said a rather tearful goodbye, Mrs. Bing at her side. Their plan had been imparted to the housekeeper, who had heartily applauded the idea. She was filled with gratitude for the Viscount, whom she hailed as the savior of her young mistress.

"Godspeed, sir, and bring ye back straightaway to take me pigeon here off. It'll be a spanking thing for her, sir, but I'll not rest easy in my bed till she be gone clean away from this place."

"Don't worry. I won't turn cat in the pan and shab off. Be back before old grumble-gizzard has even left Bath. M'mother'll see to Heather. Get her safely buckled." He lifted his beaver in salute. " 'Servant, ma'am, Heather." And he set his curricle in motion again. Chale sprung up lightly behind him, and they headed down the lane, the groom looking back curiously at the young woman who could make his master change all his plans of a sudden.

Heather stood before the house until long after the pair of them had disappeared from sight, then turned her attention to the dreams of adventure awaiting her in London. The rest of the day and evening passed in something of a daze. Heather, Ellen, and Mrs. Bing spoke of nothing but the impending escape.

As she stripped off her clothes, jumped hurriedly into a calico nightdress, and dove under the heavy woolen blankets that night in her icy bedchamber, it was not to sleep but to lie in her bed full of wonderful imaginings of the pleasures that lay before her. When at last she closed her eyes, it was to dream of London, and a young nobleman with sandy hair and twinkling blue-grey eyes.

Heather's dream was doomed to be brutally shattered the very next day. When Jurby, one of whose jobs it was to collect the post from the letter office in North Hill, came up to the house he carried a letter for Mrs. Bing. This was an unusual circumstance in itself, and Heather, who was mending her best petticoat before the kitchen fire, looked up with an interested eye. The stricken expression that crossed the housekeeper's face almost as soon as she broke the wafer on the letter made her jump up in alarm. "What is it, Bing? Is it bad news? Is it your brother in Essex, perhaps?"

"No, lamb. It isn't from Richard. It's from Bath. Yer cousin be comin' home early, Lady Margaret. The day after tomorrow, in fact. She's askin' that Jurby go with the whiskey to pick her up in Launceston."

"Day after tomorrow?" cried Heather mournfully. "But she can't! Oh, Bing, she can't! Geoff won't be back for me for another five days at least!" The stricken look on Mrs. Bing's face was completely outdone by the horror on Heather's delicate features. "If she comes back before Geoff takes me away, Bing, I shall *never* leave Heathside! I shall never go to London, or meet anyone, or have any friends, or, or *anything*, Bing! It isn't fair." To have her freedom snatched away just as it seemed within her grasp was too much. She sank down onto a chair and began to sob.

"Now, now, my little love," said the kindly old woman who had been the closest thing to a mother Heather had ever known. "I'll not let her keep ye here. There, there, love. Bing'll make it right." She was mouthing the sort of reassuring sounds she'd always given out when confronted by trouble, but now she realized suddenly that the words she had just uttered so thoughtlessly were true. She would *not* let that clutch-fisted old fidget keep her darlin' girl hidden away here any longer. The young Viscount had had a first-class idea when he thought to send the girl to his mother. She stiffened with resolution and bade her young charge to pay attention.

"Now listen to me careful, Lady Margaret. Do ye remember aught about this Lady Morpeth from yer days in Kent?"

"Well, she was very beautiful and seemed always to be smiling."

"But do you think she's a good woman as'll look after ye proper?" Her face on Heather's was very earnest.

"Yes. She was always very kind, and I think she liked me."

"Well," announced Bing with an air of finality. "Ye must go to her, child. It goes against the pluck with me to send ye, her not havin' invited ye as yet. But so I must do if ye're to have any chance at all in this life. I'll not have ye wastin' away here till ye're no more good to 'em at all, and then have ye tossed off by yer rightful family. It's to London ye must go."

"Bing! Do you think I could? Would Lady Morpeth not be very vexed with me for coming uninvited? To be sure, Geoff did seem certain that she would not mind to have me stay."

"And so ye must go, pet. But how are we to get ye there? I've enough money set by to send ye on the Mail, fer I'll not have ye travelin' on the common Stage, an' ye a lady born. But how we are to get ye to Exeter to catch it I don't know."

"I do!" piped up Ellen who had been listening to this exchange carefully. "My John."

"John Tanner? And what might he be havin' to do with this, miss?" asked Mrs. Bing, referring to the young farmer with whom Ellen had for a long time been "walking out."

"Well, you might know I finally brought him up to scratch, in a manner o' speakin'," she admitted with a healthy country blush. "We're to be married next month. He asked me last night."

"Ellen!" cried Heather, jumping up and giving her friend a solid hug. "I'm so happy for you. You'll make him a good wife."

"Aye, that I will, and so my John knows."

"It's right pleased I am fer ye, Elly," said Mrs. Bing

with a smile. "But what has yer John to do with gettin' Lady Margaret to Exeter?"

"He be goin' there tomorrow morn! In the hay cart."

"What? All the ways to Exeter? Whatever for?" asked Bing.

"Well, he *says* as how he be needful of a milch cow 'fore he brings a wife to home. That's me, in course," she added unnecessarily and with a pert little twinkle. "But if ye was to ask me, what he truly be thinkin' he's needful of is a bit of a fling off to Exeter town before I pulls in the reins, which yer may be sure I will do an' no mistake." She gave a conspiratorial smile and added, "Though I'll take good care he don't feel 'em much. But I knows well there ain't no call to go all that ways to Exeter jest to buy hisself a milch cow, fer all they got their fancy cattle fair goin' on. I daresay he ain't never been further off than Liskeard," she said with the fine sense of disdain of one who had once traveled a full ten miles farther than this to Tavistock to visit her aunt. "Why he knows sure as day that old farmer Crungett down to Linkinhorne has a right pretty little lady cow he'd be happy to part with fer a price, an' fine milk she gives, too, I'm thinkin'. But I don't begrudge my John his bit o' fun, fer it's the last time he goes to anywheres without his lady wife next and nigh him, an' that I will swear." She paused, and her grin peeked out. "An' I do like a nice bit o' cream in a mug o' tea, yer know, an' they'm do say that Devonshire cows give the best."

"Aye, that they do," agreed Mrs. Bing, but she was not to be sidetracked from the problem at hand. "Yer John is jest the man we need, I'm thinkin'. Can he be trusted to see Lady Margaret safe to Exeter? It do be a long ways."

"In course he can, Mrs. Bing!" answered Ellen indignantly. She might poke gentle fun at her prospective mate, but she bridled like a cornered wolf over her pups at the hint that anyone else might do the same. "My John be the solidest man in these parts, and well yer know it!"

"No need to flare up now, Elly. John Tanner be a fine man, and yer right, I do know it. But I be that afeared fer my lamb." She couldn't keep the worried look from her face as she gazed at Heather and wrung her apron in her hands.

"Don't be, Bing," said Heather. "I shall be all right. Really I shall. I'm sure John will take good care of me. And once I am in Exeter, what can happen, after all?"

"Oh, Missy, I wish I knew! Well now, there's nothin' fer it. Ye've no future at all if ye stay here. That's a fact. And if yer cousin is comin' back in two days, we have to get ye safe away as soon as can be. Go ye off, Elly, and ask yer John if he'll oblige us by takin' Lady Margaret with him tomorrow."

"Oh, he'll take her, all right," chirped Ellen. "I'll tell him so meself if he doubts it." She jumped down from the edge of the scarred oak table where she'd been perched, peeling potatoes into a heavy pan, untied her apron, tucked up a stray curl that had escaped her cap, and went merrily off.

Long before the sun had descended to the horizon, Heather's plans were complete, her meagre belongings were packed in a battered old valise, and she floated through her last night at Heathside. Her emotions rose and fell like the tides from excitement at the impending journey, to sadness at leaving Bing, to a healthy fear of the unknown. And through them all ran a strong current of happiness at the thought that she would soon see Geoff again, and he would be her friend.

Chapter Five

Used to rising early, as every true country girl was, Heather was wide awake almost before the sun peeked over the hills. She slipped out of the house that had been her prison for so long, and climbed up eagerly onto the hay wagon of Ellen's swain, dutifully waiting by the kitchen garden. As she settled onto the hard wooden seat, Mrs. Bing waded out of the house and handed her a small black leather purse, heavy and clinking with coins.

"I've always feared—nay hoped—that ye'd find a way to slip away like this, child. So I've been settin' a bit by each month, from the bit o' housekeepin' money the old lady gives me." The rosy face blushed a deeper red at her own daring. "An' I'll be bound she never knew, nor suspected neither, stingy though she be. Well, that's no longer here nor there, but I've said I'll not have ye, rightful daughter of a real earl, travelin' on the common Stage with all the raff 'n' draff of the countryside. No, it's the Royal Mail ye'll take to London, an' here's the money to pay fer it."

She handed Heather the purse, then blustered and fidgeted about the hay cart, bringing another rug for the girl's knees, and handing up a large basket of fruit, cheese, and pasties to eat along the way.

"Now ye're to put that money safe inside yer petticoat pocket, mind. Give the guard half a crown when ye're to London. *And*," she admonished, "ye're to take a proper hackney cab straight to Lady Morpeth's house." The stern tone dissolved in a wringing of hands. "Oh, how I do wish I could be goin' with ye, pet, jest to be sure that ye'll come to no harm." The wrinkled face wrinkled up further in a sound perilously like a sob.

Heather hopped from the cart and was immediately

buried in the warm and well-loved bosom, amid the comforting smells of green apples and fresh-baked bread. The two ladies, young and old, clung to each other a moment.

"I'll send for you, Bing," promised Heather from the depths of the ample bosom. "Just as soon as I can. You must promise to come, Bing."

"And where else should I be but with my lamb? Of course, I'll come." Her sobs had finished.

All bustle and efficiency again, Mrs. Bing shooed Heather back up onto the cart, saw her well wrapped up against the breeze, and, with several admonitions to John Tanner to be careful how he drove and not to stop at any low hedge-taverns, she saw the pair on their way.

Saddened though Heather was at taking leave of her two most steadfast friends, her excitement was enormous, and her first glimpses of the countryside beyond the bounds of her prison were too great to allow her to be depressed. The huge eyes scanned the hills, taking in every detail. White-faced cows and black-faced sheep dotted the meadows like puffs of dandelion on an overgrown lawn. Moisture still hung on the morning air and clung in droplets to the hedge veronica and cow parsley that lined their route.

John Tanner was a desultory conversationalist at the best of times, and this morning he was somewhat awed by his company. Heather tried several times to draw him into conversation, but he would answer only with a "Yes, mum," or "I don't rightly know, mum" albeit always with an engaging grin. Heather liked his open, friendly farmer's face and knew a brief moment of envy for Ellen's good fortune in attaching such a man.

She finally gave up her attempts to get him to talk and abandoned her thoughts to the delightful time she would have in London. Maybe Geoff would take her to see the Tower and the lions at Exeter 'Change. Everything would be new, and exciting, and delightful.

Such thoughts could fill only a limited number of hours, however, and the trip to Exeter was a long one. Well before that budding metropolis came into view, she had wearied of the jolting and was beginning to feel as though she had been riding under the cart instead of on it. With very little fat to cushion the bumps, she felt bruised all over by the time the twin Norman towers of the ancient cathedral came into view.

The day was far advanced when the farmer pulled his horse to a stop in front of the Post Office. Heather handed him her precious purse, and off he went to purchase her ticket and place her name on the waybill. He was back almost before she'd had time to notice the delightful little half-timbered houses clustered near the church or the bits of Roman wall still partially surrounding it.

"Here's yer ticket, mum," said John as he handed back her sadly diminished purse. "Ye'll come with me now over to the Crown and Feathers there. They'm be good people, the guard says, as'll take good care on ye till ye leave."

Heather stared. This was certainly the greatest number of words that she had ever heard the farmer string together at one time. He helped her down onto the gravel road and led her to a pleasant-looking inn across the way.

They entered a dark-beamed and cozy room presided over by a robust and rounded landlady, brushing flour from her hands.

"And what may ye be wantin', good farmer?" she asked with an undeniable hint of resolution to allow no rabble into her respectable house.

"The Young Miss here be waitin' fer the Mail, mum, an' she be needful of a good hot mug o' tea, with plenty o' sugar, mind, an' a respectable place to sit till it be time to go."

The great bulk of the woman looked past him to where Heather was trying hard not to hide, and the huge violet eyes peeked around his broad back to meet two shining blue ones nearly lost in the folds of flesh that surrounded them. Their vague hint of hostility quickly melted into something like a smile. Heather was reminded so strongly of Mrs. Bing that she smiled back, gave a shy curtsy, and said softly, "If you would be so kind, ma'am."

The landlady's heart opened to the little waiflike creature. She shooed the farmer out of her spotless room, allowing Heather to give him only a quick thank-you and a light kiss on the cheek from which he blushed scarlet, and bustled her into the coffeeroom. She settled the girl into a comfortable settle in the sunshine and went off directly to get the tea.

She was back in a wink, with a clatter of crockery and a clucking of her little cherry mouth.

"Och, child! Yer look fagged to death. Now here's yer tea, all nice an' hot. So thin an' pale as ye be, poor thing."

"You're very kind, ma'am. It smells delicious."

"Och! An' I'd not rest in my bed to send a poor child off alone on the Night Mail without a good strong cup o' tea in her, an' that's God's truth."

When Heather crossed back to the Post Office at a few minutes before eight o'clock to board the impressive maroon and black coach with "Royal Mail" picked out importantly on its side, she was rested, warm, and filled with the contentment that comes from being well cared for. She was well wrapped up in the landlady's second-best shawl, which had been pressed upon her, try though she might to refuse it, with instructions to leave it with the guard in London, who would see it safe returned.

Her fellow passengers were boarding the coach as their names were read off the waybill. A huge and puffing Mr. Nobb was wheezing his way up the steps to the outside seats atop the coach, muttered oaths and a distinct smell of stale tobacco and ale punctuating each degree of the ascent.

He was followed by a vaguely canonical-looking Mr. Ridgely and his wife. The latter was so muffled up in shawls and cloaks, mufflers and scarves, against the exigencies of an outside passage, that her cronic whining was blessedly muffled as well and her tiny person all but invisible as the huge pile of garments was assisted onto its perch.

Next on the list came Mr. Wadebrill, a stringy-looking gentleman of indeterminate age and tutorial mien, accompanied by a sturdy young fellow, obviously his pupil. Tucked under Mr. Wadebrill's arm was his traveling arsenal consisting of *Mr. Carey's Itinerary of the Great Roads of England and Wales*, 1814 edition; half a dozen handkerchiefs; a large snuffbox, recently filled; a traveling rug; two vinaigrettes; and a pillow. His pupil's arsenal was simpler, with only a slingshot projecting from his right pocket, a dozen good round pebbles in his left, a large bag of barley sugar in his hand, and a bright green apple in his

THE RELUCTANT SUITOR 43

mouth. The two of them climbed inside and settled in for the long trip.

"Yes, yes, Mrs. Hatcherly, that's me. I'm here, I'm here. No need to caterwaul after me," Mrs. Hatcherly caterwauled. She was a brown-faced and ham-handed woman, wrapped about with a strong smell of fish. She scrambled, surprisingly nimbly, up to the top of the coach.

Lastly, a pleasant-faced, round-cheeked Mrs. Beeven, climbed inside, giving the company a friendly smile. Heather followed and settled comfortably into her own corner of the coach, enjoying the luxury of the leather squabs after the rough board of Farmer Tanner's hay cart.

Through the window she watched the guard, in impressive Royal livery of scarlet and black, making his final preparations. He locked his timepiece into its pouch and strapped it securely around his waist, double-checked his time-bill, and took up his formidable array of weapons: a blunderbuss, a brace of pistols, and a cutlass. A shiver of anxiety passed through Heather as she wondered into what unknown dangers they were heading that could possibly call for such an armory. But the might looked quite capable of defending them all. She sank back to enjoy her trip.

" 'Isca Dumnoniorum, as the Romans called the city of Exeter, is the site of the oldest remaining guild-hall building in England,' " the tutor began reading in a droning voice. " 'The present building dates from 1460, though the portico is Elizabethan, together with the, . . . Master Gerald, if you please."

The boy pulled his head in from the opposite window, turning on the tutor a look of angelic innocence, as a screech came from outside. The boy no longer had his apple, the core of which had apparently just been propelled, with pinpoint accuracy, at the ostrich plume of a passing bonnet. Since the possessor of the bonnet was beneath it at the moment of impact, she was, quite naturally, not best pleased by this behavior and stalked up to the coach at once, bellowing in outraged accents.

"Here, boy! Yes, you, boy! Nasty little thing! You, sir. Are you in charge of this young ruffian? I'll have you know, sir, that this little monster . . ." The air was rent by a long blast from the guard's yard of tin, and the Royal

Mail, which waits for no one, however outraged, hurtled off in the direction of London.

Although it was already eight o'clock in the evening, it was not yet quite dark as they pulled away from Exeter, and Heather could see quite clearly the countryside outside the coach windows. After the plodding of John Tanner's old cob, the fields and hedgerows seemed to be whizzing by at an alarming rate. The four good horses, changed at frequent intervals, would see them all in to London at the earliest possible moment.

" 'The village of Clyst Honiton is noted for its church, which is typical of the sandstone architecture of this part of Devonshire.' " Mr. Wadebrill had a voice rather like an overnectared bee in the heat of a summer's day, a sort of slow, halfhearted droning, with heavy overtones of DUTY in every syllable. But mercifully, it soon grew too dark for him to read from his very thorough guidebook, and it was tucked away without the least sign of regret on anyone's part.

"Are you traveling far, dear?"

Heather realized with a start that the question was directed at her. She turned to Mrs. Beevan with a smile. "To London, ma'am."

"Oh, my! Such a long trip for a young girl on her own. Have you family there?"

"Yes, ma'am," she lied.

Mrs. Beeven's chatty nature needed no more than that. "How nice. I am going to visit my married daughter in Salisbury, you know." She was off and running. Her artless chatter carried them several miles and whiled away several hours.

By the time Charmouth was reached, all four occupants of the coach interior were fast asleep, the gentle swaying of a well-sprung coach on a good road acting like the rocking of a cradle.

The sun slanting through the window woke Heather a little before six. She was bone-cold and stiff and thankful for the extra warmth of the landlady's second-best shawl. She sat up, stretched, and wrapped it firmly about her, gazing out the window at the countryside still whizzing past.

"Breakfast stop!" announced the guard as they rolled

into Tarrant Hinton. "Twenty minutes! And mind you're back in the coach on time. The Mail doesn't wait!"

Everyone was thankful for a chance to move about a bit and stretch their legs, Heather among them. She was not particularly refreshed, however, by her "breakfast," consisting as it did of a slice of cold toast and a cup of tea too hot to drink. Precisely twenty minutes after it had stopped, the coach rumbled off again.

The countryside seemed to change little with the miles, and Heather drifted into a doze that carried her all the way to Salisbury, where she bade goodbye to Mrs. Beevan and nodded hello to Reverend Carpinkle.

By the time the luncheon stop at the White Hart at Overton arrived, she found she was developing a headache from the ceaseless swaying of the coach.

She nodded and gave a weak smile when Mr. Wadebrill and Master Gerald departed and were replaced by two middle-aged brothers, looking so exactly alike that it came as no surprise when they both fell promptly asleep, as if on cue, and began to snore in perfect harmony. The company was also augmented by the tiniest woman Heather had ever seen.

Miss Patterson took Heather to her tiny bosom at once, and regaled her for the rest of the way to London with witty sayings and sage advice on everything from the best manner of dressing a haunch of venison to how to go about finding a husband in London. It did just occur to Heather that perhaps the little spinster was not the best source for this sort of advice, but the lively little woman, with a grin a mile wide, served to happily while away the remaining hours.

It was nearing evening when the coach approached the metropolis. Heather's first glimpse of London was filled with wonder. The coach rolled over the noisy cobbled streets amid congestion that was overwhelming. The shops, their windows sparkling with goods of every description, were still open for business; the flagways were thronged with shoppers, loungers, promenaders, delivery boys, and street vendors of every conceivable sort.

Heather had never seen so many coaches, chaises, tilburies, phaetons, horses, handcarts, soldiers, sailors, fine ladies, and ragamuffins all at once. Bollards at the intersections did their best to control the teeming masses and untangle the hapless horses. Oaths filled the air as jarveys tried to wriggle their hackney carriages past donkey carts and high-perch phaetons. The guard atop the Mail Coach blew his long brass horn in every direction to try to clear a path. The cries of an old woman selling playbills and oranges mixed with that of another crying, "Apples a-baking. Fine hot sweet apples!" in a loud, musical voice.

The beautiful dome of St. Paul's glowed softly in the sharply angled rays of the setting sun, as the coach turned into the cobbled yard of The Swan with Two Necks in Lad Lane. The yard of the popular coaching inn was a busy hive, a jumble of coaches, people, mailbags, caged animals, portmanteaus, and a general air of confusion such as Heather had never ever imagined. The wild moorland of Cornwall seemed a million miles away.

Miss Patterson deftly guided her through the throng, striding (if such a thing is possible in a woman whose legs seem barely long enough to reach the ground) purposely toward the street, towing Heather after her.

"Now, Miss," she said as they reached the relative safety of the pavement, "you go off now and find yourself a nice husband, do. Here's a hackney cab to take you anywhere you want to go. Be a good girl, you hear?" The tiny thing stood on tiptoe and planted a kiss of Heather's cheek, then disappeared back into the crowd.

Heather, now truly on her own, approached the hackney driver unsurely.

"Can you take me to Clarges Street, please?"

The jarvey stopped picking his teeth and peered down at the child in the big cap. "Clarges Street, eh? That's a six-bob ride, Missy."

"Six bob?" she parroted uncomprehendingly.

"Six shillings! You got six shillings, little lady?"

"Oh," she replied, understanding at last. It seemed like a lot of money, but she was sure she had just enough to cover it. "Yes, sir, I have six shillings."

The skeptical look on his grizzled face grew. "And would you mind showin' it to me then, Missy?"

His manner struck Heather as singularly unpleasant, but she supposed it must be the custom in London to pay in advance. She gave him the money, his face cracked into a wide grin, and he said, "So it's Clarges Street, is it? Well, get you on up, then. I ain't got all night."

Throughout what Heather would always remember as an eventful ride she saw nothing more of London. Her eyes were shut tight, and she was holding onto the strap as tightly as she could manage. The carriage swayed alarmingly over the stones, swung sharply around corners, and skidded past other coaches with inches to spare. She prayed her first day in London would not also be her last.

The horses wheezed to a stop; the coach seemed to settle with a sigh in front of a pleasant house. No sooner had she alighted than the coach spun off again down the street, covering her with a fine layer of dust.

She turned to the house, momentarily taken aback by the fact that no lights seemed to be burning in any of the upstairs rooms. But at least she was here. She mounted the stairs, took a deep breath, and raised the heavy brass knocker.

Chapter Six

"I can only repeat that Lady Morpeth is presently from home and is not expected back for some days," the stately butler intoned in lofty accents, and the big oak door began to swing shut in Heather's face.

"Wait, please!" she cried, struggling to keep a desperate tone from her voice. "I am a friend of Geoffrey. Viscount Morpeth, I mean. Can you tell me where to find him? I'm sure he will help me."

The butler's wooden countenance looked genuinely alarmed. Whatever would the young master think of him if he were to send importunate country wenches round to his lodgings? "Certainly not! If his lordship wishes to see you, I am sure he will inform me of that fact." This time the door closed in earnest, and Heather was left alone on the darkened porch. Despair threatened to overwhelm her. She had nowhere to go and no money left; she was left on her own in this very overpowering city. She turned in a daze and ambled off aimlessly down the street.

She crossed Piccadilly and made her way into the Green Park. Sinking onto the fresh coolness of the grass, she began to cry quietly.

Soon she noticed a tall young man, dressed in beautiful livery of scarlet and silver, grinning down at her. She had never seen anyone quite so impressive before; his powdered and long-tailed wig made him look like the portraits of old mad King George. She remembered Ellen's brusque manner with the local fellows when they became too bold. Drying her eyes quickly and putting on her best country-wench voice, she demanded, "Whatcher lookin' at then?"

To her surprise, the footman boomed out a happy laugh. "Why, you to be sure. And might fine looking it is too."

"Well yer can jest be on about yer business, an' leave me ta mine!" she retorted, standing squarely up to him now, though she scarce reached his shoulder.

"And what might that business be, I'm askin' myself. And what's it got to do with my mistress or Viscount Morpeth, for well I know that he ain't one to dally with serving-girls."

The Ellen manner disappeared in a rush. "Oh, you know Geoff! Will you tell me where to find him? I would be so grateful. And so would he, too."

"Hold on! I might be able to help you, and then again I might not. How do I know his lordship'll be wishful to see you. You don't hardly look his type."

"I don't?" she asked before thinking. "Well, anyway, he *will* wish to see me. Really! We're very old friends. And he is arranging with his mama to take care of me. So you see, if you leave me here in the Park with nowhere to go, he will be very angry with you. Very angry indeed! You see, I'm, I'm Lady Morpeth's goddaughter!"

"Hah!" he boomed out. "And the King's your uncle, I suppose!"

She felt she had lost, and a single large teared rolled silently down her cheek.

"Here, no call for that," said the footman kindly. The wench was devilish pretty, and he would have liked a touch at her himself. But if Master Geoffrey wanted her protected, he'd better help. It didn't seem she would have mentioned Lady Morpeth in just that way if she was one of his lordship's chères-amies. Besides, she didn't have the look of one about her. Looked more like a baby, if you wanted to know. With a smile, he finally gave Heather exact directions on how to reach the Viscount's lodgings in Albany. She thanked him prettily and headed off down Piccadilly, not knowing that she had made an ally in her campaign on London.

As it happened, she hadn't far to go. Albany, elegant home to dashing London bachelors, was only a short way down Piccadilly, and she was shortly turning into its cobbled court, where flowers bloomed happily and the street sounds were blessedly muffled. She tripped across the yard and entered the building.

"Yes, miss," came a disapproving voice. "What can I do for you?"

Heather thought she had never heard anyone speak in such arctic tones. She felt frozen to the bone by the supercilious doorkeeper. When she turned to look him in the eye, his glacial gaze intensified the chill. She gathered whatever poise she might possess and said in clear tones, "I would like to see Viscount Morpeth, if you please."

The man's white hair might have been dusted with snow instead of hair powder for all the melting her words produced. The frozen eyebrows inched up a notch as a single icicle word formed on the blue lips. "Indeed?"

"Y-yes sir," she replied, trying not to shiver.

"Is his lordship expecting you?"

"Well, not precisely," she admitted. "But he will be pleased to see me, I assure you. You may tell him that I am here. My name is . . .".

Before she could finish, the iceberg spoke again. "I'm afraid that would be quite impossible. His lordship has left no instructions with me to admit any Young Person to his chambers. When he wishes to see you, I assure you that he will do so."

For the second time that evening, Heather was about to have a door closed in her face. She had no way of knowing that Albany, of all places in London, was the last at which a respectable young lady would allow herself to be seen.

She was growing desperately afraid. "But I must see Geoff. Really I must. I assure you he will be very angry if you do not let me in."

His only answer was a scowl; his snowy head loomed over her in a very menacing fashion. She cowered and would have scurried across the courtyard like a rabbit had not the door at the opposite end of the hall opened at that moment. Since she had so little to lose, she hoped she might petition whoever was coming through that door to carry a message to Geoff. Brushing past the scandalized doorkeeper, she threw herself across the tiled hall toward a large young gentleman with a friendly face.

He was addressing an unseen companion behind him and so didn't see the hurtling form fast closing on him. A furious "Here, I say!" issuing from the doorkeeper caused

THE RELUCTANT SUITOR 51

him to look around just in time to have his hand seized by a frightened-looking child with enormous eyes. He was too amazed to speak.

"Oh, sir, will you help me please? This gentleman will not let me speak to Geoff, and I must. Really I must! Viscount Morpeth, I mean. Would you be so kind as to..."

Before she could finish, the companions of her would-be savior came through the door, staring in astonishment.

"What the... Damme!" The exclamation was cut off short, and she turned to see Viscount Morpeth staring at her open-mouthed.

"Geoff!" she squealed in delight. "Oh, Geoff, thank God!" The scowl on his face stopped her in the act of throwing herself at him in her relief. "Please don't be angry with me, Geoff. I had no choice but to come to London. Truly I didn't."

"What the deuce... Oh, never mind!" he ground out, seeing the *very* interested expression of the doorkeeper. Whatever harebrained stunt Heather was up to, he couldn't leave her here in the hallway to be exposed to the stares of the curious. He grabbed her hand and pulled her rudely back through the door he had himself just entered.

She soon found herself in a comfortable and masculine sitting room, its walls crowded with sporting prints, its furniture overflowing with copies of the *Racing Calendar*, the *Turf Guide*, and *The Gentlemen's Magazine*. In short, a typical bachelor's lodgings.

"Sit down!" said Geoff in an uncharacteristically peremptory manner. She wanted to obey and looked around for a free chair, but every surface seemed to be covered with a clutter of spurs, riding crops, brandy glasses, jars of snuff, packs of cards, sets of dice, newspapers, and journals, and all the other paraphernalia of a young gentleman on the town who was sporting mad. Crossing to the chair that seemed least cluttered, she gently removed a copy of *Broughton's Rules of the Ring* and perched, gazing at her friend in some trepidation.

He seemed to become aware of the fact that his two companions were surveying the girl with clearly interested expressions. He opened his mouth to order them out, then thought better of it. He'd only compromise Heather further by being alone with her. Also, he knew for a certainty that he was in deep water and likely to need a towline soon.

The three young gentlemen were in vivid contrast to one another. Geoff introduced the large kind-looking young man to whom Heather had first applied for assistance as Courtney Blascomb, the Right Honourable the Earl of Pythe. He favored her with an engaging grin and a simple bow. He was correctly but simply dressed in a comfortably cut coat of nut-brown kerseymere, matching pantaloons, a plain yellow waistcoat, and excellent boots. A simply tied cravat set off the strong veins in his neck and the line of his pleasant square-jawed face.

The other gentleman was the Honourable Robert Ayrton. His eyes twinkled with a mixture of mischief and curiosity as he swept her a low, graceful bow. His lithe figure showed to advantage in a superb black coat of superfine, impeccably fitted black pantaloons, a white piqué waistcoat, and a neck-cloth *à la Sentimentale*. The monochromatic ensemble served to heighten his brooding and romantic good looks in the Byronic mould, complete with dark curling locks. " 'Servant, ma'am," he said with a smile.

Heather turned a prettily turned-up smile of her own to them and gave each a proper curtsy. "My lord, Mr. Ayrton, I am pleased to make your acquaintance."

They gazed at her intently, for the good manners and cultured voice belied the simple servant's dress. A few seconds of confused hesitation and Geoffrey took the plunge. "The Lady Margaret St. Vincent," he blurted out. His friends' faces turned comical in their surprise.

The Earl of Pythe gave out a startled "I say!" while Mr. Ayrton only stared. After a moment of thought, he said, "St. Vincent? Stonington, ain't it?"

"Yes, sir. The Earl of Stonington was my father."

"I say!" repeated the Earl.

Geoff had been considering how much of Heather's story to share with his friends. For all their differences, the three had been fast friends for years. From the days at Eton, when Court Blascomb had covered for the others after one of their madder adventures and saved them a caning, through Oxford, where Robin Ayrton had drilled and tutored his friends through more than one exam-

THE RELUCTANT SUITOR

ination, the three had been nearly as inseparable as musketeers under Louis the Fourteenth.

So Geoff's hesitation was short-lived. As soon as he'd heard from Heather the reason for her precipitate flight from Heathside, he poured out her whole story to his friends.

"I always said Stonington was a rascally scrub," exclaimed Mr. Ayrton with feeling. "To treat his own sister in such a shabby way! Damme if I haven't got half a mind to call the fellow out!" His black eyes flashed at the delightful prospect.

"No!" cried three voices in unison.

"Do us no good," said Geoff. "Probably wouldn't go out with you anyway. Stands to reason. Why should he? Doesn't even know you." He paused then added, "Probably a damned good shot anyway."

"Are you implying that I couldn't hit him?" Mr. Ayrton's brow darkened in a menacing manner.

"You can't help Lady Margaret that way," said the Earl calmly.

"If I kill the rotter it will help her," he pointed out reasonably. He paced energetically before the dying fire, dark eyes kindling, muttering on the iniquities of the Earl of Stonington and making no more useful suggestion whatever.

The Earl threw himself into a comfortable chair, having ruthlessly swept to the floor one card case, a tinderbox, a cricket bat, and three framed caricatures of the Regent. Hands thrust deep in his pockets and long legs stretched out before him, he stared at the floor in thought.

Heather turned a worried face on Mr. Ayrton. "If you challenge Bo to a duel he will know I'm here, and he will send my cousin to fetch me. Besides, I don't really think I should like you to kill Bo, for he is my brother, even though he has not always been very kind to me. And I *know* I shouldn't like it if he were to kill you." The look she bestowed on the young man, who was much given to thinking himself a handsome young devil, caused his ill temper to flee with a swiftness that left his lifelong friends amazed.

"Well, the first thing is to fetch your mother, Geoff," he said practically. "Where is she?"

"How the devil should I know? Got a bee in her bonnet to toddle off, I daresay."

"Morpeth?" asked the Earl.

"Dash it all, Court. You've seen the place. Would *you* go there if you didn't have to?"

"No," he admitted. "But it's not mine."

"Say!" exclaimed Mr. Ayrton. "Isn't she a friend of my mother?"

"What's that to say to anything?"

"She's gone to Oatlands. My mother, I mean. The Duchess is having some sort of a do. You know the type. Might your mother be there too?"

"Course she would!" exclaimed Geoff in triumph. "Just what she would do. Devilish fond of the Duchess and all her blasted dogs."

"But, Geoff," said Heather. "Will she have planned a long stay?"

"Don't signify if she did. Bring her back!"

"Yes," concurred the Earl.

"But you cannot, Geoff!" said Heather. "Whatever will she think of me, barging in on her uninvited, causing her to change all her plans? She'll hate me."

"Don't be a muttonhead. Why should she? Curst bore, anyway, Oatlands. Daresay she'll be glad of an excuse to leave. Fetch her tomorrow."

"Yes, do that," said Pythe solidly.

"But what shall you do with Lady Margaret in the meantime?" asked Mr. Ayrton. "She can't stay here."

"Of course she can't stay here. But what the devil am I to do with her?"

"But why can I not stay here, Geoff?"

"Why? Why?" he asked with a look of disbelief.

Mr. Ayrton gave a cough of embarrassment. "It won't do, Lady Margaret. No Young Lady of Quality should even be seen near the lodgings of an unmarried gentleman. If you stayed here your reputation would be beyond saving. We must find you someplace safe until Lady Morpeth can be fetched back."

"Oh, I see," said Heather quietly. She certainly had a lot to learn about how to go on in London.

"Got it!" said the Earl, rising like a Phoenix to his full six feet plus. "Goodie!" he stated with satisfaction. He looked at the others who were waiting for him to follow up this unusual statement of glee with his suggestion. "Goodie," he repeated clearly. Still they stared. "Mrs. Goodfellow, you dunces! My old nurse. Lives in a cottage at Crouch End, not much of a drive from here. She'll look after Lady Margaret till your mother comes back."

"Capital idea!" the others chimed in.

Not much more than an hour later Heather found herself tucked up in an enormous feather bed in a cozy cottage at Crouch End. A down quilt was pulled up to her chin, and she was spooning up thick Scotch broth while simultaneously pouring out every detail of her young life to the woman seated at her bedside.

On arrival in this picturesque corner of Hornsey, Heather had been taken aback by "Goodie." The name seemed singularly inappropriate for the wizened little old woman who had answered their knock. She was dressed in a costume all her own; a long black woolen thing, suspiciously like a priest's cassock, grown green with age at cuffs and elbows, a shiny red silk kerchief about her neck and a pristine white apron, tied in a perky bow. On her head was a tiny puff of a black cap, threaded through with red and white ribbons, perched on springy, iron-grey curls. Below the curls was a pleated, crinkled-up face dominated by a beak of a nose. She looked altogether so much like a little old witch that Heather was hard put to it to keep from peering round for her broom.

The image flashed for a second only, as the old woman creaked open her door. But it was doomed to extinction almost at once. For as soon as the brilliant blue eyes lighted on the Earl, the wrinkled up face cracked into a happy smile. And that, of course, made all the difference.

"Och! An' it's me douce lad himself!" came a voice so full and deep that Heather at first thought it must have come from a source behind the woman: the big pot on the fire perhaps, or the chimney itself, but surely not this tiny bit of a thing all but disappearing into the bear hug that the Earl was giving her.

The foursome was ushered into the cottage, and Heather was reassured to see that it was quite ordinary and comfortable, not in the least like a witch's den.

"Now sit ye down, one and all, and bide awee while I

mask the tea. It willna be but a moment." Almost at once they were sipping the fragrant brew, and the Earl began to relate Heather's story.

The pleated eyes opened wider, two bright spots of blue sparking with anger, as she learned of the treatment to which Heather had been subjected.

"Aye, 'n' it's a good lad to bring the bonny wean to me," she said with a good deal of feeling and a shake of her head that set her wisp of a cap to fluttering. She took Heather's hand in her own knarled one. "An' such a pale, skinny bairn as ye be, poor lass, for all ye are a bonny one. Ye do look a bit peaked like, an' that be something I can fix. I ken it well how to feed up a hungry child."

She shooed the gentlemen on their way. "Dinna fash yerselves over the lass while she be here, lads. I willna see her come to harm." And they were on their way.

For all the love and worry that Mrs. Bing had showered on Heather in the last few years, she could barely remember a time when she had felt so "cared for" as she did at Mrs. Goodfellow's. The old Scotswoman firmly believed in the ability of her native foods to cure all ills, both of the body and the spirit, and she served up a constant stream of skirlie, bap, finnan haddie, and buttery buns. And she listened. She encouraged the girl to tell her story completely, and Heather found herself basking in the unaccustomed attention.

Late the next day a message from Geoff informed them that he had indeed found his mother at Oatlands, where she had been visiting the Duchess of York. She remembered Heather as a big-eyed child with an impish grin and a cat's curiosity and was delighted at the prospect of having her to visit. She felt fully confident that she'd soon find her an excellent husband. She told Geoff to fetch her at once.

"So yer lad'll be here tomorrow forenoon for ye, child," said Mrs. Goodfellow with satisfaction. She gave Heather a keen glance. "Ye do be afeared yet, I see. What is it, lass?" she rumbled out in the low, rough voice Heather had come to love.

"Could I not stay here with you, Goodie? You could tell Geoff that I've decided I don't want to live with his mama." Heather, on the brink of her adventure, was afraid.

"If I judge that lad aright he, wouldna take tellin'. An' och, lass, what good in heaven would it be? Dinna ye ken, child, that it's London where ye must be? I can feed ye, an' I can love ye, but find ye a husband I cannot. And a husband is what ye must have."

Seeing the fear writ large in the girl's eyes, she reached out a knarly hand that was yet soft to the touch and stroked Heather's cheek. "Ye needna worry, child. The good lady'll have a care of ye. Ye'll ne'er agin have such a chance to be happy, child. Gang ye must, an' I'll be here praying that a douce lad'll come along for ye and make ye his glowin' bride." She tucked Heather up into the big feather bed. Tomorrow was London.

Chapter Seven

"Mrs. Bing!" flared Honoria Stapleton in a voice of doom. "WHERE IS LADY MARGARET?"

It was the day after Heather's flight from Heathside, and Miss Stapleton had just received the news. The cage of Heathside, in which she had for the last six years imprisoned her young cousin, had creaked open in her absence, and the bird had flown. Mrs. Bing had put on quite a convincing show of ignorance, despair, and overwrought emotions. She was secretly quite pleased at her performance, for she had been rehearsing this scene ever since seeing her young lady off with John Tanner.

Ellen too put up a fine facade of the servent fretting herself to pieces over the mysterious disappearance of her young mistress. The story that the two ladies had concocted for Miss Stapleton's benefit was perfect in its simplicity. Lady Margaret St. Vincent had just vanished. When they had come down to breakfast the day before, she had not appeared. They thought to let her sleep awhile. When her room had been checked it was discovered that not only was the young lady missing, but so was an old valise, her night things, and her heavy cloak.

A sort of croak seemed to issue from somewhere deep inside Honoria Stapleton's old bones. A stricken look shot across her face. She wheeled, and hurried from the room, coming as close to running as an energetic and frightened lady of sixty could manage. She charged up the stairs and into her bedchamber, emptied several jars onto her vanity in her haste to find a certain key, unlocked and jerked open a small drawer, and gave a shriek like an animal caught in the jaws of a steel trap.

"The jewels!" she howled. "My pearls! My sapphires! They're gone! The little thief has run off with my jewels!"

58

They were not, of course, her jewels at all. The magnificent black pearls and the pretty, delicate set of sapphires had belonged to Heather's mother. They were all that remained of a once-glorious collection, purchased in the main by Heather's grandfather in his travels and bestowed upon his pretty and adored daughter. All the jewelry had been left to Heather in her mother's will, but her brother had long since sold off most of it to pay his gambling debts. That they were not his to sell bothered him not at all. Selling the jewels of his undeserving little half-sister was decidedly easier than selling her out of the Funds.

For the present he was content to let the last few pieces of the collection remain at Heathside. He had somewhat hinted to his cousin Honoria that the few remaining pieces would constitute a part of her reward for her role as warder to his sister, and he rather liked the notion of their constant presence before her, like a carrot on a stick. She must never forget that it was in her best interests to keep his sister close-guarded, and above all unmarried. He wasn't really worried about her. The old woman was completely under his thumb. But the jewels served as insurance. He let them remain at Heathside.

Honoria had taken to wearing the jewelry at times. The cool beauty of the pearls, the elegant lights in the glowing sapphires, soothed away some of the bitterness of years. And even Heather had come to think of the gems as belonging to her cousin. She had suffered a severe struggle with her conscience, and a brisk talking-to by Mrs. Bing, before finally accepting her right to take away her very own property.

Miss Stapleton stood up abruptly, her petticoats crackling, as she strode to the door. Hand on the knob, she turned to the two servants. "I shall find her!" And she swept from the room.

There seemed to be no more information to be got from the house servants, and Jurby, the erstwhile coachman, had not been at Heathside on the day of Heather's disappearance. That left only Jem, the stable boy.

And here Miss Stapleton struck gold. She tracked him down sitting on a rock by the stream that bordered the west farm. A fishing pole dangled nearby while he threw small pebbles at his would-be victims, thus satisfactorily scaring them away from his hook which, in any case, held no bait.

Poor Jem had always been afraid of Miss Stapleton and probably could not have succeeded in prevarication even had it occurred to him to try. Miss Stapleton knew instinctively where to strike.

The boy was taken aback at sight of his mistress here by his stream. She bore down upon him like some spectre from a bad dream, black skirts swirling around her as she strode energetically across the meadow. She stopped dead before him, seemed to hesitate, then wreathed her beaky face in an uncomfortable smile.

"Well, Jem! And how is the fishing today?" she asked pleasantly, as though this meeting were a friendly everyday occurrence. To a more sophisticated listener, her words would certainly have rung false, but the little boy had not yet learned that people do not always mean what they say.

He gave her a toothy smile. "Oh, I ain't never catched no fish, missus. They fishes do me too mortal smart fer me."

"Oh, but I think you must be a very smart boy, Jem." Her eyes hardened as she spoke, the frozen smile still in place.

"Me, missus?" he explained in patent disbelief. "Not me, missus. Why John, he do say I be the stupidest boy that ever was." He seemed to consider a moment. "I 'spect he's right."

"John? John who?" She sensed somehow that this grubby little boy knew something about her missing cousin, but she was still trying to decide how to play this particular hand, when the boy himself removed that necessity.

"John Tanner, to be sure, missus. You know. The one as took Miss off yesterday in his hay cart," he answered innocently, greatly surprised that the mistress should ask such a silly question.

The dark eyes snapped, the thin smile pinched quickly into a frown. "Do you mean Lady Margaret? This Tanner fellow took her away yesterday?"

"Aye, missus. I seed 'em drive off meself. Real early it were."

"Where did he take her?" she spat out at the boy. Before he could answer he felt a hand close on his shoulder like a vulture's claw, and he was being shaken till his teeth rattled. "Come now, you stupid boy! Tell me where they've gone!"

Through his shaking teeth he managed to answer, "I dunno, missus. I dunno! I'll swear to that anywhen!" She let go his shoulder as suddenly as she had grabbed it, and he sat down on his rock with a thump, mud splattering, fishing pole flying and frogs hopping croakily away. She peered at him keenly, and seemed, reluctantly, to believe him.

"Where does this farmer live?" she snapped out.

The boy pointed a muddy hand across the meadow without a word. Not far from where they stood was a small but sturdy cottage of Cornish granite, pretty vines curling up its walls. A thin wisp of smoke rose from its stubby chimney.

"Hah!" she grunted and headed for the house without so much as another glance at the boy. As soon as her back was turned he scrambled to his feet, tripping only once in his haste, and took off across the meadow, heedless of where he was headed as long as it was away from the missus.

Honoria's imperious knock was answered by a round and ruddy woman in a bright yellow cap and a merrily checked apron over a sturdy fustian dress. Her eyes twinkled with good humor and curiosity. In six years at Heathside Miss Stapleton had never ventured out to visit any of the tenants and so was all but unknown, except by reputation, to the lot of them.

"This is the house of the farmer Tanner?" The statement was made a question only by the slightest lift of a brow.

"Aye, that it be, mum, but my Johnny do be gone just now. An' what would ye be wantin' with my boy, mum, if I might make so bold as to ask?"

"Ah, it is Mrs. Tanner, is it?" Honoria was making an effort to be pleasant. "I am Miss Stapleton. May I come in?"

The twinkling eyes of Ellen's future mother-in-law smiled her understanding, and she ushered her exalted visitor into a spotless sitting room. "Sit ye down, mum. No, no, mum, over here, in the good chair." She stirred up the fire and bustled about, putting the kettle to the boil. "Ye'll like a drop o' tea, I'm sure, mum." She chattered as she worked, scooping a handful of tea into a cherry-red glazed pot and setting out a plateful of fresh buns and ginger biscuits. "Ye must know my Johnny a good deal, mum, so much time as he be spendin' up to the Big House lately."

Miss Stapleton's ears pricked up. "Yes, I do think my boy be fair catched at last, an' glad I am to see it. I disremember when I seed him grin so. He be like a cat at a cream pot, mum, that he do." Here she turned a grin to her guest and gave a faintly lascivious cackle. "I been hopin' these dunnamany years that the boy'd pick hisself a good strong girl an' set about givin' me my grandchildren. I do be gettin' on meself, an' I'd like oncet to rock a wee babe agin afore I go. I'll be right proud to welcome my boy's wife, mum, that I will."

Honoria found her voice with an effort. "Mrs. Tanner, where is your son?"

"Why he do be gone to Exeter, to be sure," she replied, impressed by his adventurousness in traveling such a distance. "Gone yesterday morn, he was. Gone off to buy a cow, he do say." She twinkled mischievously and dropped her voice to a conspiratorial tone. "I do 'spect he had more reason 'n that, though. But I don't ask too many questions. 'Twere best so, mum, to be sure."

Miss Stapleton took a much needed swallow of the scalding tea, which seemed to turn to cotton in her mouth. "When will he be back?"

"Oh," said Mrs. Tanner airily, "I misdoubt I'll see him fer a week or more. Exeter do be a fair ways off, ye know. I'll not worrit myself over my Johnny. He do be a good boy."

The happy farm wife chattered on about the myriad virtues of her only son, but Honoria Stapleton had heard enough. Without another word to her hostess, she rose from Mrs. Tanner's good chair and walked wearily from the cottage.

So the girl had eloped! And with a farmer! How could I

have been such a fool, she asked herself, not to see what must have been going on under my nose? That Lady Margaret St. Vincent and John Tanner had left Heathside together, with an eye toward marriage could no longer be in doubt. And since Lady Margaret was under age and needed the consent of her guardian to be married in England, they could only have gone to Scotland. This faradiddle of the Tanner woman about Exeter was probably true as far as it went. Exeter was, after all, a major coaching town where the young pair would easily find passage north. They certainly couldn't ride all the way to Gretna Green in a farm cart.

She would not *allow* this to happen! She might well be able to stop them if she acted at once. A tenant farmer would certainly not be able to afford the charges of traveling post and probably the Mail was even beyond his touch. Honoria would hire a chaise-and-pair at Launceston. A team would, of course, be preferable for speed, but to this her purse could not be made to stretch. A pair would have to do, and all-in-all she thought it would be sufficient. She refused to believe as yet that she had lost her entire future in the actions of a silly girl whose grandfather was a merchant!

She entered the house with a brisk step and issued several orders with a bark. Mrs. Bing, on learning her mistress's destination, was only too happy to assist in speeding her off to Scotland. In less than an hour, Miss Honoria Stapleton was back in the whiskey, the faithful Jurby at the reins, speeding after the young couple she was sure was her cousin and John Tanner. She was determined to stop them.

Mrs. Bing and Ellen, all worried condescension and assistance, saw her tucked into the carriage and bade her Godspeed. As it disappeared down the lane, they turned to each other, let out simultaneous breaths of relief, and broke into happy giggles.

Chapter Eight

"Oh! You do have the Cornish roses in your cheeks! I was raised in Devonshire, you know. And it's an oft-stated fact that West Country Beauties beat all the rest to flinders. How pleased I am that you are grown so pretty."

Thus did Christina, Lady Morpeth, greet Heather on her return to Clarges Street.

"Pretty, ma'am? Me?" asked Heather amazed.

"Oh, yes, decidedly," stated Geoff's mama. "Not just in the common way, but definitely pretty. Or at least you will be when we rid you of those impossible clothes. Where did you get them, dear? Here, let me take this horrid, ugly cap."

Heather's mobcap was ruthlessly plucked away to reveal masses of raven hair falling softly past her shoulders. "Oh!" cried Lady Morpeth in genuine delight. "You are so wonderfully dark." She gave a satisfied nod of her own golden head.

In Heather's eyes, Tina Morpeth was quite simply the most beautiful creature she had ever beheld. Radiant golden curls, creamy skin that glowed pink with only the tiniest bit of help from the rouge pot, an elegant and graceful figure set off by perfect taste in dress, and a smile that could charm the birds out of the trees, or a loan out of the tightest-fisted gentleman, as it had often done in the past two years. In fact, the word charming might have been invented to describe her. Even her closest friends found it difficult to believe that the Incomparable Tina had reached the age of three-and-forty and had a full-grown son.

It was not in the lady's nature to be vain. She had been praised and petted so long for her beauty that she had simply come to accept it as a rather delightful fact of life, yet another treat to be enjoyed to the fullest. For her greatest talent by far was an ability to enjoy everyone and everything about her. And so her pleasure in having a young girl so pretty under her wing was quite genuine and raised not the tiniest spectre of jealousy in her lovely and affectionate breast. If such a thought had occurred to her at all, she would have dismissed it at once with the simple knowledge that Heather's piquant dark looks would serve as the perfect foil to her own golden beauty.

They were seated in Lady Morpeth's delightfully pretty morning room. Creamy walls were patterned with trellises, bright buttercups intertwined amongst the vines. A gracefully curved settee and gilt chairs were covered in pale straw-colored damask, and the sunlight pouring through the Austrian-draped windows made the room glow. Heather thought she'd never seen anything half so pretty. Her hostess was perfectly suited to the room in a morning dress of amber silk tissue shot with white, finished with Paris net sleeves and green velvet streamers that fluttered when she walked.

"Now," she said in a surprisingly matter-of-fact manner. "We have so much to discuss. Geoffrey, ring for tea, won't you, my darling?" Her son, who had been skulking around the room in an ominously brooding manner, complied. His mother settled onto the settee and patted it invitingly for Heather to join her.

"I'm so sorry, my lady, that I caused you to cut short your stay in the country," Heather began. She had carefully prepared her apology, but this was as far as it got.

"Oh, pooh. I was already fretting myself to flinders at Oatlands."

"Knew you would do, too," muttered Geoff. "Curst bore, Oatlands."

His mother ignored this provocation. "And since you are to stay with me for a time, you really must not call me 'my lady' in that odiously proper fashion. It makes me feel horridly *matronly*, you know. As if I should be wearing a turban! How if you were to call me 'Godmama'? I know it sounds perilously like Grandmama, which I *could* not bear, I'm sure, though I shall certainly try to, Geoffrey dear, when you decide you must make me one." She took Heather's hand and gave it an affectionate squeeze. "I do most truly think of you as a goddaughter. If you could bring yourself to call me Godmama I think it would answer delightfully."

Heather blushed and smiled. "I shall try . . . Godmama."

"There. It is quite simple, you see."

The door opened silently to admit the wooden-faced butler who had so recently turned Heather away from the door. "My lady?"

"Oh, Bellows. This is my goddaughter, who has come to pay a nice long visit." Her emerald eyes twinkled conspiratorially at Heather. The butler showed by not so much as a flick of an eyelash that he had ever seen the young woman before. "We will have some tea, I think. And some of Mrs. Jumples's almond cakes, as well. They're simply heavenly, my dear," she added to Heather. The butler all but strutted from the room.

"Now. I've been thinking how best to present you to the ton, my dear. Now that I see you again I am certain you'll make a very big splash indeed. You are not just in the current mould, and that is all to the good. The first thing we must decide . . ."

"Pardon me, my . . . uh, Godmama," Heather interrupted her. "I've been thinking too, and I have decided you really mustn't present me to the ton at all."

"But how else are we to find you a husband, dear?" asked Lady Morpeth in real confusion. To her the world outside the ton simply did not exist.

Geoffrey, who was slumping in one of the spindly gilt chairs, insofar as it was possible to slump in such a delicate and precarious piece of furniture, pricked up his ears. He'd been having second thoughts about this mad adventure ever since leaving Cornwall. It had been a good notion, he supposed, to rescue Heather from the clutches of her dastardly brother, and he rather liked the image of himself as knight-errant. The devil of it was that that sort of knight-errantry was likely to leave you with a distressed damsel on your hands. This affair looked like becoming deuced uncomfortable. Geoffrey Curwen did not at all like being made uncomfortable.

Though there was no fonder son in all England, the Viscount could not deny that his mama was sometimes more

THE RELUCTANT SUITOR 67

than a bit feather-witted. She seemed bound to come a cropper over this affair. And somewhere in the murky depths of his mind wriggled the unpleasant picture of his little Heather being sacrificed to some curst fortune hunter. He didn't like the idea at all.

Heather continued with her idea. "Perhaps you might just introduce me quietly to one or two pleasant gentlemen, ma'am. Would not that answer?" She was, in fact, inclined to think that she'd best utilize her time in London discovering some means of making her own way when she came of age and was turned off by her brother. She felt quite sure that no one would be the least interested in marrying her. But she wisely kept these conclusions to herself. "I will *not* return to Heathside, ma'am," she continued with unaccustomed determination. "And if I go to grand ton parties and such, everyone will know who I am. Bo is bound to get wind of it and send me back to Cornwall."

"Capital notion, that!" said Geoff. His mother looked at him with ill-concealed annoyance. "Meeting a few people on the quiet, I mean," he added defensively. "Get to know them. Find you a nice fellow that way. No need to puff you off to the whole ton." He felt a surge of relief at the idea.

"Fudge!" stated his mother flatly. "You simply must be properly presented, dear. If it will make you more comfortable, Geoffrey will send to Cornwall to discover if your cousin has the least idea where you have gone, though I am sure I do not see how she could. And as for your odious brother, there will be not the least problem about him, I assure you. For I have had the most famous notion! We will present you incognito!" she announced triumphantly.

"Incog . . ." sputtered Geoff.

"Under a false name! No one will have the *least* idea who you are. We will let it be known that there is some great mystery about you, and everyone will be intrigued. It will be such fun." Heather found it very difficult not to be swept along by her enthusiasm.

Her son, however, found it not at all difficult. This was even worse than before. "Of all the bacon-brained, paper-skulled, muttonheaded starts, this takes the cake! Tell you what it is, Mama. You're dicked in the nob. Got some maggot or other in your head. To try to fob such a Canterbury tale off on the ton! It's the Bank of England to a Charley's shelter that all the world and his wife'll twig it quick as the cat can lick her ear. Then we *will* be in the basket."

"Are you finished, dear?" asked Lady Morpeth patiently when this nearly indecipherable tirade had dwindled to assorted mutterings. "Because if you have, I will finish telling you my plan. You know, dear, you're acting sulky as a bear, and I do wish you'd stop because we still have much to discuss. I promise you I have hit upon the very way to go about our campaign." She returned her attention to Heather. "Now, your brother is not exactly known for his attendance at ton parties. I fancy his title still gains him admittance at *some* houses, but I have not laid eyes on him these three years and more, I assure you. He has been permanently barred from Almack's for a shocking rake, and I believe he spends his evenings in *quite* another part of town." Her tone said clearly what sort of low neighborhood the Earl was wont to frequent. "And besides, I daresay he wouldn't recognize you if you did chance to meet, for you will be quite, quite changed when we have finished."

Heather, who rather liked the idea of being quite, quite changed, had to admit the truth of this. "Well it has been more than two years since he has seen me. And he hardly looked at me even then. I don't think Bo likes me very much."

"There, you see," said Lady Morpeth briskly. "There is not the least cause to worry on his account." Geoffrey, sensing defeat, sank back into his chair. "Now, what are we to call my new goddaughter? Do you like Cassandra? No, too exotic I think. Something simpler. Hmmm. Elizabeth?"

"If you please, ma'am," said Heather, not quite realizing that this was her final surrender. "I like the name Heather."

"But we really cannot use your own name, dear."

"But it is not precisely my name, ma'am. My full name is Lady Margaret Barbara Heather St. Vincent. I have always been called Lady Margaret. No one except Grandpapa and Geoff has ever called me Heather, and it is quite my favorite name."

"Very well then, Heather. It will serve admirably, and Geoffrey will not have to struggle to learn another. And for your surname I propose Braddock. Miss Heather Braddock," she tested. "It will serve quite well, I think."

Heather repeated the name softly, trying out the sound.

"Why Braddock?" asked Geoff.

"Simple, darling. Because I have never in my entire life met anyone by the name of Braddock. Have you?"

"Can't say I have. Might be some, just the same."

"Well, it doesn't signify if there are. They won't know about Heather, and she needn't know about them. That's settled then, is it, Miss Heather Braddock?"

"Well, if you are really quite sure my . . . Godmama. But . . ." Heather's last objection was doomed to oblivion by the arrival of the tea tray, gliding in on the arm of Bellows. In addition to several of Mrs. Jumples's famous almond cakes it held an array of biscuits, gingernuts, bread and butter, seed cakes, a dish of lavender lozenges, and an exquisite *Gateau Millefleur*. Heather's eyes widened at the heavily laden tray, but she was a well-mannered young lady and so at first limited herself to an almond cake, two biscuits, and a slice of the *Gateau*.

"Bellows," said Lady Morpeth. "Please see that the pink bedroom is made quite comfortable for Miss Braddock. We will be going out shopping soon, but will dine at home."

"Very good, my lady," came the awesome reply, and the butler slid from the room.

"You know," continued his mistress, "I do not at all think that Bellows approves of me. My late husband more or less inherited him. He's been with the Morpeths for time out of mind. I shall be ever so glad, Geoffrey, when you marry. You may take him off my hands."

"Devil a bit!" answered Geoff, who found Bellows even more forbidding than did his mama.

"If you please, Godmama," said Heather in an attempt to bring the conversation back to the matter at hand. "I cannot go shopping with you. I have no money left."

"Well, I was sure you would not, dear, after Geoffrey told me your story. How could you after all? I think it was amazingly well done in you to get yourself to London at all. But there will not be the least problem about shopping, I assure you."

"But, Godmama. I cannot, I really cannot allow you to pay for me. It would be too ungrateful of me."

"Well, it wouldn't be at all terrible if I should, but the sad fact is I cannot. I have never a feather to fly with, you know," she stated happily, as though this were no problem at all. And so, for Christina Morpeth, was it not. "One certainly doesn't need money to live well, you know. I have been proving that forever. Only the *appearance* of money. It is a distinction, you must admit."

"I'm afraid I don't understand, ma'am," said Heather, who had been taught by Mrs. Bing to always pay the meagre bills at Heathside promptly.

"Well, how should you to be sure," she said sympathetically. "You've never been able to order yourself a pretty dress, I'll swear." She undertook a detailed explanation of how such things worked in London. "And so, dear," she concluded, "as long as you *appear* to be terribly wealthy and are quite arrogant (the more so the better, in fact) shopkeepers will fall over themselves to extend you any amount of credit."

"But what shall I do when the bills arrive, ma'am?"

"Why, to be sure, that is the simplest part. You send them back. Then you go in the next day and order another *very* expensive gown, or hat, or whatever," she finished with wonderful simplicity.

"Oh," said Heather as though she understood, which she certainly did not. Geoff gave his mama an admiring look.

"Told you m'mother was a knowing one," he said proudly.

"Yes, darling, I rather think I am," she said. "But now you may run along, for Heather and I have much to accomplish. You may dine with us this evening. We will outline strategy."

"Can't," he answered. "Dining with Court and Robin."

"Well, you must cancel, dear. We need you."

"Godmama," submitted Heather, "could not the Earl and Mr. Ayrton dine with us? They know my history, after all. They might give us good advice."

"What a splendid notion! They are both young men of

superior minds. You shall bring them with you, Geoffrey."

"Might not like having their plans changed for them, Mama."

"Nonsense! Why should they not? I'm sure they will like it of all things," she said, moving her only beloved son inexorably toward the door. "We shall expect the three of you at eight. Goodbye, dear." And he disappeared out the door. Viscount Morpeth knew when he was outclassed.

"Now we must go upstairs at once," said Lady Morpeth with an admirable shift in tactics. "We *must* rid you of those things you are wearing, and there is no time to be lost in putting your wardrobe in train. We'll begin, I think, with Mademoiselle Brulé. She is by far the most fashionable modiste in town. Her bills are quite outrageous. She sent me one just the other day, so I daresay she will be glad to see me. Yes, we will certainly begin with Mademoiselle Brulé. Come along, dear. We will find you something enchanting to wear." She took Heather by the hand and began pulling her gently up the stairs.

"But, Godmama. I cannot take your clothes!"

"Pooh! Whyever not? You must, dear. For you cannot expect her to see you in *that* dress and extend you any credit at all." She wrinkled up her pretty nose in distaste at the dreary gown Heather was wearing. "Most likely she would send you round to the tradesmen's entrance. No, you must look extremely elegant, very pretty, and above all wealthy."

They had reached the second floor, and a doorway was thrown open. Heather was nudged gently into a room unlike any she had ever seen, or even imagined. Her mouth gaped, eyes shining, as she took in the full magnificence of Lady Morpeth's bedchamber.

They were in a delightful garden in shades of green and violet. Heather's heavily clad feet sank nearly to the ankles in the deep green carpet. A bow window overlooked the true garden below, but there seemed to be nearly as many flowers inside as out. Every available surface carried fresh violets and white rose petals. Their delicious scent assailed her nostrils. It was the smell of Lady Morpeth herself who never used any scent but that of Devonshire violets, "For it reminds me of my childhood home, you see," she would explain to anyone commenting on this trademark.

The walls of the room were papered in gay stripes, more violets, soft, pretty, and feminine, climbing their full height. A *chaise longue* fitted perfectly into the curve of the window and was covered with a pale green moiré. A delicate vanity, billowing violet gauze skirts, perched in a corner, and a large white cockatoo looked down on it all from a flower-bedecked sconce on one wall.

But the true magnificence of the room lay in the bed, a high, wide work of art. Fresh violet petals were strewn over the expanse of its exquisitely worked silk counterpane. Extravagant lengths of the sheerest imaginable silk voile in the palest imaginable shade of violet were draped and looped up here and there to form fanciful shapes under a lattice-work canopy, entwined with vines and leaves and dripping blossoms of foamy white, deep purple, and glossy green.

Heather's eyes glowed, her hands clasped before her, as she let out a long "Ohhhhh!" Lady Morpeth spun around in delight.

"Do you like it? I am so glad! It was such fun to do, I must say, and such a pity that so few people get to see one's bedchamber. I do wish we could go back to the days when ladies held a levee each morning in their boudoirs. Georgianna Devonshire, bless her sweet soul, was the last to really get away with that, and she's been dead for years."

Lady Morpeth flitted across the room and pulled on the tail feathers of the cockatoo. To Heather's surprise, it didn't squawk. She realized it wasn't real, and began to giggle.

"Yes, isn't it the silliest thing?" exclaimed Lady Morpeth in delight as a French maid entered the room. "I was not just sure I ought to make him the bell-pull, you know, but one has to have it *somewhere,* and it did seem like fun, just for a giggle, you know." In that moment any fears Heather may have harbored about loving the lady unreservedly were banished. Who could not adore such a creature?

The lady in question had thrown open the double doors of a huge wardrobe and was pulling out gown after gown, tossing them negligently onto any convenient surface after a cursory glance.

"What a shame that I have so much pink and amber. They will never do for you." She paused in her rummaging to study the girl. "Blue, I think, and silver, and perhaps some touches of lilac or mauve." With that she disappeared among the silks and velvets and swansdown. Suddenly a breathy "Ah, yes!" seemed to issue from somewhere inside a sleeve to be followed but a moment later by Lady Morpeth herself, looking all the more charming for the disarray of her golden curls and the fact that her lace collar was askew. "It's simply perfect! Do you not agree?"

She held a lovely confection of ice-blue India muslin of the finest weave with a darker blue tattersall check woven through it. It was embroidered with sprigs of forget-me-nots around the hem, with clusters of the flowers caught at the waist with velvet ribbons. It was quite the loveliest dress Heather had ever seen.

"Simple and to the point," said her hostess with a flush of triumph. "It presents just the right image. Not too dashing, but tasteful and elegant." She turned to her maid, who was all wide-eyed curiosity about the newcomer. "Marie, this is Miss Braddock, my goddaughter. Dispose of her clothes, if you please."

The little maid twinkled with pleasure. *"Oui, madame! Tout de suite."*

Heather's clothes were instantly removed and dumped in an ignominious pile. She was roundly admonished by the little maid to remove those *sabots* from her feet. Heather did as she was bid. One look at her serviceable and much mended undergarments decided Marie that they must speedily join their comrades on the floor.

Heather turned in protest to Lady Morpeth, but that intrepid lady had disappeared once more into the vastness of the wardrobe, from whose depths now issued a series of strange shufflings and clatterings, mutterings, and triumphant "Ah hahs!". These were followed at length by a blue kid sandal, which flew out and up to land in the vicinity of the *chaise*. Its mate, which speedily followed, would have landed on Heather's head, had she not ducked in time. As it was, it only glanced off her shoulder and flipped onto the vanity, narrowly missing a jar of Denmark lotion and a rouge pot, choosing instead to land squarely in a bowl of violets. Marie unconcernedly lifted it dripping from the bowl and dropped it onto the floor beside its mate.

When at last Lady Morpeth herself emerged triumphant from the wardrobe, bearing a deep blue velvet spencer, Heather was beginning to shiver, standing in the center of the room without so much as a petticoat to protect her. The maid returned from some muttered shufflings of her own, laden down with cream-colored silken undergarments lavishly trimmed with Brussels lace, and a tamboured muslin petticoat. *"Mademoiselle, s'il vous plâit,"* she said sternly. The young lady closed her eyes and abandoned herself to her fate.

An hour later, two very lovely ladies of ton might have been seen stepping up into Lady Morpeth's smart plum-colored town carriage. The owner of the equipage, in a very fetching bonnet and cherry pelise, was accompanied by her "dear goddaughter" who, in addition to the blue muslin and the velvet spencer, now sported a pretty velvet bonnet with an up-standing poke and two curled white ostrich plumes, a flowered parasol, and blue French kid gloves. Pinned to the spencer was her mother's beautiful sapphire brooch. The entire ensemble was being carried inexorably toward Bruton Street and the salon of Mlle. Brulé.

Chapter Nine

Honoria Stapleton believed that for once luck was with her. She counted the miles as she hurried north after her fleeing cousin. That she was hard on the trail of Lady Margaret and John Tanner she would not allow herself to doubt.

She had arrived in Exeter in the early evening of the previous day, in good time to prosecute her inquiries there.

It took some time to cover the offices of all the stage-coaches that left from Exeter: The Red Rover, Regulator, Traveller, Sovereign, Telegraph, Defiance, to name but a few. Her powerful personality enabled her to easily—or if not easily at least effectively—convince the various clerks to furnish her with descriptions of all passengers departing in the last twenty-four hours. But these efforts were not destined to succeed. She turned up not a single trace of any young couple of suitable proportions and demeanor, heading anywhere at all.

Next she tried the slow-moving and inexpensive stage-wagon. Its so-called "office" consisted of a sort of shed, attached to the blacksmith's yard, and furnished with a scarred oak table, a crooked chair with torn rush seating, and two wooden benches leaning against a wall. The rickety chair was being threatened by the presence upon it of a very rotund man in a red flannel waistcoat which nearly matched his voluminous springy red hair. He rocked back and forth precariously on the two hindmost legs, alternately puffing on a long clay pipe and picking his teeth with the point of a rusty knife.

"Aye, lady. Remember 'em well," he said in reply to Miss Stapleton's inquiry. He remained seated, but in deference to her sex and station he stopped picking his teeth. " 'Twere a pretty wench. And fair determined, too." He gave a coarse laugh. "I'll wager he's one as'll live under the cat's paw, poor bloke."

A slight frown crossed Miss Stapleton's features. "What do you mean?" she demanded.

"She were jawin' at him no end 'bout wantin' to take the stagecoach. Complained the wagon were too slow. Dangerous, she called it!" He let out a belly laugh, puffing blue smoke with each bellow like a defective chimney. "If it's danger she be afeared on, she'd find more'n she bargained for on the stagecoach. Those gent-coachmen they got drivin' 'em nowadays, racing each other 'n such. Ain't nobody safe." He spit into a corner of the dusty floor for emphasis.

The light of interest in Honoria's eyes was steadily turning to triumph. A rough, nervous farmer sort of a fellow and a wisp of a serving maid was how the red waistcoat had described the young couple. Heading north. And the girl in a hurry, fearing some danger after them. "How far were they going?" she snapped out.

The mound of flannel-covered flesh lowered his chair onto all fours. Planting dimpled and dirty elbows on the scarred table, he peered keenly at the lady before him. The rusty black gown was far from new, but it wasn't fustian, that was sure. Real silk was what it was! She might be good for a touch. Worth a try, anyway. He picked up the knife and began determinedly picking at a molar. "Well now, lady. I might know that, an' then agin I might not."

Miss Stapleton's indignation was high, but he was more than a match for her. Terms were quickly agreed upon.

"The wagon only goes as far as Manchester, and that's where they were headed," he said, pocketing some coins. "But I heard the fellow sayin' as how they'd hafta count their pennies close if they were wishful o' gettin' all the way to Scotland *and* back agin."

By now she had her proof, and she allowed herself a small sigh of relief. Lady Margaret and John Tanner were eloping to Scotland on the stagewagon. A full three hundred fifty miles lay between Exeter and Gretna Green. In her hired chaise-and-pair she would easily outrace them long before the Scottish border was in sight. This she wanted to believe, was in fact desperate to believe, and so she believed.

By this time it was grown quite dark. She gave in to the necessity of a meal and a few hours' sleep in the delightful Crown and Feathers, allowing herself to be comfortably seen to by the hospitable landlady.

Very early next morning she set out in hot pursuit.

A quintet of attractive faces gethered around Lady Morpeth's dinner table and she presided over it with uncommon vivacity. She was her usual glorious self in a draped half-dress of ecru spotted lace over deep gold stain which left bare her lovely shoulders, hair *à la Madonna*, and the set of topazes she had purchased that very afternoon from Jeffrey's, jewelers to the Prince Regent, to whom she owed a small, or rather a not so small, fortune.

Heather sparkled in a simple gown of pale blue crape embroidered with silver acorns, a gossamer shawl of midnight blue Norwich silk draped elegantly across her shoulders. About her neck were her mother's beautiful sapphires. She glowed in the praise being heaped upon her by the three young gentlemen who made up the remainder of the dinner party. She had never before been the recipient of pretty compliments, and she blushed rosily as she basked in their praise.

The Earl of Pythe, a man of few words at his most garrulous, had stated simply that she looked fine indeed. For the rest of the evening he continued to smile at her very often in his friendly and reassuring way and to interject astute comments now and then in the sparsest and most direct language possible. And he enjoyed his dinner hugely.

Mr. Ayrton's compliments were of a more flowery variety and went on well past the interval in the drawing room, through the soup and into the fish, when he was at length called upon by Viscount Morpeth to stop making a damned court-card of himself and eat his dinner.

The young Viscount suffered from a curious mixture of emotions on seeing his one-time playmate. He had at first scarce been able to believe his eyes. Marie had dressed her raven hair in a Sappho, wrapped around with a silver fillet and held in place by a mother-of-pearl comb. She seemed somehow taller, older, and decidedly more self-possessed. He blinked her into focus and muttered, "I say! Heather?" The vision of cool elegance evaporated as she ran lightly across the floor and impulsively took his hand with a happy squeal.

"Oh, Geoff! Do you like it? I so hoped you would."

"Well!" he exclaimed, holding her at arm's length and studying her with wonder. "Mean to say, knew you'd turn out deuced fine once m'mother got her hands on you. But damme! Heather, you're beautiful!"

Her pale face turned the prettiest shade of pink imaginable, and she covered her confusion with a neat curtsy and a twirl around the room for his better inspection.

"And only wait until you see the other things I have ordered. You would not credit how many gowns your mama says are necessary. We've bought ever so many. And shoes, and gloves, and bonnets, and oh, everything! I'm quite in a whirl. And Godmama says we have only *begun!* I cannot imagine how I shall wear the half of them."

Mr. Ayrton had entered the room in Geoff's wake but checked at sight of Heather. "It is to be hoped that we shall be allowed to see them all if they present such a charming picture as this one," he said smoothly, smiling his appreciation at the vision she presented.

"Mr. Ayrton!" she exclaimed happily. "How glad I am you could come."

"Well, I was looking forward to meeting " 'Miss Braddock.' " He bowed gracefully over her gloved hand.

Heather bubbled up a laugh. "I suppose I must get used to answering to that now, mustn't I? I hope it won't be too difficult. Until I do, do you suppose you might call me Heather?"

"I should deem it an honor. But only if you will consent to call me Robin."

"Humph," muttered Geoffrey at his friend's fluency. He wasn't at all sure he liked such fawnings on his little Heather. The Earl of Pythe stepped forward.

"My lord," said Heather with a proper curtsy as she shook his proffered hand.

"Court," he said simply.

"I beg your pardon?"

"My name is Court," he replied with a disarming smile.

"Court," she pronounced happily and looked around at them all in great contentment.

In this happy mood the company proceeded through a fine dinner, of which Heather particularly savored the Cressy soup, two *beignets* of salmon with cucumbers, half a roast leveret in truffle sauce, a sago pudding, some *marbre* jelly, and a healthy share of a basket of meringues.

The cloth was removed at last and the servants quit the room, leaving the company with a mound of fruit, a wheel of Stilton, and some fresh wine.

"Well, gentlemen," began Lady Morpeth. "Now you must help Heather and me to plot out our campaign on London. Fortunately, Lady Scopes's ball is only two days off. You couldn't want a better debut, my dear, for everyone will be there."

"But, Godmama," breathed Heather in a voice of doom. "I don't know how to dance."

"Oh," said Lady Morpeth, who had clearly not taken this eventuality into consideration. "Oh, dear. You really must dance, you know. Are you quite sure you can't? Couldn't you try?"

"Of course I'm sure, Godmama," Heather answered, unable to keep from laughing. "I have never so much as seen anyone dance in my life."

"Hmmm. Do you suppose we could get a dancing master on such short notice, Geoffrey?"

"Damned if I know," he dutifully answered.

"There's no need, ma'am," Robin cut in. "I'm accounted a fair dancer. I'd be glad to show Heather the steps," he finished, neatly selecting some fat round grapes.

"Oh, Robin, would you?" said Heather. "I'd be so grateful."

"Don't see why there has to be such a curst hurry about the thing," muttered Geoff. "Needn't be married tomorrow, y'know. Get your feet on the ground first."

"But, darling," said his mama, "We haven't a lot of time. It does take *some* time to find an eligible husband. And it will be such fun! There will be the opera, and routs, and Venetian breakfasts . . ."

"And may we go to the theatre, Godmama?"

"Of course, darling. It is quite my favorite amusement.

I was a Pic-Nic, you know, some dozen years ago. Such fun it was," she said with a wistful sigh.

"A Pic-Nic?"

"Oh, yes. We were the very finest amateur theatrical troupe. *Everyone* belonged. Why, the very governors of Covent Garden felt threatened by us, so fine were our performances. Mr. Kemble was enraged. I'll own I was a charming Juliet. The Prince himself thought so." She shook herself out of these agreeable reminiscences and came back to the question at hand. "And of course there will be Vauxhall, and drives in the park."

"Geoff has promised to teach me to drive," said Heather.

"NO!" came back the chorus of voices as three fruit knives clattered to their plates in horror. "Whyever not?" she asked. "Do not young ladies learn to drive in London? I thought it was all the crack."

"Not from Geoff, they don't," stated the Earl. "Worst driver in London."

"Court!" blustered the offended Viscount. "Ain't as bad as all that!"

"Worse," stated the Earl with unimpaired calm.

"Why the deuce shouldn't I teach Heather to drive?" he blustered some more.

"Because she won't learn from you," the Earl answered, deftly peeling an apple.

Heather felt she should spring to the defense of her hero. "I'm sure Geoff could teach me very well!"

"I'm afraid it won't do, dear," said Lady Morpeth cheerfully. "He really is quite a hopeless driver. Hasn't the least notion how to go about it. I shouldn't like to see you put yourself in such danger."

"Well, Mama!" sputtered Geoff at this high treason, unable to say more for his indignation.

"I'll teach you, Heather," offered the Earl. "I'm a fair whip."

"None better," agreed Robin.

"Well, thank you, Court," she gave in. "I should very much like to learn. I want to be all the crack, you know."

"Don't worry, darling," said her godmama. "You will be."

"You ought to have a horse, too," continued the Earl in an unwontedly talkative vein. "Do you ride?"

"I was used to ride a lot when Grandpapa was alive. Of course, that was years ago, and I haven't been on one since. But Grandpapa said I had a good seat."

"Get you a horse," said the Viscount who was beginning to feel that this adventure, which he had, after all, begun, was being taken out of his hands entirely. He turned to his two best friends and said with unusual sarcasm, "You *do* trust me to choose her a suitable hack, I hope?"

"Of course, Geoff, of course," said Robin. "You're the best judge of horseflesh I know." He poured the Viscount some more wine.

"Thank you," muttered Geoff as he savagely hacked off a hunk of cheese.

In an attempt to turn the subject Heather said lightly, "I'm so afraid I shan't know how to behave at the ball, Godmama."

"Quite simple," Robin interjected. "You need only blush prettily and lower your eyes demurely when asked to dance. Bat your long lashes now and then, and if there is a gentleman whose attentions you particularly wish to attract, you drop your fan or reticule just where he can pick it up for you." His teasing tone was lost on Heather who was seriously alarmed at the behavior expected of her.

"Couldn't I just speak to him instead?"

"Devil a bit!" said Geoff strongly. "Do neither! Ain't the thing at all to go flirting with some curst fortune hunter."

"But surely not *every* gentleman I meet will be a fortune hunter. And besides, no one will know I have a fortune. It was your idea, after all Geoff, to bring me to London to find a husband.

"Don't mind him, dear. I can't understand at all why he is being such an old surly-boots," said his fond mama. "And there is not the least cause in the world for you to worry about how to behave. You must simply be yourself. If you do have a tiny question about something, just look around at how the other young ladies behave."

"God forbid," muttered the Viscount.

"Exactly!" said Robin, ignoring his friend's provocative remark. "Now take Lady Susan Prenderby. You couldn't want for a better example of how to go on. She's all the rage, and..."

"And a devilish silly female," finished the Earl bluntly.

Mr. Ayrton, who by this time had consumed a great deal of wine, leaped to his feet in defense of his goddess. "What the devil do you mean by that? Susan is divinity. She's perfection!"

"She's silly," returned the Earl quite placidly, munching on his cheese.

"If you weren't my best friend, Pythe, I'd call you out for such a slander on that angel, damned if I wouldn't!"

"Do you no good," said Geoff who had seen the scene played out many times before, and had even been on the receiving end of Mr. Ayrton's famous temper more than once.

"I *am* your best friend, and I wouldn't go out with you anyway," concluded the Earl. "Have some wine." Robin was still glowering menacingly at the slurs on his goddess.

"Now, Robin," soothed Lady Morpeth. "You know I really cannot allow you to call Court out in my house. You don't really want to at all, you know, so you'd best have this peach instead. Susan Prenderby is one of the sweetest and handsomest girls I know. She is just not quite in Court's style. I expect it's because she doesn't sit a horse very well. I fancy they frighten her."

"Just so," muttered the Earl disparagingly.

Robin swallowed his anger and his wine.

"'Sides, Robin," added Geoff. "No good holding old Susan P. up to Heather. Ain't in the same style at all."

"But if she's all the rage," interrupted Heather, "I should very much like to be like her. I have decided to be *terribly* fashionable, you see, for as long as I am here."

"You need have not the tiniest fear on that account, my love," reassured her godmama. "I've a strong notion you're one to set fashion rather than to follow it." She nodded her golden head in satisfaction and bit into a big juicy strawberry.

Chapter Ten

Lady Morpeth timed their entrance to Lady Scopes's ball perfectly. They were among the last guests to arrive at an affair destined to be the biggest crush of the Season. Absolutely *everyone* who mattered in the ton was present. The ballroom had been buzzing with speculation about Tina Morpeth's mysterious goddaughter, so suddenly materialized out of nowhere. The rumors of her unusual and interesting style had been thoroughly spread by the milliners and mantua-makers, just as Lady Morpeth had known they would be. The stage was well set for their entrance.

"Tina! You naughty thing!" exclaimed their hostess in a sort of *basso profundo* as she greeted them at the door. "Why have you never so much as hinted that you would be bringing out a goddaughter this season?" She turned a crackling smile to Heather as Lady Morpeth's pretty voice tinkled out some friendly rejoinder. Lady Scopes extended a large, strong hand, and Heather's more delicate one was seized in a viselike grip. "Miss Braddock, is it not? Welcome to Scopes House," she rumbled. Heather gave a pretty curtsy to the tall, magnificent, and altogether overwhelming lady.

"Thank you, Lady Scopes," she managed to say. "I appreciate your willingness to include me in your invitation on such short notice."

"Nonsense." The bass resounded in sharp contrast to Heather's soprano. "I'm always ready to have another pretty girl at my parties." Lady Scopes had no marriageable daughters. "Ah," she boomed, seeing Geoff on the steps behind his mother. "The Viscount." She shook his hand severely, causing him to wonder if he would be capable of keeping his appointment to spar with Gentleman

Jackson on the morrow. "Welcome, my lord. I think you'll find several pretty girls inside quite fainting to stand up with you." She fluttered a giant, luridly painted fan and let out what she thought was a feminine titter but which came out rather more like the roll of a kettle drum. "Off you go, then, and enjoy the dancing." Heather was relieved to feel Lady Morpeth gently nudging her into the ballroom. Geoff followed, gently nursing his right hand.

The threesome was immediately surrounded by a flurry of muslin and satin, velvet coats, and knee breeches, as friends of Lady Morpeth crowded around begging introductions to her goddaughter. Before many minutes had passed, Heather had had no fewer than three requests to stand up for the country dance then forming.

"Off with the lot of you, my good fellows!" said Mr. Ayrton, who suddenly appeared at her elbow. "You're all after the battle. The first dance is long since promised to me, is it not, Miss Braddock?" He bowed handsomely over her hand and twinkled up at her merrily.

She was relieved to see a familiar face in this crowd of strangers, and she smiled back at him warmly, giving him a little curtsy. "Why yes, I believe it is, Mr. Ayrton," she answered pertly, and the couple sailed off. Viscount Morpeth watched them go with a frown. Damned if she didn't look to be flirting! What had Robin been teaching her in those curst dancing lessons? He wandered off to find himself something sustaining to drink.

Despite Mr. Ayrton's excellent instruction, Heather felt unsure in her steps and had to concentrate on what she was about, leaving her little leisure for conversation. Mr. Ayrton, a graceful dancer, had no such problem. He grinned at his pupil with pride. "You're doing very well, you know," he reassured her.

"Oh, Robin, I'm so nervous," she admitted between steps. "I'm certain to tread on someone's toes, if I don't trip over my own skirt first."

"No such thing," he promised. "And even if you did, I daresay they're all so dazzled by your beauty they'd scarce notice."

"Now you are being perfectly ridiculous," she returned, though not without a grateful smile. "I do wish you wouldn't tease me when I am in such a flutter."

THE RELUCTANT SUITOR 85

In truth, Mr. Ayrton's compliments were far from ridiculous. Heather was looking very fine. After long and tireless search, Lady Morpeth had found a length of fine soft silk the exact violet of Heather's eyes. It was fashioned into a beautifully draped half-dress, slit down the front to reveal a petticoat of dove-grey sarcenet shot with silver. French beading and silver cord graced the hem and circled the high waist, trailing in delicate streamers almost to the floor. The gown was cut low across the bosom to reveal remarkably white shoulders and a swanlike neck, perfectly set off by her magnificent black pearls. The waves of dark hair had been caught into Grecian knots, threaded through with violet and silver ribbons.

Even the French maid had sighed her satisfaction at the finished picture. "*Mademoiselle est plus belle que la Reine Marie Antionette!*"

Heather remembered the unfortunate history of the hapless French Queen and answered dryly, "Well, I hope I do not lose my head, as I am sure to do if all this flattery continues."

Almost before the first dance was ended, she was being solicited for the next. A duke, two earls, a viscount, and an Honourable Mister were all vying for her attention. Heather thought with a giggle that she should be wearing green spectacles to save her eyes from the glare of such an august assemblage.

She could not but fear that her dancing was not yet up to the standard they might expect. She gazed around for a less daunting partner. The peers were disappointed at her choice of a very young Mr. Wesley, an eager-looking young fellow with violently projecting front teeth, wide eyes, and a perpetual anticipatory grin. He walked up to Heather on the balls of his feet, which gave him a funny sort of bounce, leaning forward like an eager puppy.

The young man wore an immensely high cravat, as though in the height of his neckcloth he might make up for his own lack of inches. His conversation consisted mostly of a string of "Yes, yes, and then . . . ?" Heather took to him at once.

"Have you been in town long, Mr. Wesley?" she said as they danced in an attempt to elicit some variation of response. He grinned at her sheepishly.

"Just this week, ma'am." He paused, his bulging eyes seeming to judge her. Apparently reassured that she would not laugh at him, he continued. "This is my first London ball."

"No really? But it is my first as well! Are you as nervous as I?" she asked ingenuously, thereby succeeding in sending young Mr. Wesley head over ears in love with her. "I scarce know where to turn in such a company. I'm sure to spill my ratafia or something on the most important dowager in the room or burst into giggles just when I should be giving my most proper curtsy. I should hate to have the whole company guffawing over my country ways."

"No one, Miss Braddock," he said with great feeling, "could laugh at you!"

And so the evening went, Heather quite unknowingly making one conquest after another. Being innocent of coaching in the simperings and flutterings expected of a young lady in her first season, she was simply herself. In the few days she had been away from Cornwall her natural sense of humor had blossomed, and she charmed everyone she met. Lady Morpeth watched in satisfaction. It was just as she had predicted. The ton had a new Incomparable. How delightful, to be sure!

Lady Morpeth was, in fact, enjoying the ball nearly as much as her goddaughter. "My love," she said to the girl halfway through the evening. "You would not credit the things I have been hearing about you! It is too delightfully funny!"

"What things, Godmama?" asked Heather uncomprehendingly.

"Well, Mrs. Rushbrooke believes you must be Black Irish, while Lady Phillimore insists that you are French. Lady Stonehouse, however, had it on *very good authority* that you are American!"

"American?"

"Oh, yes, my love. You are most certainly a Cajun, from New Orleans. Tell me, dear, how does London compare with New Orleans?" she asked, her voice rippling with mirth.

"Oh, no, Godmama! Whatever can have made her think anything so absurd?"

THE RELUCTANT SUITOR 87

"But, my dear, there is more. Just let me tell you!"

And tell her she did. Christina Morpeth had not been so amused in years. The ballroom had been ripe with speculation all evening.

"Russian royalty?!" snapped the Countess Lieven. "She most certainly is not! I would know her if she were, I *assure* you!"

"Braddock, Braddock," Lady Dartford, across the room, was muttering to a bosom bow. "There are Braddocks in Northumberland, I believe. Or no, stay." She put her finger against her massive nose. "That was Craddock. Or was it Paddock? Oh! Oh, dear me, no! It couldn't have been Paddock, could it?" And she went off into a titter of giggles behind a fan that did not yet conceal the bulk of her nose.

"Well, whoever she is, there is money there, you may depend on it," said Mrs. Hallagan to her sister-in-law. "My dear, did you but *see* those pearls she is wearing? They most certainly cost *someone* a few guineas!"

"Trade, do you think?" asked the sister-in-law in shocked accents.

"Perhaps, though I must admit the young lady's manners, at least, do not smell of the shop. Very pretty-behaved I should say."

"Certainly. There is nothing to give one a disgust of her. And there is something decidedly aristocratic about her features. That neck!" The matron sighed into her own tiers of chins, momentarily quite struck by the unfairness of fate. Lady Morpeth had heard the conversation clearly and had to walk away lest she break into unladylike giggles.

But she could not escape. Speculation drifted around the floor to meet her. The evening was capped by the odious Mrs. Drummond Burrell. She leaned her bulk toward Princess Esterhazy. "For my taste," she sniffed, "her hair is far too black to admit of respectability. And I am quite sure that no young lady with the least claim to gentility would be allowed to possess such eyes. Did you but see them, my dear? I declare, they are quite purple!"

"Humph!" snorted her very aristocratic companion. "My own great-grandmother had just such eyes, I am told, and I *assure* you, her claim to gentility was *unimpeachable!*"

It was during one of the waltzes, in which Heather had been specifically warned that she must on no account participate until she had been given permission by one of the Patronesses of Almack's, that Geoffrey wandered over to where she sat on the sidelines. He held out a dainty, stemmed glass.

"Brought you some champagne."

"Oh, thank you, Geoff. I am quite parched from so much dancing."

"Should think so!" he said gruffly. "Haven't stopped since you walked in." She drank some of the champagne, wrinkling up her nose at the fizz. "Don't drink it too fast. Go to your head." She obeyed, sipping the drink slowly and peeping at him over the rim of her glass. She was looking very pretty, flushed with her triumph, but the Viscount sat gazing out into the room.

"I'm so glad that Robin taught me to dance so well. I was terrified, you know, but I do think I'm doing all right." She got no response to this sally, so she went right to her point. "Why have you not asked me to dance, Geoff?"

"How could I?" he answered bluntly. "Had a swarm of fellows around you all evening!" He shrugged and added, half to himself. "Knew you would do, too. Devilish pretty tonight, you know."

"Do you really think so, Geoff?" she asked. A glow of pleasure crept over her such as she had not felt at any of the other pretty compliments that had been heaped on her all evening.

"Course I do," he said matter-of-factly. He gazed at her as the music began to draw to a close. It had never before fallen to the Viscount's lot to help steer an innocent young girl through the rapids of a Season with the ton. He didn't feel fitted for the job and was sure he'd land in deep water. But he felt a strong sense of responsibility for this girl that he was wont to think of almost as a younger sister.

"That fellow Peevesby, one you danced with a while ago," he began unsurely.

"Do you mean the Major?"

"Whatever he calls himself. Fellow's a rake. Oughtn't to dance with him."

"No, is he really?" she exclaimed, her eyes suddenly searching the ballroom for a sign of the Major. "I never met a rake before. How very exciting! I do hope he asks me to dance with him again!"

"Heather!" exclaimed Geoff in exasperation. "Tell you the fellow's a moulder! Done up. On the catch for a rich wife. Oughtn't to dance with him," he repeated.

Heather, who harbored more than a little of her grandfather's independence under her pretty exterior, bridled at this instance of meddling. "Major Peevesby was *most* gentlemanly, I assure you!" she said loftily. "If your mama does not object to my dancing with him, I don't see why you should."

"Just told you why," he pointed out reasonably. "M'mother don't know about him. Very smooth fellow, Peevesby."

"Yes, he is," she countered. "And as he has no way of knowing that I am possessed of a fortune, I think it very unfair in you to imply that he could have no other reason for wanting to dance with me."

"Sniffing out the territory," he replied in what she could only think of as a very vulgar way.

"Well!" she exclaimed. "At least the Major behaved very civilly to me, with very proper manners, which is more than I can say of you!"

Before the Viscount could leap to his own defense, Mr. Ayrton appeared in front of the bickering couple. "Say, Geoff! What think you of my pupil?" he asked brightly, flashing Heather his devastatingly handsome smile. "She does me proud, does she not? The boulanger is next, Heather. Shall we show them how it's done?"

She glowered another instant at Geoffrey, then turned away with what in a more experienced young lady would certainly have been called a flounce. "Thank you, Robin. I should like it of all things." The couple floated away as the Viscount glared after them.

Viscount Morpeth was not the only guest in the ballroom that evening who watched Miss Heather Braddock's progress with less than unalloyed delight. Lady Susan Prenderby had reigned as The Incomparable for the past two Seasons, and she took her crown very seriously indeed. She was the perfect example of the current fashion in beauty: guinea-gold curls atop round, pink cheeks that blushed prettily at the least provocation, a pert little nose with a delicate up-turn beneath wide eyes of a clear China-blue, and a neat rounded figure in a cloud in pink muslin. The face glowed prettily now, but it was not from a maidenly blush that she suffered. She was beginning to grow alarmingly angry.

Every one of her very particular suitors had danced with Heather Braddock this evening, and now Mr. Ayrton, *her* Mr. Ayrton, who had once threatened to throw himself in the river if she refused to wear his flowers, was dancing with her a *second* time. And he seemed to be enjoying himself hugely. His usual behavior at such a ball was to lounge sulkily against the wall and glower at Lady Susan as she moved from one partner to another. Now he seemed not even to mind that she had granted him only one waltz all evening. He was perfectly content to dance with that skinny, washed-out, gawky girl, with her oh, so innocent smile, fluttering her big purple eyes.

Lady Susan chewed meditatively on the end of one gloved finger as she watched the pair, trying hard not to stamp her foot in anger. She would not have it! Or at least she would *try* not to.

But before she could think how to stop it, her attention was claimed by Major Peevesby, the same Major Peevesby whom Geoff did not at all like. She gave him her most brilliant smile, her blue eyes sparkling dangerously. Well, she would show Mr. Robert Ayrton that she didn't need his attentions!

"Oh, have you come to dance with me, Major?" she tinkled. "How fortunate that I have this dance free." Before the Major could open his mouth, the pair of them were dancing off.

It was during the next waltz that Lady Morpeth floated back to Heather with a rather unique gentleman in tow. "Heather, my love, here is someone who has been dying to meet you the whole evening." A pronounced twinkle of amusement danced in her green eyes. "Sir Ninian Netherwold, my goddaughter, Miss Braddock."

THE RELUCTANT SUITOR

"Chahmed, my deah, chahmed," he drawled in an excrutiatingly languid and surprisingly soprano voice. Heather extended her hand. Sir Ninian looked at it a moment, as though not entirely sure what it was, then raised his own to take it. Heather had the feeling she was shaking hands with a noodle. She looked up to discover herself being surveyed through an ornate quizzing-glass which so distorted Sir Ninian's left eye that he looked like some sort of lopsided fish.

Far from being disconcerted by his scrutiny, she took the opportunity to conduct a study of her own. For all her unworldliness, she recognized him at once as what her grandfather would have labeled a "demned macaroni" and anyone else would simply call a fop of the first order.

He wore an alarming Jean de Bry coat of apricot satin, puffed out like watermelons at the shoulders, nipped in like an hourglass at the waist, and with very long, pointed tails that threatened to trip him up if he turned too quickly. Heather should not have worried. Sir Ninian had perfected the art of flicking them out of his way as well as any dowager with a court train. His canary-yellow pantaloons were cut very short and strapped down over highly varnished dancing pumps and clocked rose silk stockings. No less than a round dozen of fobs and seals dangled below a scarlet and yellow striped waistcoat. She raised her eye to a neckcloth which Sir Ninian, if asked, would have proudly drawled was known as The Netherwold Neck. Its height and intricacy made the forbidding Waterfall look simple; its starched stiffness reduced the dangerous Oriental to the status of a wilted handkerchief. Sir Ninian was very proud of it.

His hair *au coup de vent* was oiled to perfection, glistening with *huile antique*, one glossy lock drooping interestingly onto his brow. Unfortunately for the total effect, the heat of the ballroom had caused the *huile* to puddle slightly on his forehead. It hung there in a very menacing fashion threatening at any moment to dribble down one side of his face. Sir Ninian, luckily, was unaware of the impending catastrophe.

"Dew yew care to dahnce, Miss Brahhdock?" he drawled out in the fashionably bored manner he'd carried to its logical extreme. He seemed in imminent danger of falling asleep.

Heather, forcing herself to avoid the ever more pronounced twinkle in Lady Morpeth's eyes, was just able to stifle a giggle. She looked demurely at the floor to hide her incipient laughter. "Th-that is very kind of you, Sir Ni-Ninian," she spluttered out, "but I do not waltz."

His sleepy eyes opened a trifle in surprise, and the quizzing-glass came into play again. "Wahhhltz? My deah Miss Brahhdock. *I* dew noht wahhltz! So tiring, yew know. And it disarranges my cravaht. I meant, of course, the next country dahnce."

By a sad accident of fate, Heather chanced to look up just then to catch sight of the fish-eye peering at her and was sent into a paroxysm of coughing in an attempt to cover her mirth. Finally she managed to say, "Too kind, sir, but I am already engaged."

"Pity," he closed the conversation and sauntered off with a languidly mincing step, if such a thing is possible.

"You really must not laugh at Sir Ninian, dear," said Lady Morpeth through her own barely concealed mirth. "He tries so very hard, you know."

"Godmama! I didn't know where to look! Was anyone ever so absurd?"

"Well, here comes a decided contrast to Ninian to ask you to dance."

Heather turned to see the Earl of Pythe, in sober and uncomfortable-looking evening dress. "Court!" she exclaimed in delight. "I haven't seen you all evening. I thought you must have stayed away."

He gave her his charming grin. "I tried to avoid it. My mother sent for me," he stated flatly, not at all embarrassed by the notion that he was at his mother's beck and call, but clearly wishing himself otherwise. "Dance, Heather?"

"Of course, if you're sure you want to."

"I do know how, and better you than another," he answered. His boyish grin removed any trace of an insult from the remark, and the couple took the floor. It was the last dance of the evening. Heather had still not danced with Geoff.

Riding home in luxurious exhaustion, the two ladies

recounted every event of the evening, pronounced themselves entirely satisfied with their triumph, and, once home, dragged themselves happily up to bed just as the first cock crowed somewhere in the direction of Covent Garden.

Chapter Eleven

Bridgewater, Bristol, Gloucester. The towns were speeding by with soul-filling satisfaction as Honoria Stapleton hurried north. By her calculation, she could hope to catch up with the sluggish stagewagon about midday tomorrow. She was determined to catch her fleeing cousin and John Tanner before Manchester was reached. Inquiries at the various tollbooths along the way had reassured her that the gap between the two vehicles was narrowing.

In the interest of speed, she had changed horses frequently and pushed the poor postilion unmercifully. At Droitwich he rebelled.

"Look you, missus," he piped up indignantly, brushing the mud from his boots outside the George Inn. "If you feel like goin' further tonight, well you can jest *walk!* I ain't movin' no more till I've had my dinner and my sleep!"

"My good fellow," said Miss Stapleton, bristling with indignation. "I have hired this chaise, *and you,* to carry me where I wish to go!"

"Then you can UNhire me, missus. I ain't movin', and that's flat!" He stomped into the taproom. Miss Stapleton spent the night at Droitwich.

They had just crested the hill beyond Stafford next day, the road winding off into the valley before them like a girl's party ribbon, when she caught sight of the lumbering wagon ahead. It was several miles off still, ambling up out of the valley, but there could be no mistaking it. Miss Stapleton began marshaling her forces. She knew the girl might be unwilling, but she also knew she had the law on her side. If necessary she would summon the nearest magistrate who would have no choice but to hand the girl over into her custody. She would brook no opposition to what was, after all, her legal responsibility for Lady Margaret St. Vincent.

She had given orders to the postilion that as soon as the wagon was passed, he was to pull across its path, effectively blocking its further progress. This accomplished, she climbed down into the road and strode up to the indignant driver of the wagon, now lumbering to a halt.

"Now would yer *mind* movin' that cake box on wheels or whatever it is?" he bellowed. "I got me payin' passengers here 'oo've a mind to see Manchester this day."

"My good man!" Miss Stapleton bellowed back, every drop of her noble blood at her command. "You are harboring a fugitive on your wagon, and not another foot will you go until she is restored to me."

Various unpleasant and threatening sounds issued from the depths of the wagon. Hoots, jeers, catcalls were hurled at Miss Stapleton and her chaise by the impatient travelers.

"A foogitive, is it then?" asked the sunburnt driver with a spit. "An' if ye be the gaoler, I can't say as 'ow I'm surprised. 'Oo yer lookin' for, then?"

Miss Stapleton brushed past the driver and climbed up into the very lion's den. "Lady Margaret!" she called, the undeniable authority in her voice momentarily silencing the passengers. "Lady Margaret St. Vincent! You will come out this instant!" She was peering into the wagon, filled with perhaps twenty people. They were crowded in like grapes in a wine press, and smelling nearly as strongly. The canvas cover that protected them from the sun seemed disinclined to allow in enough light for Miss Stapleton to discover her cousin. Unsurprisingly, no answer came to her summons.

As the wagon didn't seem likely to begin moving again at once, a few of the passengers took advantage of the pause to climb down for a stretch of cramped limbs. It was then that Miss Stapleton learned the sad news. There was no Lady Margaret and no John Tanner on this wagon.

"Would ye be meanin' that little-bitty thing with the big farmer fella she kept callin' 'My Johnny' all the time?" asked a strapping country girl in answer to Miss Stapleton's desperate inquiries.

"Yes, yes! Where are they?"

"Got off in Birmingham, they did."

"But they bought tickets to Manchester!"

"Aye, an' you could tell she weren't 'alf pleased 'bout that neither. Got 'im to agree on a change to the Stage this mornin', she did, an' off they went jest like rich folks."

"Where were they going?"

"She did keep on 'bout Scotland," and the girl gave a good country leer.

Miss Stapleton turned on her heel, and her cake box on wheels hurried north, leaving the wagon passengers to eat its dust.

"Postilion! Spur them on!" she barked out the window. The boy looked over his shoulder in ill-concealed disgust and continued to move the horses forward at his own chosen pace. At the postilion's chosen pace they reached the village of Newcastle-under-Lyme. And here Miss Stapleton was deserted. For the shiftless boy—the one who had so quietly taken her harping and bullying for so many miles—refused to take her any further. She had no choice but to go in search of another. She managed to hire an old rattle-trap that had seen far better days. But at least the horses, and the boy, were fresh, and she was able to travel through the night.

She slept, or attempted to, across most of Lancashire. The roads were considerably worse here, rougher and narrower. Ruts like plow furrows impeded their progress, and the swaying and jolting were so severe she feared she would be seasick.

Across the Cumbrian hills, and now she was frozen as well as ill. She was hungry, cold, tired, worried, and very angry when her chaise pulled into the courtyard of the Bull and Mouth in Carlisle, only ten or so miles from the dreaded Scottish border.

She reached the village less than an hour after the little Stage that she supposed to be carrying her cousin. This was the end of the line, and she learned that her quarry had headed off toward the livery stable as soon as they arrived.

"Hired my gig, they did, milady. Oh, 'bout half an hour back, I'd say," came the words of the stablemaster in his leather apron.

"Damme," muttered Miss Stapleton loudly enough to be heard.

"Not to worry, milady. Said as how they'd be back afore nightfall. Booked their bed an' dinner over at the Bear there." He gestured across the road with a huge raw-veined arm. "If ye'd care to wait . . . ?"

Once again she plunged into the now thoroughly despised chaise, to be bolted over another ten miles of terrible road.

Gretna Green was an ugly village that had grown up around the tawdry string of "wedding chapels." As the closest Scottish town to England, it was famous the length and breadth of the country for quick, easy weddings. *Anyone* with the minimal fee could get married in Gretna Green. Miss Stapleton, as she drove into the village, was still hopelessly determined that her cousin would not be among their number.

Strictly speaking, neither the chapel nor the fee were needed. All a couple had to do in Scotland was say "We are man and wife" in the presence of a witness, and it was so. Luckily for her sanity, Miss Stapleton was not aware of this quaint law. Had she been, she would have been kneeling on the floor of her carriage praying that her cousin was not aware of it.

No sooner had the sign announcing the border sped past her window than she saw a gig drawn up outside a dirty whitewashed structure with "Cupid's Bower" painted in scroll letters over a peeling green door. "Legal Scottish Weddings—7/6." the sign concluded. The door stood ajar, as though someone had just entered. Miss Stapleton was out of her carriage before even the steps could be let down. Two strides carried her up the weed-covered path and into the little "wedding chapel."

It was clear that a service had just begun. She could see the young couple standing before a huge bearded man in shirtsleeves, leather breeches, and muddy gaiters. The groom was broad-shouldered and tall, and he peered fondly down into the face of the girl. She was tiny, reaching only to a point somewhere below his shoulder, but she stood very straight and proud. She wore a dun-colored dress and a wrinkled apron, a mobcap atop her head, and she carried a bunch of primroses, obviously picked alongside the road.

"STOP!" boomed out the voice of Miss Stapleton, startling even herself by her vehemence. The pair whirled around. The girl's eyes blazed; the young man let out a frightened squeal like a cornered animal and promptly fainted dead away.

"An' jest what do yer think yer doin'?" asked the girl, hands on hips. She spared an impatient glance at her groom on the floor, then apparently decided that first things must be dealt with first. She squared up to Miss Stapleton, standing very straight, and fired out at her again. "Well, who be you, an' what do yer want with me an' my Johnny? I'm warnin' yer now. If so be it's his mama as has sent yer after us, it'll do her no good, nor you neither. He's mine now, an' so I'll keep 'im. I won't have that ol' witch scarin' 'im no more, an' so yer kin tell 'er!"

Miss Stapleton found herself confronting two perfect strangers. As the girl's words began to sink in and she realized the enormity of her mistake, she let out a long, low wail. Then, out of her inability to discover any other suitable course of action, she fainted dead away, joining the broad-shouldered young farmer in the world of the unconscious.

Chapter Twelve

The day following Lady Scopes's ball gave Heather her first taste of the afternoon promenade in Hyde Park's Rotten Row. This daily parade of the rich, the would-be rich, and the downright shabby was at the very hub of London life. Not to be seen frequently in the Park of an afternoon was simply not to exist.

As they turned into the Park, Heather's eyes darted here and there, not wanting to miss any of the show. A flash of scarlet and a jingle of bracelets caught her attention. "Tell yer fortune, milady," came the offer from a gypsy who sidled up smelling of onions and musk. To Heather's disappointment, they drove on.

More scarlet, now laced with gold, dressed the half-pay officers, trying to look suitably warriorlike on their glossy chargers, though they no longer had a war to fight. A pair of them eagerly joined the ladies in hopes of cementing their budding acquaintanceship with the newest Incomparable. A group of their brother officers came up too, supplicants begging an introduction. Lady Morpeth's carriage was soon besieged by well-bred gentlemen astride equally well-bred horses paying pretty, well-bred compliments.

Among them was the Earl of Pythe, looking ever so much more comfortable in a fawn riding coat and top boots, atop a magnificent black gelding, than he had the previous evening in Lady Scopes's ballroom. He and Heather chatted comfortably, as old friends do.

The Earl was a country squire at heart, ill-suited to London posturings. He'd led a comfortable sporting life until the death of his father a year ago. But now that he was the Earl, his mother was insisting that he take his rightful place in the ton, make a brilliant match, and become a leader of society and a credit to his family name.

He'd managed to resist her for a whole year, but her harpings had finally worn him down. He came to London for the Season.

"She thinks I'm dangling after you," he told Heather with a sheepish grin. "Do you mind?"

"How could I mind, Court? Every girl likes to have such a handsome suitor." She twinkled up at him atop the glowing mountain of horseflesh. "But doesn't she mind? She has no idea, after all, of who I am?"

"I hinted that you were very wealthy," he admitted.

"How clever of you. Why don't we encourage her to think you really are dangling after me? Perhaps she'll leave you in peace."

"I think I will," he said, not making it clear whether he really meant to dangle after Heather, or merely to encourage his mother to think so.

Their progress through the Park had taken on something of the character of a triumphal procession, including a marquis, two noble eldest sons, and Mr. Wesley on a sad little piebald, man and horse both hopelessly dwarfed by their companions. Horses, regimentals, and young gentlemen shifted about in ever-changing patterns as the group slowly advanced.

When progress became nearly impossible due to the numbers of eager followers, Lady Morpeth shooed the gentlemen away. They grumbled and groaned, but they rode off. Several were accosted almost at once by the Haymarket goddesses who roamed among the crowd, discreetly handing out their cards to potential gentlemen customers.

The Row was so enthronged with carriages of every description that forward movement became almost impossible. Many of the passengers had descended to the gravel walks and pavements to proceed on foot. As Lady Morpeth's barouche sat hopelessly mired in a string of equipages, unable to move at all, it was approached by a middle-aged matron in a salmon-colored lustring gown, all over geraniums, and red embroideries, and a very *outré* bonnet with a high poke, a forest of curled ostrich plumes and a bouquet of bobbing silk poppies. A large bow of coquelicot ribbons was tied pertly at one ear. She was a large, puffed-up looking woman, with a sallow complexion nearly as yellow as her improbable yellow hair. Luckily, only traces of the jaundiced skin could be seen, for the lady was rouged to the eyes.

She approached with a briskness surprising in one of her inflated proportions, towing a tall, angular, and decidedly gawky young lady, with a long, horsy face, lanky hair of a mousy brown, and fine, soft eyes wholly overborne by the mountain of ruffles, flowers, and knots of ribbon that covered her person. Lady Morpeth, who had been nodding to a duchess on the other side of the Row, didn't see this odd couple approach, but turned her head with her usual ready smile at mention of her name.

"Why, yes, it *is* Lady Morpeth?" exclaimed the woman in a voice just a shade too loud for gentility. "I knew it must be so, and very pleased I am too, for I wished to make my dear Miss Wheatley here known to you."

"I beg your pardon," said Lady Morpeth. "But do I know you?"

"Well, not properly, my lady, though I daresay you have heard my name. I am Mrs. Whitecastle," she stated, as though that explained everything.

"Mrs. Whitecastle?" replied Lady Morpeth blankly.

"Oh, yes, my lady, and it's very pleased I am to meet you at last, us being such close connections and all."

"Connections?" Lady Morpeth was beginning to feel like a parrot. "I think you must be mistaken, Mrs. . . .?"

"Oh no, not at all, my lady. My great-grandmother, you see, was a Winterhalter, her father being the younger son of the Fourth Baron, as I'm sure *you* know." Mrs. Whitecastle was off and running. "And, as you also know, of course, your sister-in-law, dear kind Lady Staid, (so very kind, is she not, and such style!) well, *her* mother was second cousin to Lady *Amanda* Winterhalter, who, of course, was a Miss Healy before her marriage to the present Sixth Baron. And so, you see, her marriage made her cousin to my grandmother." The sentence had a period. The recitation, alas, did not. "And then, of course, when you, dear Lady Morpeth, married her half-brother . . . Ah, poor Lord Morpeth! So sad for you to lose him in the prime of his life, so to speak. Well, to be sure, he was a bit older than you, but there, I cannot tell you how *distrait* I was when I learned of his sad illness and death. I was positively *vaporish* for months, I promise you!" She digressed, but Mrs. Whitecastle was not one to stray from her main point for long. "So you see, my lady, that your marriage certainly made you a definite connection of the Winterhalters, to which family I am myself so closely related." She concluded the genealogy. "It is such a joy to meet you at long last. I cannot conceive how we should have gone so long without chancing to meet, can you? Ah, but then I have been forced to live very quietly since my own Mr. Whitecastle died. So lonely being a widow, is it not? I have quite longed for someone like yourself, my lady, who can understand my feelings, to discuss things with, you know. And now that I have dear Sophronia to bring out . . ." She pushed forward the awkward girl, who had been cowering in the background, whether from shyness or embarrassment could only be guessed. "Miss Wheatley, my lady," she introduced the girl, who seemed to be about Heather's own age. Miss Wheatley gave a painful curtsy in their direction. Lady Morpeth, a very kind-hearted soul, could not help smiling at the girl, so obviously suffering acute emotional pain at the behavior of her chaperone. Heather offered her hand at once.

"And I am Miss Braddock. Is this your first Season as well?"

"Yes," came the answer in a voice barely above a whisper.

"Then we have something in common. Isn't it terrifying meeting so many people and having everything be so new and, well, *different?*" She couldn't have picked a better conversational gambit for Sophronia Wheatley. For Miss Wheatley had not known a comfortable moment since the day she left behind her horses and her dogs and her father in Leicestershire. She and Heather took to each other at once.

Mrs. Whitecastle, seeing her young charge engaged in conversation with Miss Braddock, launched into her monologue again. "Dear Sophronia is the daughter of the Fourth Baron Wheatley, don't you know. Such a lovely man, the Baron, don't you find, my lady? And of course his dear daughter is a delight to me, all alone as I am. To be sure, I could wish that she were as pretty as your own dear Miss Braddock. Your goddaughter, is she not? It is so very difficult to find an eligible *parti* for a young lady such as Sophronia, with neither looks, accomplishments, nor fortune to recommend her. To be sure, I have done my best with her. I cannot tell you the *hours* we have spent with milliners and dressmakers, my lady, but I fancy our efforts are not wholly contemptible." She gave a complacent smile. Lady Morpeth, who had only with great difficulty been able to remove her gaze from the full hideousness of poor Miss Wheatley's ensemble, could not speak, but there really was no need as Mrs. Whitecastle never required a response. "But I do not despair, my lady. Oh no. I am truly flattered that the Baron has reposed such confidence in me where his only daughter is concerned. And it will serve to prod me out of my doldrums, of course, and force me to go out into society a bit more."

The monologue seemed to wind down at last. Lady Morpeth, usually complete mistress of herself in every social situation, was so struck by Mrs. Whitecastle's encroaching manners and by the sheer nerve of the woman, that she was momentarily bereft of speech. She found herself staring in horrified fascination at the outrageous bonnet so carefully perched on the overblown yellow hair, her wide emerald eyes apparently mesmerized by a very large bee trying unsuccessfully to suck a drop of nectar from a sagging silk poppy.

She was drawn from her reverie by Heather's hand placed lightly on her arm. "Godmama, it seems that Miss Wheatley rides in the Park every morning. And Geoff has promised to bring my horse soon. May I ride with her one day? Please say I may."

Sensing trouble ahead if she allowed the pushy Mrs. Whitecastle into her world by so much as an inch, Lady Morpeth was reluctant to agree. She turned to squash the idea, only to meet the pleading in Heather's eyes and the look of sad resignation in Miss Wheatley's. She meant to explain that the idea was out of the question, but what came out was, "I'm sure Heather would enjoy that, Miss Wheatley. It is kind of you to invite her." Horrified at her own words, she started to add "But . . ." when she was cut off by the brightening in Miss Wheatley's soft brown eyes and her shyly spoken "Thank you, my lady. It will be a great treat for me." She looked at her chaperone with painfully knowing eyes, and added softly, "I can meet Miss Braddock in Clarges Street, or if you prefer we can meet in the Park. There will be no need for her to ride all the way to Lowndes Square." She hoped Lady Morpeth understood that she had no wish to force Mrs. Whitecastle on them. She was simply desperate for a friend of her own age, class, and circumstances.

"Lowndes Square?" echoed Lady Morpeth.

"Oh, yes, my lady," plunged in Mrs. Whitecastle, apparently feeling she had been left out of the conversation too long. "Quite out of the world, of course, but we are tolerably comfortable there. You must come to tea one day soon, my lady. I can promise you as good a scone with your India tea as you're likely to find in all of Mayfair. And if you'd condescend to eat your mutton with us too, I'll wager you'll not be disappointed in your meal. Oh, no! I know how to serve up a proper joint, and no less than two full courses will you get at my table. If there is anything I pride myself on, my lady, it is my kitchen."

Lady Morpeth looked at Miss Wheatley again, desperate for some means of escape from this woman and her determined society. "Heather will send you word, Miss Wheatly, if she can join you." The words were gently said, but the tone was dismissive, and her next words were to her coachman, an order to drive on.

"I may ride with her, mayn't I, Godmama?" asked Heather as they pulled away. "When my horse arrives?"

Lady Morpeth gave a quick glance back to where the girl was standing, looking forlorn. As the daughter of Lord Wheatley her birth was certainly unexceptionable. Whatever was she doing with that terrible woman? Lady Morpeth vaguely remembered the Baron. A sporting gentleman, as she remembered, more at home with his horses and his dogs than with most people, not caring much for fashionable society. His daughter looked to be very much like him.

"Well, we shall see dear," she sighed. "We shall see."

Mrs. Whitecastle was not, in fact, an unknown type on the fringes of the ton. Widows living in genteel poverty filled many of the row houses in the less exalted neighborhoods skirting Mayfair. To augment her income, Mrs. Whitecastle, by virtue of her much vaunted, but certainly tenuous, connection with Lady Staid, had taken to hiring out her services as sponsor and chaperone to young ladies making their come-out.

By a close study of Debrett's and the society columns of the fashionable journals, she was able to ascertain exactly which gentlemen had daughters of marriageable age and who were unlikely to be able to find suitable chaperones from among their own sisters, aunts, and cousins. Many such gentlemen were only too willing to grab at an offer to relieve them of the burden of placing their daughters on the Marriage Mart, happily turning them over to someone seemingly well-connected in the ton.

The Fourth Baron Wheatley was just such a man. He dearly loved his daughter, and really missed her whenever he bothered to think about her. But he'd promised her mother long ago that Sophy would be given every chance to become well-established. And so off she had gone to London and Mrs. Whitecastle.

Sophy was the third young lady that had been sponsored by the intrepid woman, and she was by far the biggest fish yet caught in Mrs. Whitecastle's net. The first had been the daughter of a newly created Welsh baronet, the second the only child of a *nouveau riche* Scots coal merchant. She had married off one to the eldest son of a squire, the second to a young banker on the way up. In the process, she'd earned for herself two fat fees and siphoned off several hideous and terribly expensive gowns from the girl's wardrobe accounts.

"This is Miss Wheatley's first Season too," explained Heather in the midst of her godmama's musings. "And she hasn't any friends in London either. She seems a very good-natured girl."

"I have not the least objection to Miss Wheatley, darling, but you can see how impossible that Whitecastle woman is." But she could not deny Heather her friend. "Oh, very well, dear. Just do not, I *beg* you, invite her chaperone to Clarges Street."

Heather giggled. "She is rather an unusual lady, is she not? And I think you found her vastly entertaining, Godmama," she twinkled. "But I shan't invite her, I promise."

It was growing late, and the crush in the Park had

thinned considerably. The plum barouche turned back toward Clarges Street. No time was to be lost in making their toilettes for the evening. Heather had been plunged into the London Season with a vengeance.

Chapter Thirteen

Heather was beginning to get into the way of things in London before many days had passed. She was overwhelmed by the kindness that seemed to surround her, unaccustomed as she was to such treatment. The sun seemed always to be shining, the birds sang just for her, and she was in high gig.

Morning sunshine poured through the front windows of Morpeth House. Heather was standing at the top of the long, polished stairway, its smooth, curved mahogany glowing in the morning light. She was glowing as well in a round gown of water-green cambric, a powdering of multi-colored flowers embroidered along its hem, and a pretty Scotch-plaid fichu pinned fetchingly across her bosom. She was ready to join her godmama downstairs to greet the inevitable string of morning callers.

As her kid-shod foot touched the top step, an impish smile crossed her face. She paused, looked all around and down the stairs. No one was around, and the long, elegant banister beckoned. With a quick lift of her petticoats, she settled herself daintily onto its topmost point and pushed off.

She felt as if she were flying, sliding down, down the slick, cool mahogany, curving in a great arc as the marble floor of the hall rushed up to meet her. She gave out an elfin squeal.

There had been no trace of anyone nearby when she began her descent. Unfortunately, this was no longer true before she reached the bottom. Just after her take-off Bellows had magically appeared out of nowhere, a dark angel, to answer the determined summons of the doorbell. Heather, mid-flight as it were, broke off her squeal to find herself gazing down into the shocked faces of the Dowager

Duchess of Strothsey and Mrs. Drummond Burrell. They seemed even more comical than usual from this unusual vantage point.

There was no stopping now, though if anything could have halted her it would have been the disapproving gazes of the two ladies. Petticoats flying, pink garters showing daintily, she could only continue down, down into the abyss. Even more unfortunately, Viscount Morpeth had had the bad luck to encounter the ladies on the front steps. He looked on in horror as his protegée plunged helplessly toward ruin.

Heather landed at their aggregate scandalized feet with a little plop, an embarrassed "Oh!" and a curtsy.

"Heather! What the deuce . . ." began the Viscount.

"Good morning, Your Grace, Mrs. Drummond Burrell," she managed, trying to master an unladylike desire to giggle. "I think you'll find my godmama in the morning room. Will you excuse me?" She slipped into the front parlor barely in time to hide her laughter and promptly dissolved in a fit of mirth, rocking back and forth on the settee. Here Geoff found her, wiping her streaming eyes and holding her sides.

"Just what the devil was that all about?" he asked just as she was beginning to regain some measure of composure. One look at his stern face, so reminiscent of Mrs. Drummond Burrell's, and she was off again. "Oh, oh, Geoff! Oh, please don't make me laugh anymore!" she sputtered through her giggles. "Did you but *see* them? How absurd they are!"

The Viscount was trying very hard to maintain his stern big-brother-who-knows-better attitude, but he was helpless in the face of her continued giggles. His own face began slowly to crack into a smile, a chuckle wiggled through, and finally the dam broke. The two childhood friends laughed until their sides ached.

When the full fury of their mirth subsided, Geoff tried to admonish her once again. "Really oughtn't to act like a hobble-de-hoy schoolgirl, y'know. Ain't the thing at all. Ain't good ton."

"I'm sorry, Geoff, but how was I to know they would walk in at that very moment? I suppose I must go and speak to them now, but how I shall keep from laughing again I can't imagine."

"Well, come look at your mare first," he said with a smile.

"My mare? Geoff! You've brought her! Come. Don't just stand there. I must see her at once!" She grabbed his hand and led him out onto the street.

Standing before the door next to Geoff's glossy bay was the prettiest dapple-grey mare Heather had ever seen. She stood a little over fourteen hands high, her beautiful thoroughbred head bobbing playfully atop an arched neck. She had powerful quarters and the broad chest of the true Welsh breed. In short, she was perfect.

"Oh!" squealed Heather at sight of her, clapping her hands in delight. The next thing the Viscount realized, two arms had been thrown about his neck. "Oh, thank you, Geoff! Thank you. She's, she's . . . exquisite!"

Geoff removed her arms from his brown riding coat, quickly looking around to see if this assault had been observed. "Here! Not that, Heather. Not in the middle of Mayfair!"

"What's her name?" demanded Heather.

"Well," he hesitated. "It's, it's, well, it's Gertrude."

"Gertrude?" echoed Heather in dismay. "Oh, dear. She's no more a Gertrude than I am." She studied the horse with the eyes of a lover. "Cobweb," she said softly and with a nod of decision.

"Huh?"

"Cobweb," she repeated. "It's a much more beautiful, fairylike name for such a beautiful fairy-tale horse. You know. Like in *Midsummer Night's Dream*."

The Viscount, not being very well acquainted with Shakespeare, knew nothing of the sort, but he was willing to accept whatever Heather wanted. "Cobweb," he said, trying it out. "Deuced queer name for a horse."

"I think it's perfect," she replied.

"She's your horse." He shrugged.

"My horse," said Heather in tones of wonder. "When can I ride her? Now? Right now?"

"Now?"

"Oh, please, Geoff. I must try her out. Please come with me."

"Ask m'mother."

"C'mon then." Once again the Viscount found himself being pulled off by the hand.

Heather burst into the morning room like a whirlwind, having completely forgotten the presence of the two visitors. She checked her headlong progress on the threshold, trying to summon up her company manners. But it was no good. She was bursting with her news.

"Godmama, Geoff has brought my horse, the prettiest mare in the world. May I go for a ride on her please?"

Lady Morpeth smiled fondly. "Of course, darling. I'm sure Her Grace and Mrs. Drummond Burrell will excuse you. You must tell me how you like her paces. Geoffrey is a remarkably good judge of horseflesh, you know," she said with a faint note of surprise at the ability of her son. "How pleased I am that we ordered the riding habit after all."

The young pair went off in a happy mood.

The ability to ride a horse is one of those things one never forgets. Years may pass without practicing the art, but the muscles remember. Heather hadn't been on the newly christened Cobweb's back ten minutes before she and the horse were moving as one. The Viscount led them into the Green Park where there was likely to be little traffic at this hour. Soon the skirts of Heather's velvet riding habit were billowing in the breeze as she galloped along the path. Such freedom, such joy! Of course proper Young Ladies of Quality did *not* gallop their horses in the Park. Heather didn't know that. Even after Geoff told her, she didn't care. She would seize freedom while she could.

She pulled up and waited for Geoff to catch her, which was a matter of only a moment.

"A hoyden. That's what you are, Heather," he said, not sternly but with a fond smile and even a touch of pride.

"Yes, I'm afraid I am," she admitted with a laugh. "Geoff, her paces are perfect! Wherever did you find her? She must have been very dear."

"At Tattersall's, and she was. Very. But devil take it, can't have you riding a plodder. What would anyone think?"

THE RELUCTANT SUITOR

"I'm going to ride her every day." She sighed happily and stroked Cobweb's warm shiny neck.

Watching her ride the beautiful grey horse, Viscount Morpeth felt that for once he had done something right. Odd how much pleasure one could get from making someone else happy, he thought. Especially someone like Heather.

Remembering her promise to Miss Wheatley, Heather sent word that very afternoon begging her new friend to meet her for a ride. The answer came back promptly and positively in the form of Miss Wheatley herself.

Remembering the horribly ugly dress Sophronia Wheatley had worn in the Park the day they first met, Heather was pleasantly surprised to see the girl ride up in a severe, well-cut bronze habit of merino wool that became her much better than Mrs. Whitecastle's chosen ruffles. It was obvious that Miss Wheatley had brought her own riding habits from Leicestershire.

All traces of awkwardness were gone. She sat her horse like a queen. She seemed to be almost a part of the powerful chestnut, as the two girls bounded across the grass, kicking up clods of turf in their wake and leaving the groom that Lady Morpeth had sent to accompany them far behind. The horse was obviously from Leicestershire as well.

They were laughing when they finally slowed to a sedate trot near the well-known Cheesecake House in the centre of the Park. The exercise had given Miss Wheatley a delicate flush that helped somewhat to offset the natural sallowness of her complexion. Heather turned eyes brimming with mischief toward her. "Do you know I was informed only this morning that proper young ladies do *not* gallop their horses in the Park."

"Oh, dear," Miss Wheatley said with a nervous little laugh. "I'm afraid I shall never be the proper young lady that Papa hopes for." The laugh faded and was replaced by a vaguely frightened look. "You won't tell Mrs. Whitecastle, will you? She doesn't like me to ride at all, you know, but Papa insisted on sending my horse."

"Of course I won't."

They decided to stop for a cup of tea and one of the cheesecakes for which the little thatched hut was famous.

Heather, not having eaten a thing for at least an hour, was famished. As they sipped and nibbled they chatted more and more easily. They had a lot in common, they found. But in the most important thing, they were exact opposites. Heather was having the time of her life in London. Sophronia was miserable.

"Could you not go back to Leicestershire?" asked Heather.

The other shook her head. "It would break Papa's heart. He promised Mama, you see, that I should have every chance to become happily established, as he puts it." She gave an ironic laugh. "He thinks he's giving me such a high treat, you know. He sent Mrs. Whitecastle ever so much money for my clothes and all." She couldn't help a grimace of distaste crossing her face as she thought of all the terrible gowns hanging in the wardrobe in Lowndes Square. "I couldn't bear to disappoint him."

"Yes, I suppose families can be a problem even when they mean well," sighed Heather whose own family had definitely *not* meant well at all.

"Well, we simply must find some way to make the Season more enjoyable for you. Do you go to the opening of Almack's this week? I do hope so, for I'll tell you straight out, I could use the moral support. I'm frightened to death," said Heather in her charming straightforward manner. "I've quite disgraced myself with one of the patronesses already."

"I have no voucher," replied the other, equally straightforward. "Can you imagine anyone giving a voucher for Almack's to Mrs. Whitecastle?" Heather had to giggle when she remembered the stern face of Mrs. Drummond Burrell that very morning. Whatever would the censorious lady think of Mrs. Whitecastle and her silk poppies?

"No, I suppose not. But certainly they couldn't object to *you*. Your father is a baron, after all."

"But I cannot very well go without her, you know. I'm sure she expected to get vouchers for me. She used to talk of nothing else. But I should be so terribly awkward and embarrassed. I don't seem to fit in very well in a ballroom," she sighed.

"Nonsense. If you had a friend by you, you'd be fine. I would so like to have you there with me."

"Well, it doesn't seem possible, does it?"

Heather was thinking, twisting one inky curl abstractedly around her finger. "Tell me," she said at last. "If my godmama were able to get you a voucher, would you come?"

"Well, I shouldn't think she could, would you?"

"You don't know Godmama," said Heather with a smile. "Please say you'll come."

Miss Wheatley sighed. "Very well. If your godmother can procure vouchers for us, which I take leave to doubt, I will go. Mrs. Whitecastle will be in heaven. She has her gown all picked out." Miss Wheatley could not forbear shuddering at the memory of the gown in question.

A light of mischief came back into Heather's eyes. "Oh, I shouldn't think even Godmama would be able to get *two* vouchers. They are so *very* difficult to come by. But there will be room for you in our carriage, Miss Wheatley."

A glimmer of fun, the first Heather had seen there, stole into her companion's doelike eyes. "Please call me Sophy."

"Sophy," repeated Heather. "It's a pretty name."

"Mrs. Whitecastle calls me Sophronia," she said with a look of strong distaste. "I detest it, even if it is my real name."

Heather wrinkled up her nose. "My real name is . . . Margaret."

"Margaret? Oh, I don't think that suits you at all. You are most definitely a Heather, rather like the color of your eyes."

Both girls were now certain they were destined to be fast friends.

Chapter Fourteen

"I can't understand a word they're singing," Heather whispered to Lady Morpeth that evening as they sat in elegant splendor at the opera.

"Don't worry, darling. Neither can anyone else, I assure you. No one really comes to the opera to listen to the music, you know."

Looking around her, Heather immediately recognized the truth of this. People strolled about chatting; dowagers nodded their feathers to each other; and fashionable Cyprians held court in their boxes. No one seemed much concerned at all with the antics onstage.

And from what little she could tell, it seemed a very silly story anyway. Something about a singing parrot and the Queen of the Night. So she banished guilt and allowed herself to take in the far more entertaining show closer at hand.

She had been impressed by Lady Scopes's ballroom, but the Italian Opera House overwhelmed her. Gilt and crystal, crimson draperies and flickering candles, and pink-cheeked cherubs smiling down on it all. It was indeed wonderful, in the truest sense of the word. To be sure, it was just a *bit* garish. But then, so were most of the spectators gracing its boxes and galleries.

She was seated in the box of Lord Handy, one of Lady Morpeth's more persistent admirers. Geoffrey Curwen completed the quartet. The Viscount had grumbled only a very little about being forced to "listen to some fat prima donna warbling in some curst jibberish." A proper appreciation of a pretty opera dancer was one thing. It was, after all, expected of a fellow. To have to sit through an entire opera was something else again. He'd much rather have spent his evening tippling a few at the Daffy Club or

THE RELUCTANT SUITOR

lounging at Cribb's Parlour discussing the coming bout between Irish Dan Donnely and Jack Carter, "the Lancashire Hero." He knew there would have been no trouble at all in finding another escort for Heather if he had refused. But he had gone to the opera after all. For what reasons he was not himself quite sure.

Heather continued to gaze around contentedly, and her eye lighted presently on Sir Ninian Netherwold, looking like a French doll in a *vieux rose* satin suit with puce trimmings, his face and hands whitened with enamel, palms tinged with vermilion, and a liberal application of Bloom of Ninon on his high cheekbones. A cravat ample as a tablecloth and a huge buttonhole of pinks, geraniums, and a lily finished the vision. He looked to be in imminent danger of falling asleep as he peered out at the crowd through drooping eyelids.

He became aware of her amused gaze, though without, of course, the least suspicion that he himself might be the source of her amusement. He seemed to collect his recalcitrant muscles with an effort, as though waking them from a particularly deep sleep, rose, and gratified her with a low, slow bow. For a moment, she feared he might not rise again. He seemed to have dropped off in a doze at the nadir of his courtly effort. He did, however, manage to right himself at last. She answered him with a friendly nod, then, fearing she would disgrace herself with giggles, let her eyes move on.

The box next to Sir Ninian's contained a very jolly-tar sort of a fellow, bald, sixtyish, and looking altogether contented. He sat in solitary state, casting smiles like bullets in every direction. Heather wondered who he was.

"Oh, that is Mr. Ramsbottom," said her godmama. "Isn't he a fright? He's just back from the West Indies, I hear, and with an enormous fortune. He's looking about him for a wife. If he weren't so very old, or so very ugly, and if he had a prettier name, he might do for you."

Heather laughed and pulled her attention back to the stage, trying to make some sense out of the nonsensical story. Why can they not sing in English, she thought. At length she gave up the fight and let the admittedly lovely music of Mozart wash over her.

It was with eagerness that she greeted the interval, heralding as it did the inevitable arrival in their box of what seemed like half the eligible young bachelors in London. Among them was the Earl of Pythe, whose mama watched contentedly from across the theatre, and Mr. Ayrton. His looks across the theatre, to where Lady Susan Prenderby sat with an elderly marquis, were anything but contented. He glowered in his brooding, romantic way, while Lady Susan studiously avoided his gaze.

"Robin, dear," said Lady Morpeth. "You really mustn't look so *threatening*. You will frighten away all of our gentlemen friends."

"What the devil does she see in that coxcomb Wattlesey?" he grumbled.

"I'm sure she doesn't see anything in him at all," soothed Geoff's mother, who had, after all, been dealing with Robin Ayrton's moods for years. "What her mother sees in him, I fancy, is a marchioness's coronet for her daughter."

"But surely, Godmama," injected Heather, "Lady Susan wouldn't marry such a silly-looking old man for such a reason. She's so lovely. She could have anyone she wanted."

"She will have," said Court matter-of-factly.

Geoff, knowing Robin as he did, perceived an urgent need to change the subject. "What the devil's that there?" he asked, indicating a box directly opposite their own.

Heather spied a lady who seemed to be smiling and nodding very determinedly in their direction. It was a moment before she could decipher the face among the feathers and ribbons and paste jewels that adorned it. "It's Mrs. Whitecastle. Do look at her, Godmama."

Lady Morpeth just caught herself before she turned completely. "Oh, dear. I really mustn't notice her, you know, for then she is certain to call, and *then* what would I do? But only tell me, darling, for I am dying to know. Is she wearing poppies again?" she asked, gazing determinedly in the other direction.

"Oh, no," chuckled Heather. "She's wearing a bird. A blue jay, I think it is. Only with very long tail feathers."

"Oh, dear, I really must see it. Do tell me when she looks away."

"She won't," said Geoff. "Determined."

THE RELUCTANT SUITOR

"What is that with her?" asked Robin.

"Why that's Sophy, of course," replied Heather.

Court saw her too. "Plain," he said simply and with more than a little truth.

"Devilish plain," seconded Geoff.

Next to Mrs. Whitecastle, poor Sophronia Wheatley was buried from head to foot in a mountain of pink tulle and green feathers, all but disappearing into its froth. Her mouse-colored hair had been tortured into a pile of fuzzy ringlets caught up with pink ribbons. "Poor child," muttered Lady Morpeth who had stolen a quick glance.

"There's one destined for an ape-leader," said Robin with a shudder.

"Robin! How can you be so unkind? Sophy is a very sweet girl. Not everyone can look like Lady Susan Prenderby, you know."

"*No one* looks like Susan!" he professed, scowling in that young lady's direction.

The Earl was still staring at Miss Wheatley. "Plain," he repeated with a decided nod of the head.

"Cits," stated Geoff as though that explained it.

Heather turned on them with spirit. "It isn't Sophy's fault that that horrid, vulgar woman has bought her such awful gowns. She is daughter to a baron, and *perfectly* respectable, and I won't have you being uncivil to her. She is my friend."

With a sniff she turned to greet some new arrivals to their box. Among them was a certain Sir William Longchamps, a friend of Lord Handy. Sir William was above the medium height, with a solid, stocky build. He was not precisely handsome, being possessed of a complexion tanned and weathered by the sun and a head of springy grizzled hair retaining only traces of its original red glow. But he exuded the strong sense of confidence natural to the self-made man, and his quiet competence could not help but attract.

"Longchamps!" greeted Lord Handy with a friendly wave. "Didn't expect to see you tonight. Thought you were still in Southampton. Come in, man. Come in."

"My ship arrived sooner than I expected, so I was able to get back this afternoon. Good to see you again, Handy."

"Make you known to Lady Morpeth," continued Lord Handy. "Tina, this is Billy Longchamps. Sir William now. Packed off to India quarter of a century ago. Just came back a Nabob!"

"Not exactly that," Sir William demurred in his warm friendly voice, though in fact Lord Handy was quite right. Sir William had just returned from twenty-five years in India enormously rich. He took Lady Morpeth's proffered hand. "It is an honor, my lady. My belated condolences on the loss of your husband. I learned of his death only recently, shortly before I left India, in fact."

"That is kind of you, sir," she replied studying his face intently.

"Actually, we have met before," he went on. "But it was more than twenty-five years ago. I don't expect you'd remember."

Her face lit with a charming smile as recollection dawned.

"To be sure, I remember you very well, Sir William, though you were plain Mr. Longchamps then, were you not? We first met at Georgianna Devonshire's ball, and we danced the minuet." Her green eyes twinkled bewitchingly. "You wore a coat of claret-colored velvet and quite the most wonderful waistcoat I'd ever seen. I was convinced you were the handsomest young man in the room."

"The biggest coxcomb, I collect you mean," he responded warmly, obviously pleased by the exactitude of her recollection. "I believe I even sported a patch!"

"Well, only a very small one," she admitted. "On your left cheek." She reached up a gloved finger and lightly tapped the spot.

"Oh, dear, it should be unlawful to remind one of the extravagances of puppyhood! Though I need no reminder of the prettiest girl at the ball, in ivory satin and powdered hair, and all-over rosebuds."

"Well, Longchamps," interrupted Lord Handy, not pleased by these delightful reminiscences. "Meet the rest of the company."

"Oh, dear," said Lady Morpeth in her pretty, rippling way. "How rag-mannered of me. Now you must be terribly civil to my goddaughter, Sir William. This is Miss

Braddock." She indicated the girl, who was now surrounded by admirers, including the rakish Major Peevesby. "And this is my son, Geoffrey. Is he not splendid?"

The Viscount offered Longchamps his hand. "Don't mind m'mother, sir. Charming, y'know, but a devilish silly woman," he added in an undertone.

Sir William took his hand, but his smile still twinkled at Geoffrey's doting mama. "On the contrary, my lord. I seem to remember her as a lady of unerring judgment. She did, after all, have the good sense to marry your father. A fine man, Morpeth. I can see you're very like him."

The Viscount warmed to the charismatic gentleman, beaming with pride at the recognized likeness to his adored father. Sir William turned to Heather. His look became fixed and penetrating as he took in the long neck, the straight nose, and the long-lashed violet eyes.

"Miss Braddock, is it?" he asked, taking her hand.

"Yes, sir. I'm very pleased to meet you."

He couldn't help but stare, caught not only by her fresh beauty. The young lady was possessed of a truly remarkable resemblance to another young lady he had known some twenty-odd years ago. That girl had traveled through India with her wealthy father, one of Sir William's trading partners. In fact, Sir William had nearly married that pretty girl. For a moment it seemed to his bemused eyes that she had been reincarnated in a London opera box.

"Where do you come from, Miss Braddock?" he asked with more than cursory interest.

"From Cornwall, sir," she answered truthfully. Before his inquiries could become too particular, she turned to introduce the others. The spell was broken, and Sir William greeted the gentlemen in his usual forthright manner.

"Were you really sent off to India in disgrace, sir?" asked one.

"I was indeed. The red hair, you know. I'm much afraid I had the temperament to go with it."

"And now?" prodded Lady Morpeth.

"Well, I no longer have red hair."

"And will you be staying in England, Longchamps?" asked Lord Handy.

"Oh yes," he said softly, a smile playing about the corners of his mouth. "I believe I'll stay."

"Have you only just returned, sir?"

"Yes. I came into the title quite unexpectedly last year when my elder brother was killed at Waterloo. But until a few months ago, I found I had no reason to return to England. You must come and see my house in St. James's Square soon, my lady," he said to Lady Morpeth. "I came back and found myself stifling in the Englishness of it all, so I'm putting a few of my Indian treasures about. To make it feel more like home. I would value your opinion of my efforts. I'm told you have a flair for such things."

"That she does," beamed Lord Handy. "As she does with everything else."

"Heather, my love," she said to her goddaughter. "Was I not warning you just the other day to be wary of suitors offering Spanish coin? Well here, my dear, you have the perfect example of what I meant. You must never listen to such false flattery."

"But, Godmama, you know very well that you are never paid in *false* coin. You have much too good an eye for the real thing."

"Ah," said the oily Major Peevesby. "It appears that our delightful Miss Braddock is as clever as she is beautiful. One might say she was as bright as a newly minted—and genuine—penny."

Heather, much to Geoff's disgust, fluttered her fan in much the same way she had seen Lady Susan Prenderby do. He half expected her to come out with an "Oh, la, sir."

"Sir William," said Lady Morpeth suddenly. "I have just remembered the last time we met. It was at my betrothal ball. I had you down for the cotillion, but when the time came you had already departed. Sir William, you owe me a dance!" she decreed, tapping her fan lightly on one sleekly clad broad shoulder.

"So I do, my lady." He grinned down at her. "So I do. And you shall have it, I promise. Perhaps I was waiting for the invention of the waltz."

The musicians began to pluck tentatively once more, and the company in the box dispersed. When they were alone again and the music began in earnest, Lady Morpeth leaned toward Heather and whispered, "Well! To think that William Longchamps should return after all these years. And quite fabulously wealthy, I collect. Apparently there is no Lady Longchamps. Did you like him, darling?"

"He seems a very pleasant gentleman."

"Good. He might do very well, you know," she mused almost to herself. "Yes, he might do very well indeed."

Chapter Fifteen

It was a very dispirited Honoria Stapleton who arrived back in Cornwall. By rushing off harum-scarum after what proved to be a false scent, she feared she had lost her cousin's real trail. She was very angry with herself. She was even angrier with her cousin.

But Honoria had never been known for a lack of determination. She simply did not know how to quit. She would not do so now, when so much depended on finding the errant girl and bringing her quietly back to Heathside.

She felt certain now that Mrs. Bing must have assisted Lady Margaret in her flight and conspired to send her guardian on such a wild goose chase. In any case, she made a convenient scapegoat. Honoria Stapleton would use a bit more cunning this time. She would find out what the Bing woman knew.

Placing herself in a huge thronelike chair, one foot resting on a damask-covered footstool, she summoned her housekeeper.

"Mrs. Bing," she began in the tones of a sorely tried monarch. "I have asked you before, but you did not see fit to tell me. Now I am asking you again. Where is Lady Margaret?"

Mrs. Bing was not unprepared for this interrogation. She was quite as clever, in her home-brewed, countrified way, as Miss Stapleton. Also, Ellen had been rehearsing her for days for this inevitable confrontation. Now, facing her employer, Bing seemed to visibly shrink into her voluminous apron, her reddened hands wringing nervously before her.

"I . . . I couldn't say, ma'am," she began tentatively. "It's like I told ye, ma'am. She just . . . upped and disappeared one morning." She knew her protestations were unconvincing, but she went on. "It's that worried I am about the child, too. What coulda happened to her?"

"*I* have no idea, Mrs. Bing, but I am quite certain *you* do."

"But, ma'am..."

"Tell me, Mrs. Bing. How old are you?"

The housekeeper seemed to grow flustered at the change of topic. "Why, to be sure, ma'am, I'm ... I'm sixty."

"Just so," said Honoria, apparently satisfied. "And how long have you been at Heathside?"

"Why since ye come yerself, ma'am. Ye know that."

"So I do. This part of the country is so remote, is it not? I understand it is very difficult to secure good positions here, especially when one has a few years on one. Is that true, Mrs. Bing?" Her tone was almost casual.

The poor housekeeper's eyes widened in her red, round face, fear shining through them. "Oh, ma'am, I'd never be able to find another, not 'fore I died! Ye'd not turn me off, ma'am. Ye could not! I've nowhere at all to go," she lied, in supreme disregard for the fact that she had already made arrangements to spend the summer with her sister in Penzance until, hopefully, Heather would be able to send for her.

"Just so," repeated Miss Stapleton. "Perhaps you would care to tell me now where Lady Margaret has gone? And with whom?"

Mrs. Bing's slender control broke down completely, and she admitted it all. How Lady Margaret had been so unhappy here. How she had decided to run away, to try to support herself and maybe find some man who would make her happy. How she'd been terrified by the thought of going alone to London. How she'd chosen Bath instead, certain that she'd be able to find employment there.

The recital was very convincing, punctuated as it was with tears, wringing of hands, head-shakings, and pleas for forgiveness. "You know how persuading she could be, ma'am, with those big eyes. She begged me fer help, an' I didn't know how to say no. So I give her the money fer the coach fare to Bath, an' off she went, happy as a grig. An' I do be so worried 'bout her, ma'am."

"You might have thought of that before!" snapped Honoria. The performance had been a good one. She was convinced. With a sigh of resignation, she rose and climbed the stairs to pack her just-unpacked valise. At least, she thought, she could stay with Henrietta in Bath and be tolerably comfortable. It could have been worse.

Within the hour Honoria Stapleton was off to Bath.

Heather's friendship with Sophy Wheatley blossomed quickly. The two young ladies rode together daily, confiding many of their hopes and fears to each other. Heather learned that Sophy's father had gone into debt to give her this Season in London, a Season she hadn't wanted at all. He was counting on her marrying well, thus relieving him of the burden of support. The responsibility terrified Sophy.

Heather confided that she was also under a certain pressure to marry, and quickly. Without giving details, she made it clear that if she didn't marry within the month, she would probably be left with no means of support. They even discussed the pitiably few ways in which a Young Lady of Quality could earn her daily bread.

On this fine, bright morning, however, their chatter covered nothing quite so serious. The sunshine had combined with the heady scent of the lilacs foaming over the Green Park to make them both lighthearted. As they cantered past the resident dairy cows with their attendant, and picturesque, milkmaids, they spotted the Earl of Pythe approaching. He reined in at sight of them.

"Court!" cried Heather in delight. "I had not thought to find you abroad so early." She twinkled mischievously at him. "I thought that no fashionable gentleman rose before noon at the earliest."

"They don't," he answered neatly.

"You haven't met Sophy, yet, have you? She is my very particular friend. Miss Wheatley, the Earl of Pythe." He nodded politely at the introduction.

"My lord," mumbled Sophy in shy acknowledgment, her eyes glued to the ground.

The Earl had not changed his opinion of Miss Wheatley's worldly beauty. Plain, he told himself. But his eyes shone with interest when they came to rest on the magnificent animal she was riding. "That's quite a colt," he said, reaching out to stroke the soft ginger mane. The admiration in his voice was pronounced, and Sophy lost some of her shyness in pride.

"Yes, Baron is my joy," she said softly, giving the horse an affectionate pat. "He was foaled on my father's estate in Leicestershire."

The Earl looked up at mention of the famous hunting county. "Do you hunt, Miss Wheatley?"

"Every chance I get," she admitted. "I hope to hunt Baron this season. It will be his first."

"And you ride so very well, Sophy," put in Heather, glad to see her friend taking part in the conversation.

At that Sophy actually laughed. It transformed her face. "Well, I was born on a horse and raised in a stable, or so my papa says."

"Wheatley," mused Court. "Lord Wheatley?"

"Why, yes. Do you know Papa?"

"We've hunted together with the Cottesmore. He's one of the best men to hounds I've ever seen."

"It's his passion. Mine too, I fear."

"Perhaps we'll meet on the field next season."

"Yes, perhaps," she answered, some of her shyness returning.

"Shall we see you both at Almack's tomorrow?" he asked.

"Oh, how stupid of me," Heather chided herself. "I had nearly forgotten to tell you, Sophy. Godmama has your voucher. I can't think how I came to be so silly as to forget. Sophy will be going with us, of course, Court."

"Till tomorrow, then," he replied civilly, tipping his hat in their direction.

Heather turned to Sophy and suggested a race to the dairy barn. Waving goodbye to the Earl, they set off at a hard gallop.

He watched them go. Plain, he repeated to himself, watching Sophy Wheatley ride away. Deuced plain, but she certainly could sit a horse. Admiration was clear on his face.

The two girls reined in by the little farmhouse, Heather trailing by a length, and dismounted to refresh themselves with a tall glass of the fresh milk.

"He has kind eyes," commented Sophy.

"What? Who?"

"The Earl. He has kind eyes."

"Court? Oh, yes. He is one of the kindest gentlemen I know. What will you wear tomorrow?" she asked as they sat on a rustic bench under a tree, sipping the frothy liquid and licking off milky mustaches with relish. In reply, Sophy only rolled her eyes and gave a little moan. "Oh," breathed Heather softly as she realized the extent of the problem. Both girls lapsed momentarily into a brown study. "Well," said Heather finally. "We must work with what we have. Let's go."

"Go where?"

"Lowndes Square."

Moments later the pair of them were in Sophy's little bedchamber in the unfashionable neighborhood of identically pillared white row houses. They had been fortunate enough to find Mrs. Whitecastle out. A number of ball gowns lay on the bed; Heather stood before them in deep contemplation.

"What do you think?" asked Sophy tentatively. "They're hopeless, aren't they?"

"I wish Godmama were here. Her taste is so exquisite. Well, the pink is out, definitely." She hung the pile of frothy tulle back in the wardrobe. A buttercup-yellow taffeta and a purple-bloom satin with chenille trimmings in Pompeian Red suffered the same fate. There remained only a gown of Berlin silk in a warm taupe, lavishly trimmed with lace, flowers, and ribbons, and with an overdress of acid-green matelassé. "It will have to do," said Heather, mentally rolling up her sleeves. "We will have to *make* it do. Put it on."

Sophy, confused, did as she was told.

Heather picked up a small pair of scissors from the dresser and set to with a will as Sophy stood speechless. Off came the green overskirt, fourteen of Mrs. Whitecastle's beloved silk poppies, two dozen green chenille leaves, and a handful of ribbon knots that were looped around the hem. A poppy-red sash was discarded, as was the fall of Honiton lace at the neck.

The taupe gown now hung in bare simplicity, innocent of trimmings. Rummaging in a drawer, rather as Lady Morpeth had done when Heather herself was being outfitted, she came up with a wide sash of mahogany crape which she tied elegantly around Sophy's waist, letting the ends fall nearly to the floor.

Sitting the girl down before her, she swept the dull brown hair into a smooth chignon, caught low at the nape of the neck. To one side of her face she pinned a simple flat spray of rust and copper feathers which she'd removed from an outrageous bonnet that certainly would not miss them. She stood back to admire her handiwork.

"There!" she said in satisfaction.

Sophy rose uncertainly and crossed to the mirror. What she saw was a young lady, well, not precisely transformed—she would never be a beauty or anything like—but she looked far more attractive than at any time since her arrival in London. She gave her friend a warm embrace. "I have never had such a friend," she declared. "I shan't be quite so afraid to go tomorrow now."

"Of course you won't," said Heather bracingly. "We will support each other through the evening. Whatever do you suppose Mrs. Whitecastle will say when she sees it?"

Sophy pulled herself up to her full height, which was considerable. "I don't care what she says! Surely I may decide for myself what to wear to a ball." She paused, then added a little sheepishly, "Besides, I won't let her see it until it is too late to change."

Heather chuckled. "And don't, I beg you, let her call the hairdresser again." With that the two girls broke into delighted schoolgirl giggles and collapsed onto the bed.

The famed Daffy Club, haunt of sportsmen from every level of society, from the out-and-out Corinthian to the meanest scrub who ever won thruppence on a bet, was bustling that evening, the din tumultuous. The air was rent with the clang of pewter tankards and heavy crockery and a chorus of voices laying wagers or arguing the merits of the latest professional pugilist. A dense, curling layer of blue, rum-smelling smoke swirled in and out among the congregated Pets of the Fancy.

And above it all, in his usual drab breeches and jockey boots, sat the greatest pugilist of them all, the owner of the Daffy Club, the famous Tom Belcher. He sat quite alone, rubbing his chin with one huge-knuckled hand, as though he couldn't quite understand what all these people were doing in his parlor. Was he contemplating that memorable occasion when he had severely rearranged the features of the great Mendoza? Or perhaps considering whether to come out of retirement for a classic bout with Molyneux, the American Black? He wasn't giving away any secrets tonight as he gazed out onto his domain, looking husky as an old apple woman and seemingly contented as a mother hen watching the antics of her brood of chicks.

Three of those chicks, Viscount Morpeth, the Earl of Pythe, and Robert Ayrton, lounged at one of the scarred tables, puffing casually on long cheroots. Casually, yes—but far from contentedly. In fact, none of the three comrades seemed to be looking in particularly high spirits. They sat there, isolated from the din by their own brooding silence.

The Earl of Pythe was bored, a deadly occurrence in a man of his energies. He was sorry he'd given in to the incessant nagging of his intrepid mama to come to London. He hated all the folderol of the ton, with its balls and routs and such. To compound her crime, his mother had insisted on introducing to his notice any number of simpering, milk-and-water misses, prodding him to dance with this heiress, or to take that earl's daughter for a drive, till he was sure he'd go crazy with it.

"They'll have to slap me in a straight-waistcoat and clap me into Bedlam before long," he groaned to his friends. "She's got me running all over town, helter-skelter. Got to get out of London, or she'll have me done to a cow's thumb."

"Good notion, that," piped up Robin. "Getting out of town, I mean. Can't stand the place!" For emphasis he gave his head a severe shake, causing one ebony curl to fall across his brow. It was lucky there were no females in the Daffy Club for he looked quite irresistible.

Had Robin's friends been in a more perceptive frame of mind they might have exhibited some surprise at his desire to leave town in the middle of the Season. He was, of the three, the most addicted to town pursuits, even exhibiting on occasion telltale signs of incipient dandyism.

"Why the devil does she allow that gimlet-eyed old square-toes, Wattlesey, to drive her all over town in that

THE RELUCTANT SUITOR

deuced ugly curricle of his?" he went on, giving them a clue to the source of his ill humor.

"Who?" asked Geoff who was also sporting a long face.

"Susey! Lady Susan. *My* Susey! What the devil does she mean by it? He's a silly old court-card, for all he's a marquis."

"He's got the gingerbread, though," Geoff pointed out. "Rich as Croesus, they say."

"Those greys he drives are plodders," added Court. "Showy, but not a leg between 'em."

"Oh, the devil take his greys! What do I care about his greys? But she *can't* want him! I heard her myself calling him a silly old noddy. Last season."

"Changed her mind," said Geoff with a lamentable want of tact. "Had her nose put out of joint by Heather's success, I'll wager. Ain't used to taking a back seat. Decided she'd better settle on someone before they stop offering. Susan's no dummy."

Robin, his regrettable temper already sorely tried by the sight of his goddess being tooled around the Park that afternoon by Lord Wattlesey, and his anger fueled by the several tankards of Daffy he'd consumed, was out of his chair like a shot, grasping at the lapels of the Viscount's bottle-green coat.

"How dare you cast such slurs on that angel, Morpeth! I'll see you across twenty yards at Paddington Green before I'll let you malign her. Damned if I won't!"

"Give over, Robin," said Court imperturbably. "You know he won't go out with you. And if you try to mill him down he'll only draw your cork for you. Outweighs you by a stone."

Geoff had managed to loose himself from his friend's grasp, a not too difficult task, as he had had much practice of it. "Daresay it's all a hum, anyway, y'know. Old Susan'll do better for herself than that old puff-guts."

Robin sat heavily in his chair. "But it won't be me. Her mother'll see to that," he grumbled, despair writ large on his face.

"Got to get out of town," repeated Court. "We'll go down to Great Pythe, then off to Epsom for the races. What d'you say?"

"Capital notion," answered Robin. "We'll go in the morning."

"Can't," said Geoff, causing two pairs of eyes to round on him.

"Why not?"

"Heather," he stated simply.

"Well, what about Heather?"

"Can't go off and leave her. Got no more notion than a baby how to go on. Every John Doe and Richard Roe in town after her. *And* that curst Peevesby fellow. Damned rake. Have to keep an eye on him. And on her."

"Your mother'll see to Heather. Very knacky one, your mother. Said so yourself," said Court.

"Well, she ain't!" said Geoff with amazing discernment. "Thought she was, but she ain't. Likely to let Heather fall into every sort of scrape and start. Hasn't kept Peevesby away, has she? Or that rum captain What's-his-name. Or that curst puppy, Wesley."

"She's trying to find her a husband," Court pointed out. "It's why you brought her here, ain't it? To find a husband?"

"Leave it to your mother to settle," added Robin.

"Makes me mad as Bedlam to see her blushing and fluttering for a bunch of damned fortune hunters, especially Peevesby. Heather deserves better."

"So warn her," said Robin with an offhanded gesture.

"Already did," Geoff admitted ruefully. "She took it in snuff."

"I shouldn't be surprised. She may be green, but Heather's got plenty of sense in her cockloft. She'll be all right. We'll leave tomorrow." Court considered the matter settled.

"No. Can't." The Viscount was being unwontedly mulish.

The trio relapsed into silence, the Viscount's two friends eyeing him thoughtfully. It wasn't at all like the comfort-loving Geoffrey Curwen to put himself much about for anyone, especially a chit of a girl to whom he wasn't even related.

But even this intriguing situation could not hold their attention for long. They all three fell to brooding over their individual problems and muttering in a round.

THE RELUCTANT SUITOR

"Damndest thing about mothers, y'know," grumbled Court.

"Land herself in the basket, sure as cheek," followed Geoff.

"As ramshackle an old caper merchant as ever was," followed Robin.

"Says it's my duty to take my proper place."

"Ain't up to snuff at all."

"Bracket-faced old bobbing block."

"Curst bore!"

"Green girl!"

"Twiddle-poop!"

Chapter Sixteen

"Oh, yes, my love," said Lady Morpeth with satisfaction as she surveyed Heather next evening. "I am glad we settled on blue. Oh I know most girls in their first Season wear white, but it does make one look so *insipid!* Definitely not in your style. But you look charmingly. And so does Sophy, of course. I shall be quite proud." She turned her charming smile on Miss Wheatley. Sophy, knowing herself so improved in the simple taupe gown, was feeling considerably less nervous than was her wont before a ball, and Lady Morpeth was almost able to bewitch her into thinking that she really was attractive.

The three of them were on the point of departing for Almack's, Shrine of the Ton. They were awaiting only the arrival of Geoffrey who had grudgingly consented to accompany them.

Heather's "blue" which Lady Morpeth had just approved was a devastatingly fetching creation of Andalusian silk, cut on severely simple lines and falling in elegant folds from a high waist. Long kid gloves in palest dove grey, satin slippers, and a wispy Austrian scarf abetted the total effect. The gown was devoid of ornament excepting only Heather's exquisite black pearls and the shimmering light of excitement in her glowing eyes.

Despite her finery she still felt perilously like a child playing dress-up. The feeling was augmented by the arrival of the Viscount looking more than a little uncomfortable in the knee breeches and silk stockings that were still *de rigeur* at Almack's, his *chapeau bras* tucked properly under his arm.

"Why, Geoff, how very odd you look," blurted out Heather with regrettable impetuosity. She was sorry at once as she saw the hurt in his eyes. He had been thinking that he looked deuced fine. For a young man inclined to be careless of his appearance, he had gone to great lengths over his toilette this evening. "But very elegant," she hurried on. "It is just that I have never seen you look so . . . well, so *formal*. And I don't *think* you are precisely comfortable, though you look *very* fine."

He seemed willing to accept her implied apology. In fact, he was finding it increasingly difficult to be annoyed with Heather at all, especially when she looked so deuced pretty and gazed up at him in that totally bewitching way. He grinned down at her. "Deuced uncomfortable if you want the truth. Not used to wearing such a puppet-rig. I say, Mama! You're looking fine as fivepence! Devilish pretty dress, that."

"Thank you, darling," she said, unconsciously smoothing the folds of her russet crape gown, and twitching her gold net scarf into an even more fetching position on her white shoulders.

"Hallo, Miss Wheatley. You here?" he said to Sophy, seeming to see her for the first time. They had met frequently of late due to the girls' close friendship, so that Sophy, nervous though she was, was not knocked too far off her stride by this offhanded greeting.

"Good evening, my lord."

He favored her with a pensive gaze. "You look different," he said after a moment.

"Thank you, my lord," she answered enigmatically and not without a twinkle in her soft brown eyes.

"Come," said Lady Morpeth. "We're a bit late, and you know quite well that that odious Willis will not let us in if we arrive after eleven."

"Just a minute." Geoff turned a somewhat sheepish grin to Heather. "First night at Almack's and all. Special occasion. Bought you something." He reached into his pocket and pulled out a small velvet box. "Trumpery stuff, but thought you might like 'em."

"Oh, Geoff!" she sighed ecstatically as she saw the beautiful pair of eardrops, the large black pearls a perfect match to her necklace.

Having had some experience of Heather's invariable reaction to such largesse, Geoff instinctively held up his two hands to ward off the impetuous assault upon his person he felt sure was forthcoming. But apparently Heather was too overcome even for this.

"Oh, Geoff!" she repeated. "They're beautiful! But I really cannot take them. They must have cost you ever so much, and with all your debts . . ."

"Dash it all, Heather!" he cursed, shooting an embarrassed glance at Sophy. "I ain't so behindhand with the world that I can't afford to buy you a piece of trumpery jewelry if I want to."

"Well, I don't expect you can really, but, oh, Geoff, thank you! Thank you!" The Viscount's premonition of the mayhem to be directed against his carefully tied cravat had been correct. His vigilance, unfortunately, had been allowed to lapse prematurely, and Heather flung herself at him and gave him a fierce hug which he had, perforce, to return or be knocked off his feet. Oddly enough, his first thought was not for his damaged neckcloth.

"Yes, yes, children," Lady Morpeth's matter-of-fact tones pulled the couple apart. "That was very prettily done of you, Geoffrey. The pearls are exactly what Heather needs. Did you have them from Love's or from Jeffrey's? No, never mind. We really must be on our way or give up the idea entirely. Almack's waits for no one."

After one more short delay for Heather to put on the new eardrops they were on their way. A very few minutes found them in King Street, mounting the steps and surrendering their precious vouchers to Mr. Willis, the eagle-eyed doorkeeper past whom *no one* without a voucher could pass. As they entered the rooms a clock somewhere in the distance chimed eleven, and they heard the front door close with an aristocratic and very final thud.

The entire ton seemed to be in attendance this evening. Across the room lounged Sir Ninian Netherwold, looking like a walking pincushion, from all the buckram wadding in his chartreuse velvet coat.

Lady Cowper talked at Maria Sefton in one corner, waving her fan back and forth like the wings of a bird in flight, snapping shut with each period and comma. The amiable Lady Sefton just stood there, a sort of hoisted-up look in her figure and her eyes bulging slightly as though pleading for someone to please loosen her corset lacings.

Heather and Sophy were surrounded almost at once by

THE RELUCTANT SUITOR

Heather's usual court. She immediately embarked on her plan to insure Sophy of a constant string of partners by the simple expedient of cajoling her own admirers into standing up with her friend. She managed it so skillfully they scarce realized they were being maneuvered. Only when her friend had been carried off on the arm of a handsome captain did Heather bestow her hand on a young baronet to join the set then forming.

It is often said that imitation is the sincerest form of flattery. If that is so, and if Heather had been a less modest young lady, she would have been very flattered indeed by much of the coterie of celebrants who had the cachet of Almack's vouchers. With a solid two weeks behind her as the newest Incomparable, Heather had turned fashion upside down.

The clouds of pink, white, and yellow muslin that had bedecked young ladies for several seasons had given way to a preponderance of blue and violet, colors associated with Heather Braddock. Rouge pots had been abandoned in favor of milk baths and rice powder in an attempt to emulate her "interesting pallor," and brows and lashes seemed everywhere longer and darker.

"Well, Tina. I hope you are satisfied!" said Lady Barrie to Lady Morpeth early in the morning. Her own daughter was making her come-out this Season and had caught the "Heather mania." "I'll have you know, Tina, that my Bella has practically refused to eat anything at all this week past except biscuits and soda water. It has put my cook quite in the dismals. But Bella insists she must become as slender as Miss Braddock."

"But Bella has such a charming figure!"

"Well, I do wish you would tell her so," said the lady archly to her long-time friend. "That is not the worst of it, you know. Only listen, Do you know M. Maupré, the French emigré who is an absolute wizard of a *corsetier?*" she asked with an unconscious heave of a magnificent bosom that owed rather more to that gentleman's art than to nature. "Well, Amanda Wythe finally agreed to have him fashion one of his exquisite 'bosom bows' for her Catherine. The poor child is so painfully flat, you know, and has been suffering torments from it. And he does make them of the best French wax. Amazingly realistic.

Well, now she has it, the girl positively refuses to wear the thing! And all because your goddaughter has no bosom to speak of. Apparently it is all the crack nowadays to be built like a young boy!" She very nearly harumphed at her dear friend.

"Well I did think she'd take," said Lady Morpeth matter-of-factly.

"Take! Tina, you know very well that young lady has taken the ton by storm. You knew she would do, too," added Lady Barrie shrewdly. "I really don't know where it will end, and I only hope you are *quite* satisfied, Tina."

"Oh, I am Augusta, I am," she replied with a smile.

The next dance chanced to be a waltz, and as neither Heather nor Sophy had been approved for waltzing, they were returned to their chaperone. Geoff and the Earl of Pythe soon joined them, freeing Lady Morpeth to float off on the arm of Lord Handy.

"Oh, Court," said Heather happily. "Isn't it all grand? I don't think I've ever seen so elegant a gathering."

The Earl gave her his engaging grin and turned an expectant gaze toward her friend.

"Good evening, my lord," said Sophy in her soft, shy voice.

His look turned to temporary bewilderment. "I'm sorry, I don't . . ." he began, then cut himself off abruptly. "Good God! Miss Wheatley! I . . . I . . ." He trailed off in confusion. The girls, realizing that he had not recognized the new Sophy at first, were delighted. But Sophy saw his embarrassment, and despite her natural shyness, instinctively came to his rescue.

"Do you go to Epsom for the races, my lord? My father has a promising filly running that may prove interesting."

"A filly, is it?" he recovered himself. "Good blood?"

"Oh, yes. She's out of Asparagus and Cathy Darling. I've had much of the raising of her myself." The conversational gambit worked, and the two fell into a lively discussion of thoroughbreds and bloodlines.

Heather, seeing her friend happily situated, turned to Geoff. "Whatever is the matter with Robin this evening?" She looked across the room to where that young gentleman was propping up the wall with a scowl. "He's looking grumpy as a bear with a sore head."

"Lady Susan," he explained. "If you ask me, Robin's getting to be a curst bore over that girl. Used to be always ready for a lark, y'know. Now he's a regular grumbletonian."

"Perhaps she doesn't know how very unhappy she is making him. Perhaps if I told her . . ."

"Can't do that, Heather. Ain't the thing at all. 'Sides, none of your affair. Make a dashed cake of yourself."

"Pooh! As though I should care for that if it would make Robin happy."

"Well, it wouldn't. Fights his own battles, Robin."

"Well, he doesn't seem to be winning this one," she said with her usual practicality. "How can she see him looking *so* and not be kinder to him?"

"Jealous," he answered shrewdly.

"Of whom? As though Robin would ever look at another girl!"

"Jealous of you, I'll wager."

"That is the greatest piece of nonsense ever I heard! Whyever should she be jealous of me?"

Geoffrey looked at his Heather with some wonder. She really did not understand how she could rouse jealousy in anyone's breast. She was so deuced innocent in the ways of the world.

The appearance of Major Peevesby bearing down on them from across the room interrupted these deep thoughts.

"Damn the fellow!" muttered Geoff. "If it ain't just like him to turn up when he's least wanted."

"Why, it's Major Peevesby!" exclaimed Heather. "You see, Geoff. I told you he was perfectly unexceptionable. I must have been right for he wouldn't be accepted at Almack's otherwise."

"Much you know. Damned commoner. Too smooth by half."

Her eyes kindled, but the arrival of the Major put a period to her protest. She turned on him a dazzling smile. "Good evening, Major Peevesby."

"Miss Braddock," he answered with a rakish kiss of her hand. "My lord," he greeted Geoff. "I believe they will shortly be beginning the quadrille, Miss Braddock. May I hope for your charming company on the floor?"

"Very prettily said, Major, and I should like it of all things. You will excuse us, my lord?" she said to Geoff, a challenge in her eyes. He could do no more than offer a slight bow and watch them walk off. He soon joined Robin Ayrton at his station against the wall, matching him scowl for scowl.

Heather moved gracefully from partner to partner. The German waltz had become so popular with the ton that it was played rather more frequently than quadrilles and country dances, even at Almack's. And so, for all her popularity, it wasn't long before Heather found herself on the sidelines again. This time she didn't have Sophy beside her, as Court had asked permission for her to waltz. So far from feeling left out by this occurrence, Heather rejoiced over her friend's success.

"You know, Godmama, I did think Court and Sophy would deal admirably together for they have so much in common. I expect it only needed a chance for him to *see* her, if you know what I mean."

"I know precisely what you mean, darling. Why, I could myself scarce credit how altered dear Sophy looks. You have worked a miracle there."

"Well, it only needed discarding all that gaudy nonsense she was always covered with."

"And who would have thought you'd turn out such a matchmaker?"

"Well, their suitability seemed quite obvious to me, though I daresay his mama will not agree. If only Sophy need not go back to that silly woman. Even I can see that such a chaperone is like to ruin all her chances."

"I've been thinking much the same thing myself. And Sophy is such a sweet girl. I have come to like her excessively. So I've been thinking we had best have her to stay in Clarges Street. She really cannot remain with that Whitecastle woman."

"Oh, Godmama! Do you mean it? Would you really invite her? I would like it ever so much!"

"Well, I thought you might, darling, so I have already written to her papa apprising him of the situation. I'm certain he can have not the least idea what sort of woman Mrs. Whitecastle is. I'm sure he will make no objection to Sophy finishing the Season with us."

"Oh, thank you, Godmama!" Heather caught herself only just in time from inflicting the same sort of damage on her godmama's coiffure as she had earlier bestowed on Geoffrey's cravat and contented herself with glowing in a happy and very captivating way.

For her part, Sophy was enjoying herself more than she had ever thought possible at a London ball. She'd had several partners, and she was not even *too* embarrassed by the niggling thought that many of them asked her to please Heather. It was true, of course, but many of the gentlemen were pleasantly surprised to discover that Miss Wheatley, though no more than passable in terms of beauty, had a good deal of sensible conversation and was not above listening to a fellow once in awhile, unlike most young ladies of their acquaintance.

The Earl of Pythe, in particular, was much struck by her almost encyclopedic knowledge of hunting, horse breeding, and farming, which almost matched his own. Their conversation would scarcely have struck an eavesdropper as romantic, peppered as it was with "bog spavins," "cross-breeding," and "land reclamation." But they seemed quite content with it.

As Heather watched them happily, and just a bit smugly, the Countess Lieven sailed up to her in all the glory that only several pounds of diamonds distributed haphazardly about one's person can bestow. She was on the arm of Sir William Longchamps, who beamed fondly on both Heather and Lady Morpeth.

"Miss Braddock, you do not waltz," said the Countess in heavily accented English. "May I present Sir William Longchamps to you as a most desirable partner."

"Oh, may I really?" beamed Heather at this official permission to waltz. "I should like it of all things." Sir William gave her hand an affectionate pat, and they moved onto the floor.

Lady Morpeth watched them go with mixed feelings, though she would not have owned to any emotion other than pure delight. Since their meeting at the opera, Sir William had been frequently in Clarges Street. He had driven the ladies in the Park, had escorted them to a gala at Vauxhall, and generally made up one of their court whenever they appeared in public. He had, in short, shown Heather a flattering degree of attention.

Tina Morpeth, from the simple fact that she had never in her life been outshone, had never experienced jealousy. And so she did not at first recognize the unhappy emotion that surged through her as Sir William led Heather onto the floor. She genuinely cared for Heather, and she wanted to see her happily settled. She had decided quite early on that Sir William would make Heather the perfect husband. He was so disgustingly wealthy that there was no danger he would fritter away her fortune. And the girl really was so terribly innocent. Lady Morpeth had herself married a man older than herself, and she knew that such an arrangement often answered perfectly. Things seemed to be going along swimmingly, and Tina Morpeth wanted to feel overjoyed. She was, therefore, distressed and more than a little confused by the waves of despondency that seemed to attack her as Heather and Sir William wheeled about the room.

The waltzing couple was chatting comfortably. Heather had come to like Sir William immensely. "I'm so grateful, Sir William, that you asked me to waltz," she confided. "I've never done it in public, you know, and I was afraid I would be terribly nervous. But I am always so comfortable with you."

"Well, I rather thought you might find me easier going than that Wesley puppy. I fancy he was about to make a try at you himself."

"Then I am doubly grateful. He is a very sweet boy, of course, and always treats me with the greatest respect. But he is just the tiniest bit difficult to converse with. I'm afraid he hasn't much to say for himself, and I always seem to run out of topics before the orchestra runs out of music. And he is so persistent."

"Calf love, but no need to worry yourself over it. We all suffer it at some point, but most of us get over it soon enough." His eyes unconsciously strayed to where Lady Morpeth was smiling her bewitching smile at a Royal Duke. He flicked them back to Heather at once.

"That is a most uncommonly lovely necklace, my dear. I don't believe I've ever seen another quite like it," he said nonchalantly. His air of casualness was feigned, for he knew quite well that there was only one such necklace in the world, with that distinctive jade clasp. He had himself sold it to a trading partner long ago, the same man who was father to the delightfully pretty girl to whom Heather bore so marked a resemblance.

He had been curious about Heather ever since their first meeting, and he was not without resources when it came to seeking information. He had put certain questions to his man of business, and certain investigations had been put in train. As a result, he knew that that pretty girl of long ago had married the widowed Earl of Stonington, had given birth to a daughter, and had died shortly thereafter.

Heather was blithely unaware of any ulterior motives behind Sir William's offhand remark "It is quite my favorite thing. It belonged to my mother, you see, and I have so little left that was hers. She died when I was very young." The simple words, coupled with the piquant face that mirrored her mother's, provided the final proof that Miss Heather Braddock and the Lady Margaret St. Vincent were, indeed, one and the same. But the question remained: why the deception? He would have to make one or two further inquiries, he decided. He gave the girl a smile, and they waltzed on.

Heather's success continued. She danced the boulanger with Mr. Wesley, a country dance with Court, and the great Mr. Brummell himself stood up with her for the quadrille. Geoff felt quite smug when at last he succeeded in carrying her off for a waltz, particularly as it was being besought by Major Peevesby.

Heather had a natural talent for dancing, and her light step showed to perfection in the waltz. Viscount Morpeth could lay no claims to a similar grace, but was able to acquit himself tolerably well. But dancing with Heather seemed the easiest thing in the world somehow. He scarce had to lead her, so light was she in his arms. Like a feather, he thought.

As for Heather, she had never enjoyed a dance more, wishing only that it could continue on and on. She seemed to fit quite perfectly in Geoff's arms, floating dreamily. It had to end, of course, and she passed on to another, but the glow of that waltz stayed with her.

Before long the last waltz of the evening was announced, and Heather favored Robin Ayrton with her hand. He had danced with no other lady all evening except for a single country dance with Lady Susan, during the whole of which they bickered like children and glared at each other.

"You know, Robin," ventured Heather as they spun gracefully. "I'm not sure it's such a good idea to let Lady Susan see that you care so *very* much with whom she dances."

"Well, I do care! D'you know she wouldn't even waltz with me! Walked off with that rake Peevesby right under my nose."

"I know, and it was not at all kind in her to do so. But I am persuaded, you know, that she has grown so very used to your devotion that she rather takes it for granted Perhaps she feels she can treat you with impunity without risking the loss of your affection."

Mr. Ayrton seemed struck by this novel, and very astute, notion. "If I thought that . . ." he began. He turned quickly to where Lady Susan, dressed in what was virtually the only pink gown in the room, was waltzing with the Major. She had, in fact, been discreetly watching him as well, but at his glance she at once turned a laughing face to her partner, flirting outrageously.

"By God! I believe you're right! The heartless baggage!"

"Oh, no, Robin! Not heartless. She's only a little put out, I think. Geoff believes she is jealous, and she would not be if she didn't care for you."

"D'you think so? I'll own Geoff tried to tell me much the same thing the other night."

"I'm certain of it. And I can't but think that if you could bring yourself to act as though you didn't care quite so much, she would treat you with more kindness. Godmama says that ladies never want anything so much as when they think they're losing it, and she is very clever about such things."

"I always said Lady M. was a knacky one, and I'm dashed if she ain't in the right of it this time. What that girl needs is a lesson!" His eyes glittered. "And I believe I'll start giving it to her right now."

Before Heather knew what to expect his hand tightened about her waist, and he wheeled her into an elegant variation on the basic steps, complete with spins, dips, and flourishes. She kept up easily, prettily flushed from her exertions. When she looked up into his handsome dark eyes they twinkled in a flirtatious and exceedingly romantic manner. She almost caught her breath at the force of that look.

She had never danced a dance quite like this one! Had she been at leisure to consider the matter, she might have decided that, for all Robin's virtuosity and romantic good looks, she much preferred dancing with Geoff. But for now, all her powers of concentration were required to keep up with her partner.

The effect of the waltzing pair was not lost on its desired target. Lady Susan turned pale, set her pretty mouth in a pout, recovered almost at once, and favored the Major with a totally devastating smile. Experienced as he was with women, he failed to note the brittleness in her light laugh or the flash of anger behind her fluttering lashes. He was pleasantly surprised at this flattering degree of attention from one he had come to think of as an unconquerable citadel. They spun off in a cloud of pink gauze and knee breeches.

The beautiful spectacle of Robin and Heather was also keenly noticed by Viscount Morpeth. A matched set! he thought grimly. He could not but admire the two ebony hands swaying in time to the music. He had never seen two people look so well together. Heather could do worse. A lot worse. The thought did not comfort him.

There was one other dancer on the floor who took special note of the spinning pair. Lady Morpeth, in the arms of Sir William Longchamps, was also struck by the handsomeness of the picture. She glanced quickly at her partner, wondering if he might be jealous, and ready, though not precisely willing, to reassure him that Robert Ayrton was no rival. But Sir William scarce seemed to notice the younger pair. Instead, he was peering down into a pair of melting green eyes, a boyish smile on his middle-aged lips. She gave herself up to the enjoyment of the dance.

The music and the evening soared to a conclusion, swelling, spinning, in a flash of color and movement. Each player prepared to move his or her own drama onto another stage, to be resolved another time.

Chapter Seventeen

"More tea, dear?" Henrietta Wardwell asked her sister in a pleasant voice, exactly as she had done little more than a fortnight before. "Or perhaps another slice of toast?" Miss Honoria Stapleton shook her head absently in reply.

They were dallying over their breakfast in the sunny front parlor of Mrs. Wardwell's Milsom Street lodgings—its comfort did not extend to a breakfast room—and considering how best to attack the day, each in her own fashion.

Mrs. Wardwell, who, though not precisely witless might have been reasonably flattered by the term untutored, was yet wise enough to notice that something was decidedly amiss with her formidable elder sister. Why, yesterday she had eaten only one scone with clotted cream and had barely tasted the lovely Bath buns procured especially for her. And today she slumped—yes, slumped! for there really could be no other word for it—in a chair gazing out with apparently unseeing eyes onto the street below.

"What is wrong, dear?" asked Mrs. Wardwell in her soft voice.

"You know very well what is wrong, Henrietta!" Miss Stapleton snapped back, though her usual fire was lacking. Her energy, her drive, even her great store of ideas, seemed to have run dry. In the three days since she had returned to Bath, she had exhausted every means available to her for locating her errant cousin. Every agency specializing in the placing of domestic servants had been checked. Copies of the *Bath Guardian* had been scanned for positions that Lady Margaret might have inquired about. Nearly every shop in town—and there were many, as Miss Stapleton knew to her pain—had been visited on the chance that her cousin had become a shopgirl. No trace of Lady Margaret St. Vincent had been found. The black pearls and sapphires she had "stolen" from Heathside had not turned up in any pawnshop. The trail was cold.

"I don't know where else to look, Henrietta." Miss Stapleton gave out a long, almost resigned sigh. "I suppose there is nothing for it but to notify the Earl."

"Notify the Earl?" asked Henrietta with a shudder. "Is he not certain to be very angry?"

"Well, of course he is! You have, perhaps, a better suggestion?"

"Well, no, of course I would not, for you know, sister, that I never have clever ideas like you. But perhaps . . . Honoria? What is it, dear?"

This question was brought about by an abrupt change in Miss Stapleton's demeanor. From a forlorn posture, chin on hand, she stiffened ramrod straight and stared intently out the window, the tiniest hint of a smile beginning at one corner of her thin line of mouth. Crossing the street below her was a servant-girl in a fustian dress and clean white apron. Her pattens clicked along the paving stones as she walked lightly down the street. "Lady Margaret," said Miss Stapleton on a sigh. She was out of her chair and hurrying across the room at once.

"Sister?" began Mrs. Wardwell.

She might have saved her breath, for Honoria Stapleton had no time for explanations. Grabbing a shawl and ramming a bonnet onto her head, she hurried down the stairs and into the street.

The little figure in the big cap, a basket of dazzling white linen swinging on her arm, was headed down the hill some fifty yards ahead. The girl, supremely unaware that anyone was following her, moved quickly and confidently, looking neither right nor left and obviously following an oft-traveled route. Down the hill into Union Passage she strode, her basket swaying lightly.

Miss Stapleton dodged in and out among the fashionable shoppers and saunterers and had to struggle to keep the girl in sight. In a burst of energy, she narrowed the gap between them considerably. By the time the girl had negotiated the busy crossing at Cheap Street and neared the colonnaded entrance into Abbey Church-yard, the older woman was nearly upon her. And then she disappeared.

Miss Stapleton stood under the pillared arch looking about for sign of the girl. She caught a glimpse of a mobcap and basket crossing the yard and passing into a building and quickly followed only to be denied entrance at the service door of the King's and Queen's Baths.

"You must be a mite confused-like, ma'am," said the doorkeeper. "This here's the staff door. You'll find the bathers entrance round the corner there. They'll take good care for you there."

"I wish to speak to the girl who just came in here."

"Well, now, there be a lot o' girls comin' in here, ma'am, an all of them proper employees. Now if you'll go round to the proper door, one of them'll be happy to help you." The voice was kind but quite firm. Miss Stapleton could do no more than follow these instructions.

Music drifted from the open windows of the Pump Room as she passed. She turned a corner and negotiated the throng of sedan chairs, Bath chairs, and pedestrians passing in and out of the elegant main entrance to the Baths.

"Good morning, madam," said the matron at the door in cheery accents. "And what will you have, this morning?" She ran a practiced eye over Miss Stapleton's harassed face. The lady's bonnet was askew due to the unseemly haste with which it had been put on, and one end of her shawl had been trailing in the dirt. Her face was flushed from her headlong rush after the girl she believed to be her cousin. "Is it to be pumping or the vapor baths? You're suffering the headache a little, I'll wager, and perhaps a touch of the gout. But never fear, we'll soon have you put to rights."

"There is nothing whatever wrong with me," answered the flurried Miss Stapleton. "I wish merely to speak to a young lady I believe to be employed here."

The matron's eyebrow raised a trifle. This one seemed like to be a problem. "And what would the young woman's name be, madam?"

The question threw Miss Stapleton momentarily off-balance. "Well, of course I don't know what she's calling her-

THE RELUCTANT SUITOR 147

self. But it is vitally important that I speak to her at once."

The matron was not inexperienced at handling reluctant old ladies assigned by their doctors to take the waters but unwilling to go meekly. To be sure, this was a story she had not yet encountered. A right twitty one, she mentally stigmatized Miss Stapleton.

"Perhaps, madam, if you were to step inside you'd find the young person in question. I'll summon a guide to assist you."

"Yes, yes. Thank you, that is precisely what I must do."

"Your name, madam? Just for my book, you understand."

Miss Stapleton granted the request, and her name was inscribed in the large register in a firm hand.

The ring of a silver bell summoned a stout, middle-aged woman. She was huge, with arms like sledgehammers and hands like melons. She smelled of soap and steam, her face glistening damply like shiny leather.

"Ah, Martha," said the matron. "Miss Stapleton here wishes to look around the Baths for a certain young woman employee. Will you see to her yourself, if you please?" Martha, offering Miss Stapleton a clumsy curtsy, had no trouble whatever in translating the matron's arch tone into "a right twitty one and like to prove difficult." She was not worried. Twitty old ladies were Martha's specialty.

"This way please, madam." Off she went with Miss Stapleton in tow.

They passed first into the ladies robing room. The walls reverberated with the babble of high-pitched voices as grand ladies divested themselves of their silks and muslins in favor of voluminous bathing gowns. The babble gave up detailed accounts of this lady's rheumatism in the shoulder, that one's sciatica in the hip, and numerous cases of gout, nervous complaints, and digestive troubles. Young maids scurried about bringing towels and handkerchiefs, vinaigrettes, and nosegays, all considered essential accoutrements in the Bath. Miss Stapleton peered closely into each girl's face but without success.

"She must be inside," she told Martha. "I shall look in the vapor room."

"An excellent idea, madam. I'll just help you into a bathing gown."

"But I do not wish to bathe."

"Of course not, madam," said Martha in her best humoring voice. "But we really cannot allow ladies in street gowns into the bathing area. All that dust, you understand, and you would surely spoil your pretty gown."

"Oh, very well," Miss Stapleton gave in.

She was speedily disrobed and re-covered from chin to toes in one of the singularly unattractive ochre flannel bathing dresses. She followed Martha into a tiled vapor room, oblivious to the towels draped over the guide's arm and the determined light in her eye.

"Now if you'll just sit here, madam, where it's nice and warm." She indicated a strange open-fronted boxlike structure with a comfortable-looking seat inside. The room was permeated with a smell like rusted nails. "You'll be able to see all the girls in this section from here."

As there was no place else to sit, and the heat of the room was causing Miss Stapleton to wilt slightly, she gladly took the seat. In a twinkling, the front of the box swung shut. Miss Stapleton's entire person, except for her astonished head, disappeared from view.

"What . . . here! Guide! What are you doing? Open this . . . this box at once!" she sputtered indignantly.

"Now, now, madam," Martha soothed. "We mustn't let ourselves be overset. The treatments work best when we are quite calm."

"I don't wish for any treatment. I only wish to find my cous . . . that girl!"

But Martha had left the room after opening the bottom of Miss Stapleton's vapor bath to allow the steam from the hot springs to pour in. Honoria found that the best she could do was to try to sit perfectly still. The tiniest movement was an effort and seemed to intensify the almost unbearable heat. Perspiration began to pour down her arms. Only her sharp black eyes moved, darting about the room. Several other patients were being scalded nearby and attendants scurried about. None escaped her scrutiny, but none proved to be Lady Margaret St. Vincent.

When the intrepid Martha returned at last, Honoria Stapleton was feeling rather too much like a puddle to allow her indignation full rein. She let out no more than a single "harumph" as the box was opened and she was assisted to her feet.

Almost immediately she found herself poured onto a long marble table. It's glassy surface felt like ice through her thin flannel covering. Every attempt at protest was ruthlessly squelched by the indefatigable Martha, and for the next quarter of an hour she was pummeled, pounded, and prodded into something that felt very like a pile of jelly. She was rapidly losing the ability, if not the will, to resist this cavalier treatment.

"There now, madam. We're beginning to feel more the thing now, aren't we?" said the guide in a sprightly voice that jarred with her glistening bulk and raw power.

"No, *we* are not!" came the feeble but still spirited reply.

"Well, no doubt you're worried about your young friend. Come along to the Bath, and perhaps we'll find her there."

Not knowing what else to do, Miss Stapleton pulled herself up and followed. They passed out into the glittering sunshine that streamed onto the Queen's Bath. The creamy-yellow walls gleamed and reflected in the green bubbling water.

Somehow—she never quite knew how it happened—Miss Stapleton found herself straightway in the big bubbling cauldron of the Bath, parboiling with the rest of the invalid frolickers, some splashing about happily, others just letting the seething brew ooze over their poor old muscles. She still had had not the slightest glimpse of the girl she had followed here.

After nearly an hour in this stewpot, and after she had somehow been convinced to drink two whole glasses of the vile stuff, she was allowed to pull herself dripping from the Bath, feeling distinctly like a pickle, and looking rather like one as well.

Martha led her off to the pumping room and sat her down on a wooden bench with a high back. Miss Stapleton leaned back and closed her eyes. "Oh, dear," said Martha with a shrewd look. "I fancy we still have the headache a bit."

"No, no!" said Miss Stapleton as quickly as she could. "But I must find Margaret."

"Margaret, is it? And what does this Margaret of yours look like, madam?"

Miss Stapleton gave her a brief description of her runaway cousin in a faint voice.

"Well now, madam. Why did you not say so before? I fancy you must mean our Meggy. She's a pumper, being new to the baths. Why, we'll have her in this very room before many more minutes have passed. I'll go and fetch her myself."

She was still staring at Miss Stapleton in her diagnostic way. A more observant patient might have heard her mutter, "Too much heat, I fancy." She crossed to a large oak cupboard and returned with what looked like a wide-brimmed sunbonnet with the entire crown removed. "Now you just put on this nice bonnet, madam," she instructed her recalcitrant patient.

"Whatever for?"

"Oh, just to shade your face, you know," said Martha enigmatically. She placed the hat on the damp head. Miss Stapleton was somehow unable to consider the question of why she should need a crownless hat to shade her face when she was back indoors.

A moment later a tiny servant-girl tripped into the room. Dark ringlets curled damply from under a big cap, and she had huge smiling eyes. "You wanted to see me, mum? I'm Meggy."

Standing before her was a complete stranger. Oh, to be sure, there was some resemblance to Lady Margaret, but it was, at best, a fleeting one. Yet Miss Stapleton could not deny that this was the girl she had rushed headlong down Milsom Street after. She slumped back onto her bench, her face showing alarming signs of wrinkling up like a baby's. She had reached the end of the line.

Meggy, new as she was to employment in the Baths, was learning her lessons quickly from Martha. She fluttered about her patient, clucking and cooing reassuringly about the headache and how she'd feel more the thing presently. She adjusted Honoria's crownless bonnet a bit, made her comfortable on her bench, then took up her position at the pump.

THE RELUCTANT SUITOR 151

Miss Stapleton did not hear the slight creak of the pump as the girl lifted the handle. She sat on her bench in a sodden lump. The ugly yellow flannel wrapping was plastered to her sides; little trickles of perspiration dribbled down her face. She felt miserable.

The next thing she knew, a torrent of icy water had been unceremoniously dumped onto the top of her head. The best treatment available in the Queen's Bath at Bath was concluded.

Chapter Eighteen

Miss Sophronia Wheatley's move to Clarges Street was accomplished without incident. Well, that is perhaps not a precise statement of fact. It was certainly accomplished, but not without some understandable perturbation on the part of Mrs. Whitecastle which manifested itself in several attacks of the vapors, a few instances of the hurling of curses worthy of a Billingsgate fishwife at her ertswhile charge, and one solemn promise of immediate court action to be taken against "that insidious Lady Morpeth" for depriving Mrs. Whitecastle of her livelihood. But Sophy did, at length, find herself settled into the comfortable bedchamber next to Heather's, having willingly and quite thoroughly shaken the dust of Lowndes Square from her shoes.

Lady Morpeth, of course, proposed shopping as their first priority. "For I really cannot have you appearing under my auspices in the dreadful gowns that woman chose for you. My reputation would be quite ruined."

But Sophy proved surprisingly recalcitrant on this point. Her allowance was nearly gone, and she refused to buy so much as a ribbon on credit. "My father has already assumed far too large a burden in sending me to London. I will not add to his worries by having a single bill arrive on his desk, ma'am. I am persuaded you will understand my position."

"Well of course you must do what you think best, dear," she answered with a perplexed look that stated quite clearly that she understood not at all. "But what then is to be done? I really think *something* must be done about your clothes."

"Godmama," chimed in Heather. "Do you remember Lady Beveredge saying only the other day what incredible

THE RELUCTANT SUITOR 153

bargains can be got at Grafton House? Muslins at only three and six the yard, she said, and silks, and all manner of things."

"I think," began Sophy, "that my remaining money might stretch to having one or two simple gowns made up. I have been to Grafton House—Mrs. Whitecastle positively haunts the place—and it truly is amazing the bargains one can find there."

"Well, what a lark!" cried Lady Morpeth. "And you know, Sophy dear, I have just remembered a lovely rust velvet bonnet I bought last week that does not suit me in the least. It is just the thing for your coloring. Yes, and those chamois gloves that make me look positively insipid. They would suit you admirably."

"And, Godmama, do you not think that Sophy's yellow taffeta could be dyed down to make a pretty underskirt? With a nice ochre muslin over it . . ."

"And some chocolate-colored ribbons!"

"Stop!" cried Sophy through the laughter bubbling up at their enthusiasm.

"Come. Get your bonnets, my dears. We'll be on our way at once," said Lady Morpeth. "I have been longing this age to visit Grafton House. Why I heard only last week that they have some of the new bugle beading from Paris. It is just the thing for my new silk spencer. And perhaps I could use some silk stockings, and maybe some handkerchiefs, and . . ."

A laughing and helpless Sophy was ushered out the door.

"Well!" sighed Lady Morpeth throwing herself into a chair. It was some hours later, and they were just returned from their shopping quite laden down with packages and parcels of every description. "I think we have earned a cup of tea, don't you, my dears? How wonderfully prudent we have been, to be sure. Geoffrey will be pleased, for he has been after me to practice just such economies as we have been up to today."

The two young ladies tactfully refrained from pointing out to her that only through their diligent efforts was she restrained from purchasing a sable muff in the middle of an unseasonably warm spring, a painted fan that she thought "amazingly ugly but such a bargain at only six shillings," and some chamois gloves identical to the pair she had just bestowed on Sophy that morning.

Their tea arrived, together with a quantity of watercress sandwiches, almond cakes, ratafia biscuits, Italian rusks, and a treacle tart—all of which Heather dispatched with great relish—and the afternoon post. There was a letter for Sophy from her father, all apology for having stabled her so long with Mrs. Whitecastle, calling her a fine filly, and praising her for kicking over her traces and bolting.

Heather had a letter as well. "Oh, Godmama, the most famous thing! It's from Bing. Only think! Cousin Honoria thinks I am gone to Bath, and has gone to look for me. It's the perfect answer, of course, because she quite likes Bath and will not in the least mind having to be there," she said, completely unaware of the enormity of her cousin's suffering in the famous spa town. "And I'm sure she won't tell Bo I'm missing if she thinks there is the least chance of finding me. He would be so very angry, you see, and not even Cousin Honoria likes to face him when he is angry."

They had by this time let Sophy into the whole of Heather's story, so this happily proclaimed news made perfect sense to her. The two girls laughed over it.

Lady Morpeth, however, barely seemed to hear. She was dejectedly shuffling through a large stack of mail, a *moue* of distaste marring her pretty mouth.

"What is it, Godmama? Have you had bad news?"

"What, dear?" she said with a start. She replaced the slightly worried frown with her bright smile. "Oh, no. It is nothing of the least importance, I assure you." She dropped the pile of mail onto a table nearby. "Have another biscuit, dear."

"It won't do, Mama," said Viscount Morpeth next morning. "Won't do at all."

His mother was seated at a pretty satinwood desk in Queen Anne style in the sunny-yellow morning room. She looked like a young girl in a jonquil sprig muslin gown, her hair tied loosely back with a ribbon and shining like new corn. The only element of the picture that jarred was

THE RELUCTANT SUITOR

the expression on her pretty face. It was that of a very harried lady.

Before her on the desk sat an alarmingly high pile of odd-size bits of paper. She contemplated the pile as though it were a snake about to jump up and bite her, or at the very least to wrap itself around her pretty neck and strangle her.

The papers in the pile were bills: bills for candles and bills for coals, bills for shoes and gloves and bonnets, perfumes and lotions, green peas and pineapples.

Lady Morpeth's tastes were extravagant. The jointure left her by her husband, unfortunately, was not. And her understanding of the laws of economics was just the tiniest bit sketchy. Consequently, she had been in debt ever since her husband's death. And the creditors who had always been so obliging were becoming alarmingly persistent in their demands for payment.

And now, to add to her sense of injury, she was being lectured by her son—yes, Geoffrey!—on the wisdom of spending less money. He had just come from a more than ordinarily Black Monday at Tattersall's. Moreover, he had had several colloquies with his man of business recently and was quite shocked to discover how close to the edge he'd been treading. He might not yet be in danger of landing in Marshalsea Prison, but if he didn't put the brakes to his spending, and soon, he might well lose Morpeth, his estate in Northumberland. He might feel no qualms about stigmatizing the place as a curst drafty pile, but, dash it all, there had been Curwens at Morpeth forever! It wouldn't sit well with him to be the one to lose it. And so he was quite bent on reform, and like all converts he wished his mama to see the light as well.

"I'll tell you what it is, Mama. Have to cut back, retrench, whatever you call it. I'm nearly in the basket myself, y'know. Haven't got the ready and rhino to bail you out, and that's a fact."

"As though I would ask it of you!" she replied with great indignation. "But I'm sure you can have no notion what it costs to run this house, darling. I'm persuaded you would be quite shocked if you knew. And I have *tried* to practice economy these past months. Indeed, you cannot guess the strain it places on one. I'm sure I look positively *hagged* from the worry of it all." She snuck a surreptitious look at herself in the pier glass over the fireplace, something she seemed to be doing much more often than usual of late. "Anyway, I *did* tell Mrs. Jumples that we are not to have potpourri in all the Chinese bowls anymore, for do you *know* how shockingly dear dried rose petals have become? It is quite scandalous, and I'm sure I don't understand it at all. But I have quite determined to content myself with fresh violets, instead," she finished, beaming with pride at the enormity of her sacrifice.

"Violets, Mama?"

"Yes. I send Jem into Devonshire for them. Well, you know that they grow the most beautiful violets in Devonshire, darling. *And,*" she added triumphantly, "I have instructed him to bring back some clotted cream and those ginger biscuits you like so well. So you can see that by having him accomplish two or three errands in one trip I am being remarkably thrifty."

The Viscount ran his fingers ruthlessly through his sandy hair. "Violets from Devonshire," he muttered in his new-found economic zeal. He ruffled helplessly through the pile of bills. "Good God, Mama! Three hundred and fifty guineas for a dress?"

"Well not precisely a dress, dear. A court gown of watered silk and Mechlin. Very becoming. I *could* not appear at Carlton House in a shabby gown!"

"Thing is, Mama, where's the blunt to come from?"

"I have not the least idea, darling, " she admitted. "But I shan't have you worrying about my little problems. I'll come about. You'll see. I always do."

The miracle, of course was that somehow she always did. The Viscount heartily wished he knew the trick of it. He might make good advantage of it himself.

It was just as the Viscount was on the point of leaving his mother's house that same morning that he was confronted by a somewhat disheveled Heather, the now familiar purple sparks of anger flashing in her eyes, and her cheeks flushed with martial fire. She was followed into the house by Robin Ayrton, who had been taking her for a drive. Just now, he was looking a little out of his depth.

Flinging her gloves onto the hall table in disgust, she

THE RELUCTANT SUITOR 157

spied the Viscount and pounced. "Geoff! It is the most infamous thing! I would not have believed it possible! One would think we were still living in the Dark Ages! Something must be instantly done!"

"What the deuce . . . ?" began the Viscount.

Robin noticed the very interested servants hovering about the hall, and ushered an indignant Heather and a bewildered Geoffrey into the front parlor.

"That poor little boy!" cried Heather, ruthlessly removing her bonnet with total disregard for the fetching hair style on which Marie had expended so much effort. "And no one would do *anything!* It is infamous!"

"What little boy? What the devil are you talking about?"

Heather would have answered, but Robin, quite rightly suspecting that only further confusion could result from any explanation she might attempt while her emotions were still so heated, intervened. "A Climbing-Boy," he explained succinctly. "We encountered one on the street awaiting his master."

"And, Geoffrey," cried Heather, unable to keep silent. "He is only seven years old! I could not believe my eyes when I saw him, for the poor thing was coughing dreadfully, and his little eyes were all sore and red, and he had burns all over his feet, and when I asked him why he went up the chimneys when they made him so ill, he said that his master would beat him if he didn't, and he said that when he got stuck in the flue, that horrid man prodded him with a stick with a big nail in the end or lit fires under him to force him up, and he has to sleep on a pile of rags in a filthy taproom, and there is no one to care anything about him at all, except that the Sweep will care if he dies because then he will have to buy another boy and train him as well, and it would probably cost him a great deal of money, and . . ."

"Hold it!" cried Geoff, effectively bringing this rush of words to a halt. "Can't make head nor tail out of a thing you're saying, Heather. Calm down, now. Robin, tell me what it's all about."

Robin sighed, as if in preparation for reliving some unpleasant ordeal. "We were driving down Curzon Street, on our way from the Park, you know. We got bogged down by a milk cart. That's when she saw him."

"Yes," cut in Heather. "He was sitting on the pavement on a big bag of soot with his poor little face all black and crying dreadfully."

"Heather!" said Geoff with a look that silenced her. Robin continued his narrative.

"Well, nothing would do but that Heather should jump down from the curricle and ask him what was the matter and what was his name and such. Then she took out her handkerchief and wiped his tears." He paused, remembering the scene, which had not left him unmoved.

"His name is Timmy," said Heather, "and he lives in Tothill Fields in a horrid tavern run by his master's brother."

"She did get him to stop crying," said Robin. "but then the Sweep came back and started scolding him for a lazy, good-for-nothing boy. That's when Heather lit into *him*. She gave him a regular bear-garden jaw, too, I can tell you. Wish you could have heard her," he finished with a note of pride.

"Well, I'm afraid quite a lot of people did hear me," she said.

The Viscount, who had seated himself and was listening as patiently as he could, felt sure somehow that worse was now to come. "Indeed, I did not mean to cause a scene," she continued. "But I was so very angry, and the Sweep was so odious, and then so many people stopped to see what all the fuss was about. I expect it was because of the crowd that the constable arrived."

"Constable!" cried Geoff, then sank his head into his hands with a moan.

"Yes!" said Heather. "And he was just as odious as the Sweep! For, Geoffrey, only think! He said I may not take Timmy away with me. He said that that poor little boy must go with the Sweep because he is his legal master, and then he said something about indentures and apprentices and all sorts of legal nonsense. But how *could* he send the boy back to someone who beats him?"

"Well, but mean to say, it's the law, y'know. Shouldn't have interfered, Heather. Shouldn't have caused a scene. Constable and all. Not good ton."

"Pooh! As though I should care for that!" she said in exasperation. "And besides, he is *not* his legal master. Timmy's a foundling and that odious Sweep actually *kidnapped* him from the woman who was caring for him. He has no rights over him at all. But that odious constable would not listen. He said Timmy was lying because he didn't like to go up the chimneys—and one can scarce blame the poor thing for that—but I know he was *not* lying."

"That's when I brought her away," Robin summed up. He was feeling rather guilty about the whole affair and hoping his friend wouldn't blame him too much for letting Heather involve herself in it.

"Yes, and I did not at all *wish* to come away!" she continued with a reproachful look at Robin. "And I saw that odious Sweep take Timmy off again, and he kicked him and made him carry a big heavy bag of soot while he himself carried only one little brush! But I shan't let him continue to treat the boy so. He must be instantly rescued. Geoff, do you know a tavern in Tothill Fields called the Flapping Crow? That is where we must go for him."

"Go for him . . . rescue . . . ?" sputtered the Viscount in disbelief. "Devil a bit, Heather! Of all the muttonheaded starts! Tothill Fields, indeed!"

"But Geoff, you could not wish to leave him there to suffer!"

"No business of ours. None at all."

"How can you say so? I had thought better of you, Geoff!" Her face was flushed again. "Will you really not rescue him for me? Must I do it alone?"

"No, I will not! And Heather, you are *not* to be thinking of going to Tothill Fields either, or anywhere near!" he finished in a very plausible imitation of his late father. Responsibility had wrought some subtle changes in Viscount Morpeth.

Heather, caught off guard by the sternness of his tone, saw the impossibility of further argument. That is not to say she had given in, but she didn't see him changing his mind just now, when he was obviously in a pet, so she decided on equivocation. "Well, I shan't do anything you would think really wrong, Geoff," she said rashly, easily convincing herself that he would see the absolute rightness of her actions once the boy was safe.

"Good!" he exclaimed, rising from his seat, pounding his curly beaver savagely onto his head, and striding toward the door. Robin rose to accompany him.

"Shall I see you at Osterley tomorrow!" he asked Heather brightly in an attempt to lighten the atmosphere.

"What? Oh, oh yes, Robin. We shall all be there, of course."

"Then I shall beg the first waltz of you now, before the pack gets to you."

She had the grace to smile then. "Of course, Robin. I should be delighted."

The Viscount's scowl only deepened. "You coming, Robin?" he snapped, and the two young gentlemen quitted the room.

Heather remained in her chair, thinking, and she soon began to form a plan. How vexatious that she had to go to Almack's tonight. And tomorrow was Lady Jersey's party at Osterley. She was learning that in some ways she had no more freedom of movement in London than she had had at Heathside.

But she would not forget the Climbing-Boy. She had promised him that she would not. She would rescue him from his odious master.

Chapter Nineteen

Robin Ayrton's hopes were riding high. It was all he could do to follow Heather's advice concerning Lady Susan Prenderby. He longed to throw himself at her feet, swear lifelong fealty, shower her with kisses. However, he'd tried most of things already at one time or another, and they hadn't seemed to produce the desired results. Heather's plan, on the other hand, seemed to be working admirably.

Robin had not spoken to Susan with anything more than common civility in days. He had written her no poems, sent her no flowers. He had not asked her to dance whenever they chanced to be at the same ball, nor had he stood by broodingly watching her. Instead he had put on a great show of nonchalance and perfect enjoyment of the company of others, especially Miss Heather Braddock.

Lady Susan was piqued. Robin had always been her most faithful, her most devoted admirer. She had always believed that if she so much as crooked a finger, he would be at her side. Now he seemed not even to care.

Seemed, of course was the operative word. In reality he cared desperately. But he saw clearly that this new approach might well succeed where others had failed. Only this afternoon in the Park, Susan had given him her most dazzling smile. He'd returned only a civil nod and ridden off in the opposite direction. But he was sure he could feel those China-blue eyes following him across the Park.

And tonight he would see her again at Lady Jersey's masquerade. He dressed himself with even more than his usual care, his fingers shaking nervously as he arranged his neckcloth *à la* Byron. He curled his glossy locks into their most romantic mode, stuck a loo-mask into his pocket, and strode eagerly down the stairs.

Mr. Ayrton's valet, vaguely confused by the unwontedly

161

cheerful demeanor of his young gentleman, a gentleman he knew to have a singularly undependable temper, watched him go with a bewildered shake of his head.

It wasn't like the Earl of Pythe to fuss over his appearance. Clean linen, a well-brushed coat, the simplest of neckcloths, were usually the height of his requirements. So his valet was somewhat amused by his lordship's antics this evening. He changed his coat once, his waistcoat twice. He dallied over the choice of a pearl or a topaz to wear in the folds of an *Irlandais* neckcloth. And he was whistling.

Court had never expected to enjoy the season so much, forced on him as it had been by his mother. Most of the young ladies he'd met had done nothing to change that expectation. But then it turned out that there were actually one or two girls around who a fellow could really talk to. Like Miss Wheatley, for instance. A bright girl, that. She knew everything about horses and riding. She knew an awful lot about farming and breeding as well. And the oddest thing! Damned if she didn't seem to be getting prettier!

Court wondered if Miss Wheatley would be at Lady Jersey's masquerade tonight. Not that it would affect him, of course, but a fellow liked an intelligent conversation now and then.

He carefully positioned his curly beaver on his well-brushed head, took up a black silk domino—his concession to going in costume—and headed for his carriage. His valet smiled broadly at his retreating back.

Viscount Morpeth was thinking. He was also frowning. He stared at his own scowling face in the mirror as he struggled valiantly with his neckcloth. Five earlier attempts at the *Sentimentale* lay on the floor. Dashed if I'm not turning into a curst Dandy, he was thinking. Going to parties and routs and stupid balls every night of the week just to keep an eye on a silly chit of a girl who don't mean anything to me anyway.

Bidding, the Viscount's impeccable and implacable valet, looked on complacently. He was more than a little surprised, but altogether pleased, by the changes he had observed in his master of late. It was high time the young gentleman took a proper interest in the activities of the

THE RELUCTANT SUITOR

ton and particularly in his own appearance. Whatever had caused such a change—and the shrewd Bidding had his own ideas about that—it was all to the good as far as the valet was concerned.

Tonight it was to be Lady Jersey's masquerade. Well, he'd be dashed if he'd dress up as a pirate or some curst Turkish pasha or other. With one last scowl and a final twitch at his neckcloth, he set out.

The Running Dog was a convivial tavern. It catered mostly to butlers and valets and other superior servants of the fashionable inhabitants of Mayfair. The three gentlemen's gentlemen of the three young gentlemen now on their respective ways to Osterley were regulars at the Dog. They were also long-time cronies who'd passed many an evening in earnest discussion of the antics of their masters. The conversation this night was destined to be particularly interesting, peppered as it would be with accounts of their gentlemen's odd behavior and fueled by rampant speculation as to the causes.

The three of them settled themselves comfortably, drank thirstily of the publican's best heavy-wet, and began their surmises.

The *crème de la* ton was on its way to Osterley, Lady Jersey's beautiful country estate, which lay at no great distance from the metropolis. Masquerades were perhaps not *quite* the thing, but Lady Jersey, on whom the title "Queen Sarah" had not been lightly bestowed, sat so firmly on her throne as the leader of Society that she could get away with anything. Even the starchiest of matrons didn't want to miss this *al fresco* evening which promised to be a high point of the Season.

A long line of carriages made its way out of town, its occupants in merry mood. In a few weeks even the most indefatigable social butterflies would begin to slacken their pace, their wings drooping with fatigue. By the time the summer heat descended on London, the Season would have ground to a halt, dead of its own boredom.

But tonight, a lovely moonlit evening in May, the ton was still ready to be amused at itself, eager to do justice to lobster patties and chilled champagne, and willing to be diverted by the lavish entertainment Lady Jersey had promised.

There was to be rowing on the ornamental water for those so inclined, a carousel on the lawn, dancing in the Long Gallery, and a theatrical performance in front of the semicircular garden house. At midnight there would be fireworks, after which the company would unmask and continue their merrymaking until near dawn.

Sally Jersey, with her usual superb timing, had chosen the perfect point in the Season for her soiree. Flirtations begun weeks ago were coming to fruition. Young men were almost on the point of declarations of affection and offers of a more permanent relationship. Almost, but not quite. And so the air crackled with expectancy and buzzed with rumors of soon-to-be alliances and misalliances.

Heather had elected to attend the party as a fairy princess, "for that is exactly what I feel like, you know," and floated up to the pillared and porticoed entrance in a cloud of silver gauze and blue ribbons, gossamer wings floating after her and Lady Morpeth's diamond tiara twinkling in her dusky curls.

Strolling beside her was Diana, the Huntress—alias Miss Sophy Wheatley—and a lovely lady dressed in a style of a quarter century ago. Lady Morpeth, for what reason she couldn't have said, had decided to go as herself as a girl. She was gratified to discover that the ivory satin dress she'd unearthed in a trunk in the attic, the one embroidered all over with rosebuds that she'd worn to the Duchess of Devonshire's ball all those years ago, still fit her to perfection. Her golden curls glistened under a light dusting of powder. She looked half her age.

They entered the marble paved hall, resplendent with the best of Robert Adam's classical elegance of design, and relinquished their wraps to an attendant footman. No sooner had they crossed the threshold than three gentlemen came from three directions to meet them.

Through the door to their right Viscount Morpeth had been conveniently munching on a macaroon in the dining room. When he saw them enter, he wondered offhandedly if someone had suddenly lit more candles in the hall. It seemed so much brighter than a moment before.

Through the door to their left, the Earl of Pythe had

been studiously viewing the paintings in the drawing room—though he couldn't tell a Tintoretto from a Turner—and casually glancing every few seconds toward the hall. At their entrance, a Sir Joshua Reynolds portrait was abandoned without regret for a much more animated face.

From the double doors facing them, Sir William Longchamps emerged from the Gallery. He looked at Lady Morpeth, blinked, and looked again. For a moment it seemed that he was once again a young man of five-and-twenty, falling in love at first sight with Tina Hadley.

"Hallo, Heather . . . ," "Evening, Miss Wheatley . . . ," "Tina!" began the three gentlemen in one voice.

"Geoff . . . ," "My lord . . . ," "William . . . ," came the simultaneous replies.

This hopeful conversation was soon on more solid ground, and greetings were accomplished all around. Donning loo-masks of varying degrees of elegance, the group passed into the Long Gallery. This magnificent chamber was already buzzing with mandarins and sultans, sailors and gypsies, and ladies and gentlemen in dominoes of every description. The whole world seemed to have made the trip from London.

Some of the company strolled out into the grounds where hundreds of lights winked in the trees and torches lit the paths like in a fairyland. Others sauntered the length of the room, sipping champagne and admiring the fine collection of paintings and each other. The green walls shimmered in the light from dozens of candles in elaborately carved and gilt girandoles and ormolu wall sconces. Everyone seemed to be smiling.

Almost as soon as the party from Morpeth House had entered the room, a gentlemen whose black mask did nothing whatever to hide his romantic good looks, approached them with long strides. Robin Ayrton greeted them lightly.

"That you, Heather? It must be, for you're nearly the prettiest girl in the room."

"But I collect there is at least one who you find prettier," she teased.

Robin grinned. "Is she looking this way?" he asked in a rough undertone.

Heather looked around for some sign of Lady Susan Prenderby. "I can't see her. Where is she?"

"Over there. By that pagoda or whatever it is. The shepherdess à la Marie Antoinette."

Then Heather saw her, looking extraordinarily picturesque in a prettily looped-up damask gown that had certainly never seen a meadow, much less a sheep, and holding a long crooked staff trailing silk ribbons.

"Yes, she is looking, Robin," whispered Heather. "I feel sure she hasn't taken her eyes off you since you entered the room. No. Don't look. I think you must keep her guessing just the tiniest bit longer."

Robin sighed. "Well, come dance with me, then."

The Viscount had overheard much of this whispered conference and was inordinately pleased by it. He'd always known, of course, that Robin was nutty on old Susey P., but he didn't like the way the fellow'd been looking at Heather lately. The devil of it was that he was so deuced handsome. How could any girl keep from tripping into love with him? And Heather hadn't got any defenses, he was sure. He didn't want her hurt. So he was relieved beyond measure by this brother-sister type scheming.

"Take yourself off, Ayrton," he cut in just as Heather was about to set off on Robin's arm. "She's going on the carousel with me."

"I am?" asked Heather in surprise and delight.

"Yes." There was an unusual note of stubbornness behind the word, but he was smiling as he took her hand from Robin's and pulled her out onto the lawn. She didn't seem to mind.

From that point on the evening became an idyll for Heather. A shifting mirage of images of Geoffrey lifting her onto a creamy white carousel horse as if she were a wisp of air. Geoffrey rowing her on the obsidian sheet of water, sending ripples across a silvery moon river while a palely glowing swan glided by. Geoffrey scaling the wall of the kitchen garden to fetch her some strawberries and both of them collapsing into giggles as the irate gardener who had been standing guard against just such an eventuality chased him vocally away brandishing a hoe. Heather thought she had never been so happy in her life.

And the evening was made complete when she discovered that her little attempts at matchmaking were paying off. It seemed that the happiness of all her most particular friends was now assured.

It was while she and Geoff were dutifully touring the magnificent State Rooms, marveling at the rich red Gobelins in the Tapestry Room, giggling over the overdone opulence of the State Bed with its gilt crown and its halo of artificial flowers, that they happened on a touching and altogether satisfying scene in the Etruscan Dressing Room, which was painted all over like Mr. Wedgewood's pottery.

Sophy Wheatley and the Earl of Pythe had wandered in some time earlier. They commented somewhat awkwardly on the uniqueness of the decor then, quite suddenly it seemed, found themselves staring soulfully into each other's eyes, the painted Roman figures quite forgotten, each of them speechless at what they could plainly read in the face of the other.

Without a word Court raised both of Sophy's hands to his lips, his eyes never leaving hers. In that moment, as a radiant smile lit her face, Sophy Wheatley became the most beautiful woman in the world.

When Heather and Geoff appeared at the doorway, checking on the threshold, the lovestruck couple were seated on a pair of japanned chairs pulled well into a corner out of the candlelight. They were still holding hands and talking in low murmurs. Heather could make out only a few words of which phrases like "Will your father like me, dearest Sophy?" and "Whatever will your mama say, Court darling?" were characteristic. It was enough.

"That's all right then," murmured Heather with great satisfaction as she led Geoff silently away.

It was much later in the evening when Heather was strolling through the grounds with Robin, Geoff having finally defected to the library for a game of cards, that the final happiness was granted.

The grounds of Osterley were filled with nooks and crannies convenient for rendezvous and romantic dallyings of every sort, and many of Lady Jersey's guests were taking advantage of them. The Greek Temple of Pan was one of the most attractive, and it was here that Lady Susan Prenderby was endeavoring to fight off the advances of the Marquis of Wattlesey.

Susan was a dutiful girl—as least when it suited her to be—and she had tried very hard this evening to follow her mama's command to bring the Marquis up to scratch. She quite liked the notion of being a marchioness, but would have much preferred the title without this particular husband. She gave her suitor a sidelong glance. He was not a gentleman calculated to inspire dreams of romance in a young lady's breast. A figure on the portly side, a complexion on the ruddy side, a constitution on the gouty side, and a head decidedly on the balding side—he was, in fact, bald as a billiard ball, excepting only a longish, lanky grey fringe—would have been a kind description of Lord Wattlesey.

Susan wasn't at all sure she could bear with what she knew she would have to bear if she married the Marquis, and she was in the Temple of Pan to find out. There were negative indications very early on.

"Ah, my little pigeon," he clucked, patting her hand affectionately. Then suddenly he lunged. Susan, with wonderful foresight, ducked, and the sloppy kiss landed somewhere in the vicinity of her left ear.

"My lord!" she exclaimed with a pettish scold.

"Such a pretty pigeon as it is!" He lunged again. His aim was improving, and the kiss hit her cheek, his beaky nose landing squarely in one China-blue eye.

"Sir!" she cried, struggling to escape his grasp and trying to reach her beribboned shepherdess's staff.

"No, no, my pigeon. I'll have you, you know. You shan't fly away." This time he was dead on, and Lady Susan found herself quite thoroughly kissed. Disgustingly so.

"Oh!" she cried in anger, and somehow managed to stamp a foot. She had her answer. She certainly was not willing to pay *this* price for her coronet. "Will you let me go you . . . you . . ."

The invective she sought was destined to go unfound, for it was at that moment that Heather and Robin chanced to pass the Temple of Pan. The fireworks which were not scheduled to go off for an hour or more began to fire prematurely in Robert Ayrton's head, their sparks shooting from his wonderful eyes. Three long strides carried him to the errant Marquis. That aging roué was much

THE RELUCTANT SUITOR 169

surprised to find his feet quite suddenly leave the ground and himself quite suddenly out on the grass. He blustered and puffed and wheezed his indignation, a heated challenge rising to his lips. One solid look at Robin's flashing eyes, however, caused him to think better of it. My Lord of Wattlesey instantly retired from the lists.

"And now I shall deal with *you!*" said Robin, advancing on Susan with a very purposeful look.

"Oh, Mr. Ayrton," she fluttered, trying vainly to straighten her golden curls, which had fallen into beguiling disarray. "How very glad I am that you arrived when you did. He was being so very disagreeable and I . . ."

"Minx!" he cut her off. "It's high time you learned to accept the consequences of your flirting!" For the second time in the last quarter of an hour, Lady Susan Prenderby found herself quite thoroughly kissed. Wonderfully so! She wondered absently why the fireworks had been set off early.

"Mr. Ayrton!" she managed to gasp out before he silenced her with another kiss. "Oh!" He kissed her yet again. "Oh . . . Robin!"

When at last he came up for air, he was still wearing a stern expression, but there was something like magic in his eyes. "From now on, Susan, when you allow a gentleman to kiss you, *I* will be the gentleman."

"But I didn't allow him to kiss me," she began hotly, but her protests were cut off by another crushing kiss. "Oh, Robin," she sighed at last. "He was so awful, but I . . . I didn't think you cared anymore. I thought . . ."

"Susey," he answered, his voice gruff with emotion. "I have never looked at any woman but you. And from now on, you will never look at any man but me. Is that clear?"

She peeped up at him from under her long golden lashes, then sank her pretty head onto his shoulder. "Yes. Oh, *yes*, Robin!"

Heather smiled. "That's all right then," she said to herself, feeling understandably smug. She turned happily toward the house.

Heather returned to the dancing in the Long Gallery. She waltzed with Captain Johnsdale, quadrilled with Major Peevesby, and country-danced with a rotund Lord Greensley and with poor moonstruck Mr. Wesley, all of whom were at great pains to let her see through their disguises. Mr. Wesley, his hopes high, led her out onto the small porch to breathe in the sweetly romantic air. Then he dutifully went off to get her a glass of champagne.

She gazed happily up at the stars. The moonlight twinkling on her diamond tiara and gossamer wings made her glow with an ethereal loveliness. She strolled idly along the porch, humming softly with the music.

It was then that the evening began to fall apart.

"How now, fair spirit! Whither wander you?" came an oozing voice behind her. Pleased at the pretty Shakespearean allusion, she turned with a ready smile.

A tall gentleman stood leaning negligently in the doorway, surveying her keenly. His black domino did nothing to conceal a once-fine figure now beginning to run to fat, or an ensemble that tended toward a peacocky sort of showiness. She knew he'd been watching her a good part of the evening.

"Over hill, over dale . . ." she began, then stopped abruptly. The gentleman had reached up to remove his black loo-mask, and Heather found herself staring straight into the eyes of her half-brother.

Years of depravity had not been able to completely destroy the handsome face, so like his father's, but its ravages were clearly apparent in the puffiness about the cold grey eyes and the deep lines of dissipation around the mouth. He was favoring her with a crooked smile that had gone a long way toward insuring his reputation as a rake of the first order, but Heather could detect no trace of warmth behind it. There was no sign of recognition in his eyes.

The orchestra had just struck up a waltz, and he reached for her hand. "Sound, music!" he continued in Shakespearean vein. "Come my Queen, take hands with me."

Heather was too taken aback to protest and very much too much afraid to speak for fear that he would recognize her voice. Indeed, she was quite sure that had she tried to, no sound would have issued from her lips. There was, besides, a determined light in the Earl's eyes and a quite insistent pressure on her hand that made it clear he didn't intend to let her go. She cursed the casualness of a masquerade that allowed a gentleman to dance with someone to whom he had not been introduced, all the while blessing the mask which hid her face from his intense gaze.

Please, she was chanting to herself, please don't let him know me.

Bo swept her into the waltz, holding her a bit closer than was strictly acceptable. He tried several stratagems to get her to speak, but she remained resolutely mum throughout the dance. He was intrigued, not only by her silence and her obvious beauty, imperfectly hidden by the silver mask, but by the trembling he could feel quite clearly through the thin gauze of her gown. She seemed afraid of him, a circumstance he had always found seductive. He held her closer, her trembling increased, and he smiled.

The Earl of Stonington, so wrapped up in his partner, was not overly aware of the other merrymakers in the room. Two of them, however, were very much aware of him. Sir William Longchamps had just come from the refreshment room. The glass of champagne from which he was sipping stopped midway to his lips when he spotted Heather and her partner. He no longer had any doubts as to Heather's identity and her circumstances, and he had no trouble recognizing the infamous Earl of Stonington, who had been recently pointed out to him. The girl was in the arms of the half-brother who had used her so ill. He must rescue her at once.

Lady Morpeth saw the pair from where she was dancing with Lord Handy. She went pale, murmured "Oh, dear," and managed to steer her partner so that they should finish the dance quite near to Heather and her brother.

Before the last note had faded, two grim-visaged rescuers descended on them, to Heather's very great relief.

"Miss Braddock," said Sir William with a reassuring smile, gently but decisively removing her hand from her brother's. "Our dance next, I believe."

"Y-yes, I . . . I believe it is," she managed to say so softly she could barely be heard. She allowed Sir William to carry her off.

The Earl had no time even to scowl after them.

"Stonington!" chirped Lady Morpeth, effectively captivating his attention while Heather made good her escape. He peered at her for a long moment, then smiled his cold, crooked smile.

"I believe it's Tina Morpeth under that so-fetching mask. Am I not right?"

She laughed in her pretty rippling way, one eye on Sir William and Heather across the room. "I suppose I must be flattered by your recognition, my lord, for it has been quite three years since you have laid eyes on me, I'm sure. One had quite given up hope of seeing you at ton parties."

His half-closed eyes touched with suspicion, for he knew well that Lady Morpeth, and indeed most of the ton, felt no great love for him and his kind. "It seems that I am not always welcome."

"Yes, one has heard that you are grown very naughty. A shocking rake, in fact. I wonder Lady Jersey should have asked you tonight."

"Ah, but Sally's a rogue, you know. And I fancy I've convinced her I'm bent on reform."

"You, my lord?" she exclaimed with an arch smile.

"Yes, I promise you. I shall be coming into a great deal of money soon. It's time I thought of marrying. Stonington must have an heir, of course."

"Marry! Well! I thought never to see that day! Had I any hopeful young daughters, I should take very good care to keep them from your sight."

"Ah, but if they looked like you, I should surely find them. Tell me, lovely Tina, who is that girl I was just dancing with?"

"Who?"

"Braddock, I think the name was."

"Oh, yes, Miss Braddock," she answered, trying to maintain a casual tone. "My goddaughter. The family's wretchedly impoverished, so I thought to give the girl the treat of a Season in town."

"She seems a pretty girl from what I can tell. Carries herself well, nice hair. Good blood there, I should think."

Lady Morpeth could not forbear laughing. "Would you? You sound as if you are judging a brood mare, my lord!"

"The two are not so very different."

She tried to ignore this remark, feeling her way in a very touchy conversation. "She's a sweet child of course, and I quite dote on her, but I've nearly given up all hope of establishing her creditably. With no dowry, no name of any importance, nor any notable blood, nothing, in fact, in her background to recommend her, well . . ." She let the sentence trail off.

"Of course the blood is vitally important," he muttered almost to himself.

"You know, Stonington, if your reputation weren't so entirely shocking, and if I didn't know the case to be hopeless, I might make a push for you for the girl," she teased. "There's no denying it would be a brilliant match for her." She gave a great sigh. "But alas, I fear I shall have to send her home again. I believe the local Squire's younger son has offered. She is certainly beneath the touch of a Stonington."

His eyes strayed to his unrecognized sister. There was something about the girl, the way she held her head, perhaps, or that long neck, that seemed vaguely familiar, and definitely aristocratic. There *was* good blood there. He'd bet on it. And he would take care to find out if he was right.

Heather couldn't stop shaking. Sir William was being very solicitous, very reassuring, though of course she had no idea that he understood the seriousness of the predicament from which he had just rescued her. She must get hold of herself!

By concentrating very firmly on the movements of the dance, she managed to regain some measure of composure. She told herself sternly not to be a ninny-hammer, and that she should be pleased by her confrontation with Bo. She had actually danced with him, and he had not recognized her. Of course, she was masked, but she could not but feel she'd passed some sort of a test. By the end of the dance she was very nearly feeling herself again.

Her sense of triumph did not, however, extend to the folly of tempting fate, and she took great care to avoid her brother for what remained of the evening. Midnight neared, and with it the time for the removing of masks. She daren't face Bo without the pretty silver shield. She went in search of her godmother.

Lady Morpeth found herself suffering from mixed emotions. She was terribly grateful to Sir William for his timely rescue of Heather, but she couldn't help wondering as to his motives. He couldn't know, after all, that the man in the black domino was Heather's wicked half-brother. And she couldn't deny a feeling of jealousy at the eagerness with which he had plucked her from the arms of a known rake. She even acknowledged her jealousy with a rueful sigh. For tonight, strolling with him under the stars, waltzing with him in the candlelight, Tina Morpeth had admitted to herself that she was head over ears in love with William Longchamps.

The fireworks were just beginning to sparkle over the water when Heather found her godmother and Sophy. Barely had the last pinwheel wheeled and the last rocket showered its colored cloud of sparks into the midnight sky than their carriage began the lengthy trip back to town. The carriage so full of expectant chatter only a few hours before was now subdued. Sophy, glowing with silent happiness, was lost in her own pleasant dreams. Lady Morpeth, the picture of Heather on William Longchamps arm engraved on her mind, was blue-deviled. And Heather, who fancied she could still feel a pair of cold grey eyes studying her intently, was frightened.

Chapter Twenty

Heather was a resilient young lady. It took much of the night, lying in the darkness with her mind full of unpleasant thoughts and images, but by the time the chambermaid had tiptoed into her bedchamber next morning to draw back the turquoise damask hangings around her bed, she had quite talked herself out of her fright of the previous evening. In fact, she could now look on the whole incident as rather convenient. A natural desire to avoid any possibility of further contact with her brother would offer a handy excuse for crying off a projected evening at Vauxhall tonight. She quite liked going to the famous pleasure garden, but she had something quite different she must do this night.

The day was bright and by afternoon had turned almost sultry. Sophy went for a drive to Richmond with Court, leaving Heather and her godmama alone in the pink saloon, languidly dallying over their tea.

Lady Morpeth, fretting into her teacup, broke their brooding silence. "The time has grown so dreadfully short. I made sure I would have you married long since, my dear, but we've scarcely a week remaining till your birthday. Whatever is to be done?"

Heather didn't know how to answer. She could not admit to this wonderful lady who had been so kind to her that she had turned down several attractive proposals in the last pair of weeks. She had been surprised and flattered by the offers, but she couldn't bring herself to accept any of them. She suspected rather strongly that she was harboring a stubbornly romantic streak in her nature, for her first thought on hearing each proposal was, "But I don't love him." And the only man she had ever *wanted* to marry didn't want to marry her.

She also didn't feel she could tell Lady Morpeth that she'd been spending her afternoons lately in a search for employment. She knew that in less than a week now she would be irrevocably cast onto her own devices. Dressed in her Heathside clothes she had visited a number of agencies specializing in the placing of domestic personnel. Then changing to her simplest cambric gown and bonnet, she'd spoken to many a shopkeeper who might be looking for an assistant. And every day she made an exhaustive study of the "Positions Offered" columns of the newspapers. She had, in fact, posted off a letter that very morning to an elderly lady in the Midlands who was seeking a paid companion.

One other problem was weighing heavily on her mind. Much as she loved and admired her charming "godmama," that lady's *laissez-faire* attitude toward bills was not Heather's. She had been feeling terribly guilty about the staggering bills she'd managed to run up in just under a month. She was determined to pay them all by herself, no matter how long it took her.

She didn't feel she could impart any of this to Lady Morpeth, so all she said was "You mustn't worry about me, Godmama. I shall be all right."

"But that is just it, dear. I'm afraid you shan't be. And who *is* to worry about you?"

Any answer Heather might have dredged up from the bottom of her mind was cut off by the silent entrance of Bellows.

"Sir William Longchamps, my lady," he intoned. The gentleman in question entered hard on the butler's words. The faces of both ladies brightened at once.

"Good afternoon, my dears," he exclaimed with a broad smile. "Do you know, everytime I walk into this house I am once again amazed by the presence of so much beauty within it."

"And any gentleman who pays such pretty compliments," said Lady Morpeth happily, "will ever be welcome at its doors."

This light banter went on for some few moments, the ladies' moods growing miraculously lighter almost by the minute. It was brought to a stop only by the arrival of the Viscount.

He was a bit worried about what had happened last night at Osterley and had even given up an afternoon's shooting at Manton's Gallery with his sporting cronies to discuss the situation with Heather and his mother. And so his mood was *not* brightened by seeing Sir William here yet again. The fellow seemed to run tame in the house. He had to admit that he liked and admired Sir William, but ever since his mama had mentioned the man as a prospective husband for Heather, he had found no pleasure in his company.

"Hallo, sir," he said, shaking Sir William's hand. "Didn't think to find you here."

"Your mother will tell you I'm underfoot at all hours. Make quite a nuisance of myself, I'm sure."

"Nonsense, William," assured Lady Morpeth.

"Well, this time I've come to take Heather for a drive. I'm trying out some new greys she'll like to see."

Heather's smile brightened at the prospect, for she really couldn't bear the thought of sitting here prevaricating to Lady Morpeth. In a very few minutes she had donned a pretty jaconet pelerine and a quite captivating villager hat of chip straw, fetched a Chinese sunshade, and floated out the door on Sir William's arm.

The couple they left behind them sank into an unaccustomed gloom, not really so unaccustomed in recent days.

"William looked very cheerful today, don't you think, dear?" Lady Morpeth remarked absently. "Almost . . . expectant."

"What d'you mean, Mama?"

"Well, you saw yourself how worried and attentive he was to Heather last night. I fear, I mean I *hope*, that he's made up his mind to offer for her." She was trying hard for her usual perky tone. It came out so brittle it threatened to shatter like fine crystal at any moment. "Why else would he have asked her to go driving in that very particular way?"

"You really think so, Mama?" The Viscount slumped lower into his chair and brooded.

Sir William's phaeton entered the Park by the Stanhope Gate, the greys stepping proudly and confidently. Instead of heading for Rotten Row, where the afternoon promenade was just beginning, he turned off along the Serpentine. The afternoon sun glinted off the unmoving water in golden lights. Heather looked up in surprise at their direction.

"Should you mind it very much, Heather, if we avoided the crowd? I have something I should like to discuss with you, and you know how impossible conversation is in the midst of that lot." He waved disparagingly in a vaguely southerly direction,

"Of course not, Sir William, but what is it you wish to discuss?"

He turned to study her face where smudgy purple shadows under her big eyes testified to her sleepless night. "You look tired, my dear."

"Only a very little. I slept ill last night."

"Yes. I rather expected you would."

Her eyes flew to his face in curiosity. How could he know that, she wondered. Sir William saw that he must explain. The story was not a complicated one. He related it simply and straightforwardly, explaining how struck he had been by her resemblance to a girl from his past, how, his curiosity piqued, he'd begun asking questions until he learned that Heather Braddock was Lady Margaret St. Vincent.

"You are remarkably like your mother, you know."

She sat silently awhile in thought, digesting this new and startling discovery. Then she spoke. "Then you must know about Bo as well," she said suddenly, remembering last evening.

"Yes," he answered grimly. "I know all about your half-brother."

" And that is why you rescued me last night! Oh, Sir William, thank you for that! How badly I wanted to thank you last night, but of course I could not."

"I'm glad I was there to help. From what I have heard of your brother, he has not the easiest of tempers and would not be pleased to find you in London."

"I don't think he knows I have run away."

"He will, and we must decide what is to be done."

"Done? What do you mean?"

"You haven't much time left, Heather. You must marry at once. Have you a partiality for any of your suitors?"

THE RELUCTANT SUITOR

Heather, to her great chagrin, blushed fiercely as an image of a shock of sandy hair falling down over blue-grey eyes leaped into her mind. "N-no," she said softly.

"That's a pity, for I don't put much faith in marriages of convenience. But in these very unusual circumstances, I suppose there is no other answer."

"But I—I don't wish to marry, Sir William. I shall do very well without my brother's fortune. I am quite strong, and I can work."

A scowl crossed his face. "That is nonsense, Heather." He looked at her closely. "And I think you know it is nonsense. Besides, it is not your brother's fortune. It is yours. Your grandfather wanted you to have what he had worked so hard for, not your half-brother, who is no kin to your grandfather, after all. Now tell me true, Heather. Have you had no offers? I own I should find that hard to believe."

She wanted to lie, but somehow she could not. He was so kind. "Yes, I have," she admitted.

"Well then. You must choose one of them, my dear. Who is to be the lucky man?" The pain in her face grew acute, and she did not answer. He softened at sight of her. "Heather, promise me that you will at least consider one of them."

She hesitated a long time. "Very well. I will consider."

He gave her an avuncular smile. "It pains me to counsel you to be thinking of a marriage without love. You see, I hope to marry for love myself, very soon."

She turned in her seat with a little bounce. "You do? To whom? Oh, Sir William, you must tell me. She will be the luckiest woman in England."

His smile grew. "I hope she thinks so. You see, I'm not sure the lady returns my regard. I thought perhaps you could tell me."

"Me? But how could I . . ." She broke off as the obvious finally became visible. "Godmama! Of course! How blind I have been not to see it all along. But it is perfect! You are just right for each other. And how happy I am for you both!"

"So you think there is a chance for me?"

"Oh, yes. Yes, I do. You must know that she has been positively moped lately, and I think it is because she feels you are about to offer for . . . for some other lady. But she simply *glows* whenever you are around. When did you know? Have you loved her a long time?"

"Oh, yes," he sighed. "A very long time, indeed."

Heather, as romantic at heart as any other young lady, would give him no rest until he had told the whole story. He told her about a moonstruck young man, a younger son with neither fortune nor title in his future, who had fallen hopelessly in love with the Incomparable Tina Hadley. She had never known, of course. He dared not approach her. And she was soon snapped up by the more dashing Lord Morpeth and given the sort of title and position she deserved.

Poor Billy Longchamps had gone on a binge—one might say a rampage—through every gaming hall, gin shop, and dive in London in an attempt to forget her twinkling green eyes. But it hadn't helped, and he made no demur when his father took the decision to ship him off to India.

He'd met many attractive women since—had even been on the point of offering marriage once or twice—but a dream that had not dimmed at all in twenty-five years had always stopped him.

Earlier this year he'd learned that Tina Morpeth was a widow. It took him less than a fortnight to pack up his life and hurry home to see if fate would offer him a second chance.

"It's just like a novel," said Heather with glowing eyes. "A romantic novel."

Sir William laughed. "I suppose it would seem romantic to you, but I can tell you it's devilish uncomfortable being a romantic hero when you don't know whether or not the book has a happy ending. I might be playing in a tragedy."

"Oh, but it will have a happy ending. I know it will."

"Well, I can but hope."

"Only wait until Geoff hears!"

"Well, he shan't just yet. I hereby charge you, Heather, to mention this to no one. Not to Geoff, or to Miss Wheatley, and certainly not to Tina. I have only told you so that you might perhaps find out how the lady feels. Discreetly, you know."

"Of course, Sir William. I'm sure I can, too."

"Good. I must go out of town in the morning for some two or three days. Perhaps when I return I shall have the courage to put my fate to the touch." The boy-in-love note left his voice, and he became the stern uncle again. "And you, Heather, must keep your promise to seriously consider a proposal of marriage. You really have no other acceptable choice." She only nodded, and they rode on in silence awhile.

"Am I really like my mother, Sir William?" she asked at length.

He gave her an affectionate smile. "Very like."

Christina Morpeth's emotions had been suffering from severe instability of late. And now, from the conversation she was having with Heather, she didn't know what to think. But mostly, through the grey clouds that seem to have invaded her mind, there began to glow a tiny ray of hope.

It seemed that Sir William knew all about Heather, about her grandfather and the will, and especially about her half-brother. Had, in fact, known for some time. So it had not been jealousy, but merely his great kindness that had prompted him to rescue her last evening. And now the girl was telling her that William was leaving town for a few days. Her heart plummeted at the thought of not seeing him, then flew sky-high again as another realization intruded. If, knowing that Heather's birthday was so near, he would still go out of town, it could only mean that he had no intention of offering for her himself. Tina Morpeth beamed all over her pretty face.

"You do like him, don't you, Godmama?" Heather injected the question into the conversation as casually as she could.

"Like him? Of course I like him, darling. How could one not like him?" she replied, trying unsuccessfully to sound equally casual. She paused, a warmer, pinker glow overspreading her already glowing features. "I think he is the kindest, most wonderful man I've ever known," she added in a very different voice.

"That's all right then," said Heather enigmatically and skipped out of Lady Morpeth's bedchamber where her godmama was dressing for the theatre. Down the hall Sophy was nervously preparing herself for the ordeal of dinner with her future mother-in-law, the formidable Dowager Countess of Pythe.

And so the whole "family" at Morpeth House would be conveniently out tonight. Heather set about completing her own plans.

Chapter Twenty-one

Tothill Fields was a neighborhood unlike any Heather had ever seen, and she devoutly hoped never to see another like it. She made her way slowly along the dark, noxious street, searching for the Flapping Crow. The hackney driver had resolutely refused to take her into the infamous Rookery, so named for its teeming, squabbling, noisy inhabitants, so she had alighted and plunged into its murky depths on foot.

Some instinct had told her she mustn't go to Tothill Fields as a Young Lady of Quality. Geoff's chagrin at the idea of her going at all had been so great that she gathered it was not an altogether respectable place. Also, in the heat of her argument with the Sweep, she had made the tactical error of mentioning her name. She hoped he would not recognize her.

So she had donned the fustian dress and mobcap, apron and *sabots*, that Marie had so ruthlessly removed from her that day that seemed so long ago.

As she picked her way along the vile streets she thought about what she would do with the Climbing-Boy once she had rescued him. Now that she saw the neighborhood where he lived, she banished every doubt about the rightness of that rescue. He must be got speedily out of Tothill Fields, and, if his master was not to find him, out of London as well. Heather thought perhaps he could go up to Morpeth to work as a stableboy. Or if not that, she felt sure Court and Sophy would be willing to find a place for him at Great Pythe. Timmy would be safe and well cared for.

The stench issuing from the doorways and open sewers as she passed threatened to knock her over. But her attention was soon called upon to the extent that she all but forgot the stink.

She saw almost at once that even in her servant's fustian she was severely overdressed for Tothill Fields. The women lounging in doorways, many of them with a squalling infant in one hand and a bottle of Blue Ruin in the other, were mostly in rags. Their hands came up in a begging gesture as she passed, almost unthinkingly, as though in automatic response to a stranger, but without any real hope of success. Their whinings of "Give us a shilling, love," and "'Alf a crown fer the baby?" were dull and seemed to lack conviction. Heather didn't find them frightening. She found them terribly sad.

Before she reached the tavern, she'd also been accosted by several drunken revelers of the masculine gender, grabbing, pinching, and begging for favors. But a put-on brusqueness combined with her swifter feet enabled her to elude them. Even the men didn't frighten her. She found them pitiable.

And everywhere were the children: young, old, tall, short, all of them terribly thin and dressed in rags with match-stick legs and hollow, sunken eyes. She never thought to see so many heart-wrenching children, begging for farthings and ha'pennies. It made her angry that they should have to beg for coins. It made her angry that she had none to give.

She found The Crow by sound before she caught sight of it, a din of voices, some raised in bawdy song, of drunken arguments, of clanging tankards, and, surprisingly, of laughter. She turned the corner, and the glow of light spilling from its open doorway seemed a welcoming beacon. She approached cautiously but steadily, peeped inside, then took a deep breath and plunged into the melee.

It took her eyes a moment to adjust to the glare. She quickly scanned the room for sign of the boy. The place was overflowing with the ragged slum dwellers of Tothill Fields, throwing away their pitifully few pennies on the dubious pleasure of a slug of Stingo, Blue Ruin, or Strip-Me-Naked, then passing out onto the piles of straw with which the corners of the room were lavishly furnished.

She also saw a table full of what the locals stigmatized as "Swells," well-dressed and well-breeched gentlemen of

THE RELUCTANT SUITOR 185

low tastes who found their amusement among the drunks and wenches of the slums, then went happily home to their comfortable beds in the sweeter-smelling sections of town. They were tossing back the fiery cheap gin with the best of the rest and adding more than their fair share to the general din.

Finally she saw Timmy. He was perched on a stool in a corner of the room, staring out miserably onto the rowdy scene, his little head nodding now and then with sleep. Heather made straight for him.

Arms shot out at her as she traversed the room. Drunken faces loomed before her with leering grins. Sweaty palms grabbed and pawed. But she brushed them off and kept going. When she was near the boy on his stool, her progress was stopped by a wool-clad arm being thrown about her waist. She quickly found herself sitting in the lap of one of the "Swells."

"Well, here's a pretty bird, and no mistake!" said the gentleman in a voice thick with gin and some other quality Heather didn't recognize. But she had no leisure to puzzle it out.

For the second time in as many nights, Heather found herself confronting her half-brother. There was a stubble of dark beard on his chin, and the ruddy glow of the cheap gin on his puffy face, but the man was undoubtedly Beauregard St. Vincent, Earl of Stonington. And now, for the first time in this adventure, she was afraid. She began to tremble.

"Ah, the sparrow is shivering!" said Bo. "It's a cold sparrow. It needs something to warm its little heart."

She felt a bottle being placed against her lips, her head tilted back. She was forced to drink. The fiery liquid burned all the way down to her stomach, and she began to cough violently. Her brother began to laugh. "Ah, sparrow. The best thing for a cough is a little more medicine." He lifted the bottle again, but she managed to twist her head away.

"Maybe it wants to buy its own, Bo," said one of his laughing cronies, flipping a shiny coin in the air. Bo caught it and grinned a lascivious grin.

"Well, is it an expensive sparrow?" He dropped the coin down the front of her dress, and she wriggled involuntarily as it touched her bare skin. The gentlemen roared with laughter.

"Doesn't our little bird like its pretty shilling?" roared Bo. "Maybe I'd better fish it out."

His free arm went up and grabbed the top of her dress as though he would rip it off in one swift pull.

"No, no, please! Don't, I beg you! Pray, let go. Please leave me alone," she cried, trying to struggle from his grasp.

The voice fell like pure music into the cacophany of the room. The "Swells" all stopped their laughing and stared at the source of the cultured accents. The most intensive stare came from Beauregard St. Vincent, Earl of Stonington. Realization slowly dawned in his hard grey eyes, and he reached up to pluck off the enveloping mobcap that hid the raven hair and shaded the white brow.

Heather's huge violet eyes widened in fear as she felt his arm tighten about her waist. He looked at her in disbelief, the range of emotions racing through him clearly telegraphed on his face. Then she was thrust away like a poisonous snake, the thrust carrying her flying across the room. He stood and glared at her, panting with the strength of his emotion. His surprise, disbelief, chagrin, and loathing had all, in that moment, distilled into one overpowering emotion—rage. His face turned purple with it; his hands, white-knuckled from clutching his chair, trembled with it; he ground his teeth with it, then unlocked them enough to speak.

"The Lady Margaret St. Vincent, is it not?" he gritted out in a parody of civility.

She scurried to her feet and backed against the wall as her brother descended on her malevolently.

"Stonington!" The word cut through the brutal atmosphere like lightning, halting Bo in his advance. Heather's eyes flew to the doorway from which the sound had come. The figure there was in silhouette; she could not see the face. But for Heather there could never be any mistaking Geoffrey Curwen, Viscount Morpeth.

Geoff took in the situation at a glance and knew that there was little hope of getting Heather out of there safely. Their one chance lay in creating a diversion among the crowd, and the best way of doing that, the Viscount well

THE RELUCTANT SUITOR   187

knew, was a mill. A regular turn-up just might do the trick.

Pounding his beaver well down onto his head to shade his face—he had no wish to be recognized—he plunged into the room, made straight for Bo, and in the words of Gentleman Jackson, "planted him a facer." Bo, caught off guard, fell to his knees, and Geoff began flailing about in all directions and throwing furniture around to very good effect. Soon nobody knew who was hitting whom, or why, but it was a grand mill, and everyone seemed to be thoroughly enjoying it.

Geoff, amid his defensive flailings, wondered idly why Stonington, who severely outweighed him, hadn't yet tipped him a settler. Bo had, in fact, tried to do just that, but his reflexes were dulled by liquor and the blow he'd already received. Before he could get fully to his feet, his sister, realizing what he was about, had grabbed a handy chair and entered the fray, with her brother as her first victim. One solid blow and the Earl of Stonington was out of the fight.

Geoff managed to work his way to Heather's side. "Outside!" he barked over the din and crash. "Go on! There's a hackney. Be right out!"

She grabbed Timmy, who had been sitting wide-eyed on his stool watching the scene with obvious delight, and dashed for the door, ducking wild blows, flying bottles, and splintering furniture all the way. They gained the street and hopped into the hackney. Within two minutes, with the raging storm inside at its peak, Geoff had jumped in after them, and they were bowling away toward Mayfair. From behind them came the sounds of breaking glass, the approaching whistles of the Charleys, and assorted cries of "Watch! Watch!"

The Viscount was still breathing hard; his head was bleeding from a cut, and he was alarmingly angry. In a few moments he was breathing well enough to spit out one word.

"Damme!"

"Geoff, you're hurt!" cried Heather, seeing the trickle of blood, and a bruise on his jaw that was beginning to turn very interesting colors and swell unattractively. She pulled a handkerchief from her sleeve and began to daub at the cut, but he pushed her ruthlessly away.

"What the devil did you mean by it, Heather? Of all the cabbage-headed starts! Pig-headed mulish female! Serve you right if I hadn't found you!"

Before Heather could react to this panegyric, the ragamuffin beside her sprang to her defense. "Shut yer potato trap, guv'nor," he began hotly, piping out the feisty words in an oddly sweet soprano. He sprang from his seat and began waving his tiny fists in the Viscount's direction. "She be a rum sort, an' I'll lump yer jolly for you, if you 'urt 'er."

Heather stared at the boy in some confusion. Geoff lost a bit of his anger in amusement at the boy's antics. "Stubble it, young thatchgallows," he said sternly.

If there was one thing Timmy's short, difficult life had taught him it was how to recognize the voice of authority and when to bow to it. He stubbled it. "And don't be talking flash in front of Heather," continued Geoff, "or I'll draw *your* cork for you."

"Geoff, he's only a little boy," said Heather, placing a hand both protective and restraining on the boy's shoulder. "You must not frighten him."

The Viscount could see that, despite his feisty words, the boy was very small and painfully thin. And he was trembling. "You're not to worry, Timmy," soothed Heather. "Geoff won't let anyone hurt you now, and neither will I."

"But what if Jock comes for me?" he asked, his terror of the Sweep apparent in his eyes.

"Won't know where you've gone," said Geoff.

"When we get home you shall have a proper supper, and I'll bet Mrs. Jumples will have some barley sugar for you too," said Heather comfortingly.

As the boy peeked out the window and realized that they had left Tothill Fields behind and he was really safe away, some of his natural animation returned. He gave himself up to enjoying the novelty of riding in a hack with a couple of bang-up swells and remembering the glorious fight he'd just witnessed.

"Cor! Weren't it 'arf a mill, though!" he said. "I'll cap downright I never seed such a rare dust-up."

"Geoff," Heather injected. "However did you find us?"

"Knew you'd cried off Vauxhall. Knew why too, I *thought*. Figured you'd be moped to death all on your own, so went round to see you, cheer you up, y'know." This was said with a great sense of ill-usage. The Viscount's charitable impulses had been few, and he was hurt by the idea that one of them should go unheralded. "Got to Clarges Street to learn you'd sherried off. What else was I to think? Damned maid kept jabbering at me in her curst parlez-vous. Couldn't make head nor tail out of it. But I did manage to understand you'd gone off alone, in a hack, and wearing that damned ugly dress. Ought to be more careful, Heather, very bad ton, that. Anyway, nowhere else you could have gone but after this rascally scrub here. Damned if you weren't always the most mulish girl! Once get a notion in your head. Well, had to go after you. Nothing else to do."

The Viscount was secretly quite pleased, and only a little surprised, at the rapidity with which he'd figured out just where Heather had gone. He'd been having to do such a damned lot of thinking lately, his wits must be getting sharper from all the exercise. He wondered idly where it would all lead, and if he'd be reading books next.

"Geoff, you were so splendid! I was sure I would never get out of that tavern, never see you again. I would never have thought of starting that fight. It was terribly clever of you."

"Clever?" asked the Viscount, wondering whether the epithet could be taken as a compliment. Once he decided that it could be, he found he quite liked the notion of being clever. It was a new sensation. "Clever," he repeated with a nod.

"Guv'nor," piped up Timmy. "Where're you taking me? Someplace Jock won't never find me?"

Geoff looked at him blankly. "How the devil should I know? She saved you. Ask her!"

The boy turned an expectant face to Heather.

"Well, I thought perhaps you would know, Geoff," she said.

Even the cleverest of fellows must sometimes suffer moments of regression. "Ask m'mother," the Viscount regressed.

Chapter Twenty-two

The hour was far advanced before Heather finally dragged herself up to bed. She had seen Timmy washed (against his vociferous protests) and well-fed, and his poor burnt feet salved and bandaged. He was then dressed in the hall-boy's voluminous nightshirt and tucked up by Mrs. Jumples own hand in a truckle-bed set up in her own room.

When Court and Sophy arrived back in Clarges Street and were treated to the story of Heather's very interesting and highly irregular adventures of the evening, Court offered to take the boy down to Great Pythe first thing in the morning. Heather breathed a sigh of relief. She need not worry longer about the Climbing-Boy. Would that all her problems were so readily solved.

Despite her intense exhaustion, she slept badly. So many thoughts and fears were scrambling around in her head, jostling each other for her attention while she became more then ever confused. She tried to sink further into the soft feather bed, deeper under the comforting down quilt.

When finally she drifted into an uneasy doze, it was to a vision of a garishly painted and decorated stage, brightly lit with smoky candles. Cavorting about the stage were several gentlemen in comical ballet skirts, among them Major Peevesby, Mr. Wesley, and others of her admirers. Weird music accompanied their high-kicking antics, and she realized that they were singing—or rather chanting—in a syncopated rhythm. "Miss Braddock, Miss Braddock, come marry me do," were the words.

Below the ungainly dancers, Lady Morpeth, in flowing robes and twinkling with diamonds and pearls, directed their steps, moving them here and there with a beringed hand and a light laugh. Heather tried to signal for her to

THE RELUCTANT SUITOR 191

stop, but found she couldn't move. She was tied to her chair with ropes of black pearls and a spider web of imported lace. Another chant came from just behind her ear, Sir William Longchamps intoning, "Which one is it to be?"

The scene shifted as her attention flew back to the stage. A giant bottle of Blue Ruin, long ragged strips hanging from its neck, stood center stage like a maypole. Groups of beggars weaved slowly around it, singing "Give us a shilling, love." The children turned to stare at her. They didn't smile and their eyes were dull, without expression.

From offstage came a clanging sound, like the clashing of swords. Two horses rode into the yellow light. Geoff, all in white armor, was fighting desperately with a Black Knight, broadswords ringing in her ears. Geoff fell. The Black Knight went after the hollow-eyed children. When the last one had been cut down and he stood alone on the stage, the Knight turned slowly to her box. Staring from the helmet were two huge cold grey eyes, her brother's. They seemed to turn to ice, to beckon to her, and a voice reverberated from the depths of the armor. "Lady Margaret St. Vincent, is it not?"

Heather awoke with a little scream. She was trembling. The darkness behind the heavy damask bed hangings was oppressive, and she jumped from her bed, jarred fully awake as the chill of the room hit her.

The fire had not yet been made up; it was very early. But she was thankful to see that the room already glowed rosily with early-morning light. She threw a wrapper about her shoulders and crossed to the window. She looked out onto a reassuringly normal London morning.

Street criers and delivery boys were already filling the street, even at this early hour. She flung open the window, and their musical cries floated up to meet her.

"Dust-O!" came the dustman, shuffling along beside his cart and its pair of shuffling horses.

"Hot loaves! Fresh hot loaves!" The baker's boy drifted into sight, his huge basket balancing on his small head. Heather fancied she could smell the fresh warm bread as he passed.

She turned back into the room. The convulsive trembling of the dream had stopped, and she was beginning to relax. But the images were still vivid in her mind. She looked around the pretty room, at the fresh flowers on a side table, at the comfortable fire waiting to be lit. Everything was so easy here, so undemanding. But she couldn't think any longer. There was never any time. And think she must.

She picked up her reticule from the bureau and dumped the contents onto its glowing satinwood surface. There was just under a guinea left of the pin money her godmama had lent her. It was enough.

She dressed quickly in a sensible cambric dress, then donned the grey cloak she'd brought from Cornwall. She sat down again and scribbled a hasty note, sprinkled it with sand, and propped it against the mirror. In another five minutes she was down the stairs, out the door, and hailing a hackney.

"But where the devil *is* she?" The Viscount's question held more than a note of desperation. He thrust his fingers savagely through his hair, which was already in a sorry state, and began what was probably his five-hundredth traversing of the room. His eyes were red-rimmed from worry and lack of sleep, his clothes were rumpled, and his entire person considerably disheveled.

He was in his rooms in Albany, and his two best friends were with him. It had been nearly two days since Heather had disappeared so mysteriously from Clarges Street. Alas for her good intentions, the note she had so thoughtfully left for her godmama was at this moment quite firmly lodged between the bureau where she had placed it and the wall. The swinging of her grey cloak as she hurriedly left the room had knocked it there, and there it still lay.

The Viscount's first reaction to Heather's disappearance had, quite naturally, been to think of her brother. He was sure Stonington had carried her off, and his mind was filled with dark visions of that blasted rotter tying her to a bedpost somewhere, locking a door, and throwing away the key. Or worse.

But a visit to the Flapping Crow, somewhat the worse for wear but open for business as usual, had elicited the information that the Earl had preceded him there by less than an hour, posting a reward of a hundred pounds for information about the girl who had been there the night before. So Stonington couldn't have her.

Peevesby! The damned scoundrel's abducted her! I'll call him to account for this, damned if I won't! Such was the direction his thoughts took next. But a chance encounter with the Major at Tattersall's doomed the idea at the outset. To be sure, the Major seemed in unusually cheerful spirits, but he most certainly was not on his way to Gretna Green, or even France, with an unwilling, or even a willing, bride-to-be.

After a hurried conference in Clarges Street, Sophy offered to call on their female friends and, by discreet questioning, try to discover if Heather had sought a haven with any of them. Chale, Geoff's groom, was posted off to Cornwall straightway to see if she had perhaps returned to Bing. And Lady Morpeth fretted a great deal. She had come to love Heather as though she really were her goddaughter. She racked her brain for some clue to her direction. And, as heartily as she hoped the girl was safe, she also hoped it was merely coincidence that she had left on the same day as Sir William Longchamps.

They had come up with nothing but dead ends. And the Viscount was nearly sick with worry. His mind was filled with Heather, her body broken and lying in a ditch, or Heather, alone and afraid, wandering the streets of London. Or worst of all, Heather in the arms of some damned fortune hunter that Geoff didn't even know about.

"Y'know Geoff," Robin intruded into his thoughts. "It don't seem like Heather to go off like that without a word."

"It's smoky," added Court. "Very smoky."

"I *know* it's smoky! Why the devil d'you think I'm making myself sick with wondering where she is? The thing is, she's so helpless, so damned innocent."

"Well, but she's learned a deal since she's come to town, you know," said Robin.

Geoff ignored this remark. Now slumped in a chair, he looked around his cluttered room, an image of a wide-eyed girl in a big mobcap filling his mind. "D'you remember how tiny and pathetic she looked that first night she came here? Sat in that very chair. Looked at me with those big purple eyes and asked me why she couldn't stay here with me." He shook his head slowly, an expression of unusual tenderness on his face.

"And we took her to Goodie," said Court unthinkingly.

A moment passed, then three pairs of eyes shot up in understanding.

"Goodie!" shouted Geoff, triumph in his voice. Without another word he was on his feet and out the door, calling loudly for his curricle and bays. "And I mean NOW!"

It was already dark when Geoffrey tooled his curricle up Crouch Hill and pulled up before Mrs. Goodfellow's door.

"Och, an' it's yer douce lad himself," rumbled the old nurse in her endearingly low voice, as she turned from the window.

"Geoff?" exclaimed Heather, looking up in surprise. As the Viscount had, unhappily, been figuring rather prominently in her thoughts the last two days, it didn't occur to her that her "douce lad" could be anyone else.

"Aye, lass, it's himself. An' he don't look best pleased if I know aught about it." The little woman, rightly suspecting that the young man now pounding on her door was very near to breaking it down, scurried to slide back the bolt. He burst into the room as though thrown by some unseen giant hand, caught his balance and his hat, and glared at Heather, sitting demurely before the fire with some mending in her lap.

"Heather!" he growled. "So you *are* here!"

"Of course I'm here, Geoff, just as I said I should be."

"Said you'd be?"

"In my note. I'm not so ungrateful to your mama that I should leave her to worry about me. But I had to get away, Geoff. Really I did."

"There was no note," he said in cold, even tones.

"Of course there was a note. Did Godmama not find it?" she asked. "I am sorry if she has been worried, but you can see that there was no need. I am quite all right." She spoke calmly, almost matter-of-factly. Had the Viscount not been prey to such waves of relief and anger he might have noticed her strange detachment and a certain look of resignation in her face. But he was far too glad to see the face to study it too closely.

"Heather. You are coming home with me. Right now!" he exclaimed in a voice that would brook no opposition.

But Heather was disinclined to offer any. "Very well," she replied in that oddly dispassionate voice, neatly folding her mending and setting it aside. "I had planned to come tomorrow in any case, so you may save me the hackney fare. I'll get my cloak."

In the short moment she was gone, Mrs. Goodfellow studied the young man who was filling her parlor with such unbridled emotion. Arms folded uncompromisingly across her diminutive breast, she looked up and down, causing him to fidget uncomfortably, then gave a little grunt that appeared to signal her satisfaction with what she saw.

Heather returned and bent to take a fond farewell of the old nurse. "Thank you, Goodie," she said earnestly. "Thank you so much for . . . for being a haven." She turned to the Viscount, her eyes dull opaque pools. "Shall we go?"

Goodie saw them on their way, then slid home the bolt on the door, a thoughtful look on her face, and gave a hopeful nod of her wise old head.

The ride from Crouch End was accomplished in almost total silence. But Heather was accorded a somewhat warmer welcome once she was in Clarges Street. Sophy was out, but Lady Morpeth was all fluttering kindness and affectionate remonstrances followed by lavish forgiveness. The offending note was discovered behind the bureau, and the trio settled into the parlor over tea.

"I have something I must tell you both," Heather began. Lady Morpeth looked at her closely. The girl looked drawn, haggard even, but surprisingly resolute. A little of the sheen of innocence had fallen away to be replaced by a shadow of wisdom. "I'm terribly sorry that you were worried about me. I would not have had that happen. But I had to go away. To think. You have been so very kind to me, but the time had come to deal with my future. I knew I could never make any decisions here in this house, where everything was so easy. Well, now I have thought, and I have come to a decision." This was quite a new Heather. This was an adult.

"I have seen my brother," she continued. "Really seen

him. I have seen the way he lives, what he has become. Once I was almost convinced that Bo had more right to Grandpapa's fortune than I had. But now I can see that, given the chance, he'll squander away a fortune that Grandpapa worked long and hard for. It won't last very long in Bo's hands, and it will not be used to any good purposes, that is certain. I don't want that to happen." Her voice faded as the memory of the tavern in Tothill Fields invaded her thoughts. Then, with an almost visible effort, she pulled herself together again. "So I have decided that Sir William was right. I must marry."

"William?" said Lady Morpeth in a small voice.

Heather went on. "I have decided to accept an offer."

"What offer?" blurted out Geoff tactlessly. "I didn't know you'd had any."

For the first time in her recitation, Heather allowed a flash of anger to spark her eyes. "It seems there are *some* gentlemen who do not consider that marriage to me would be a lifelong chore! Mr. Wesley for one."

"That puppy!"

"Mr. Wesley is very nice," she retorted, then returned to the flat, uninterested voice she had been using before her outburst. "Of course, he is very young. A better choice might be Captain Johnsdale . . ."

"Coxcomb!"

' . . . but I think he only offered because I am so fashionable. He thought it was expected of him, you know. But he looked terrified that I might accept. Now Lord Greensley . . ."

"Windbag!"

" . . . is very kind, and treats me with a great deal of civility, but he does seem a bit old and set in his ways, and I don't think I could bear with his cigars. So I suppose it will have to be Major Peevesby."

"Peevesby!" shouted Geoff, jumping out of his chair, pulling off his Belcher handkerchief with a painful tug, and throwing it to the floor in disgust. "That scoundrel? That rake? That . . . that . . . *commoner?*"

"He accords me a great deal more respect than you do, my lord," said Heather with great hauteur.

"Don't call me my lord!"

"Very well . . . sir!"

THE RELUCTANT SUITOR 197

"Peevesby's nothing but a damned fortune hunter! A rakehell. A regular Captain Sharp! He's as bad as your brother! Worse! I won't have it!"

"You! You won't have it! And what, pray, do *you* have to say to the matter?"

"I'll marry you myself!" he said.

She answered him in arctic tones. "I thank you very much, *my lord*, for your *very flattering* offer, but I no longer wish to marry you."

"It don't signify if you do or not," he yelled back. "You have to marry someone, and I won't have you throwing yourself away on that rotter Peevesby!"

Heather was now very flushed and alarmingly angry. "So far am I from wishing to marry you, I don't even wish to *see* you again! I would rather marry *anyone* than you! I'd rather marry a . . . a . . . a toad!" Her hard-won composure had snapped during this tirade. She covered her face to hide the tears overflowing her liquid eyes and ran from the room.

As Lady Morpeth watched this little battle, her mouth first fell open in absolute amazement. Before long, it snapped firmly shut in anger at herself for having been so blind to the truth for so long. Finally it curved up into a delightfully satisfied smile. Yes, there were a few rough edges to be smoothed out as yet, but it looked as though everything was in a way to being very comfortably worked out at last. How delightful, to be sure.

Geoffrey slumped back into his chair, sank his head onto his chest, and refused to say another word.

Alas for Heather's carefully worked out plans. Twice had Major Peevesby offered for her hand; twice she had refused. Now she had changed her mind. But when she sent a note around to the Major's lodgings next morning begging him to call, it was only to see it returned with the intelligence that the Major was out of town and not expected back for some time. In fact, as she soon learned, during the two days she had been in Crouch End, Major Peevesby, who had been growing more and more desperate as his creditors grew more and more persistent, had successfully wooed and won the very homely daughter of a very rich banker and had carried her off to Gretna

Green this very morning before she could change her mind.

It also turned out that Mr. Wesley had been summoned back to Essex by a father who still saw him as an errant schoolboy. And Lord Greensley was laid up with a quite vicious and unromantic attack of the gout.

That seemed to leave the field clear for Captain Johnsdale. And had the dashing Captain known how dramatically his chances of winning the beautiful Miss Braddock had risen, literally overnight, he might well have recalled that his godfather in Ireland was on the verge of death and in immediate need of his consoling presence.

"Well, darling." said Lady Morpeth happily after receiving these doleful tidings. "It seems to come back down to Geoffrey after all, does it not?"

Heather, curled up in a window seat in the morning room, staring out at the bright sunshine that accorded ill with her mood, was looking blue as megrim. "Please do not tease me, Godmama. I said such awful things to him! I am quite sure he must hate me for it. And even though he did offer, he doesn't in the least wish to marry me, you know. He told me so weeks ago, when I first asked him."

"You asked him?"

Heather hung her head. "Yes. I'm afraid I did."

"Oh, dear. That was not at all a wise move, darling. But you were a great deal younger then, were you not, for all it has scarce been a month." she said wisely. "And I rather fancy that what he actually said was that he didn't wish to marry *anyone*. Am I right?"

"Well, yes. But I'm sure he hasn't changed his mind."

"Nevertheless, he *has* offered, and in front of me. And I have not the least intention of letting him forget it."

"Oh, please, Godmama! I wish you will not speak of it."

"Not speak of it?" She pushed a chair to the window and sat herself down facing Heather, taking the girl's two hands in her own. "Now listen to me, Heather. Yesterday you came into this room fired with determination not to let your odious brother destroy what had taken so long to build. You realized, quite rightly, just how your grandfather's entire fortune would slip through his fingers and dwindle away to nothing. Are you now ready to turn around and hand it to him without even a struggle because of some missish scruples? I had thought better of you, dear." The harsh words did not come easily to her lips, but she had instinctively known that the only way to reach Heather in her present mood was through her pride.

The girl bridled up again at the picture of her half-brother brought so forcefully to mind. "No!" she exclaimed firmly. "I will *not* give in to him. I cannot, now. If . . . if Geoff asks me again, I . . . I will marry him!"

A slow smile came into Lady Morpeth's pretty face, and she sat back with a great deal of satisfaction. "Oh, he'll ask."

Chapter Twenty-three

Geoffrey did indeed repeat his offer of marriage, in the most formal of terms and with an expression of deep hurt in his eyes. Heather, staring resolutely at the floor, accepted in equally formal terms, mouthing such horridly proper and altogether silly phrases as "truly sensible of the honor you do me, sir," and "no greater felicity than the privilege of being your wife."

That settled, there remained only the question of where the wedding was to take place. The when had already been decided—as quickly as possible. The legality of any English wedding while Heather was yet under age would certainly be contested by her half-brother; the marriage easily set aside. Yet there was something so innately distasteful about the idea of a Scottish wedding and the inevitable ostracizing from the ton which would result. Gretna Green marriages were definitely *not* good ton.

"Still, you know, my dears, I really can see no alternative," said Lady Morpeth. "Scotland it will have to be if we are to foil your odious brother. It is fortunate that your seat is in the north, Geoffrey, although I'm sure I never thought to be grateful for *anything* about Morpeth! We will write the notice to the *Gazette* simply to read, 'The couple were married from the groom's home in Northumberland.' They needn't know how *far* from your home. And, after all, the border is only some thirty miles."

She chattered on in this bright manner a few minutes more, seemingly oblivious to the lack of response from either of her listeners, and in a very short time their plans were complete. Geoff was sent off to Albany to prepare for the long journey, and the two ladies went upstairs to their own packing, Lady Morpeth bouncing with energy and gaiety, Heather dragging herself up every step.

With a strong sense of the ironic, Heather watched one beautiful gown after another being wrapped in silver paper and placed lovingly in her trunks. She need never again worry about how to pay for them. She would soon be able to buy as many new gowns as ever she wanted. The thought gave her no pleasure, for she knew she would never to able to buy the only thing she really wanted, the love of her soon-to-be husband.

"Oh, Heather," said Sophy with a sigh from her perch on the bed. "I wish I were going with you. I have never had a friend like you, and I should dearly love to be at your wedding."

"Well, I shall certainly be at yours," she answered with an attempt at lightness. She gave Sophy an affectionate smile that helped to buoy her own depressed spirits. "For now, you have more important things to do than bustle off to Scotland. I'm sure you will enjoy yourself vastly at Great Pythe."

"Well, I think I may, but I shall be quaking in my boots, you know. What with the housekeeper showing me all over that ancient edifice, and Lady Pythe regaling me with the details of all Court's favorite foods, and all the servants positively *weighing* me."

"Quaking in your boots? More like quaking with laughter, I should think. And with happiness. Have you any idea how you are *glowing* with it?"

Sophy, who was looking remarkably pretty lately, blushed. "I *am* deliriously happy, and I know how much I have you to thank for it. But, Heather, I do so wish that you were happier." She gave her friend a long, serious look. "You've made the right decision, you know."

Heather looked out the window a moment before answering quietly, "I hope so."

Sophy put a hand softly on her shoulder. "You'll be happy, Heather. I know you will." The two friends stood a long while in silence, gazing out on London, while the maid bustled about behind them.

Before another two hours had passed, a small cavalcade pulled away from Clarges Street, heading north: a well-sprung chaise with two fashionable ladies, a second chaise with two fashionable servants and an immense pile of luggage, and alongside, on a fine chestnut, a fashionable and sullen viscount.

Sir William Longchamps, hurried by love, completed his business with dispatch and hurried back to town. He stopped in St. James's Square only long enough to change from his travel-stained attire, taking extraordinary care with his toilette, and set out for Clarges Street with something less than his usual self-assurance but with high hopes.

He was surprised and disappointed to learn that he had missed the impressive departure of the whole family by no more than a few hours. But he was distinctly pleased by the rest of what he learned.

A surprisingly talkative Bellows confided that it seemed that Master Geoffrey and their Young Miss had decided to make a match of it, and he even, wonder of wonders smiled as he handed Sir William the note Lady Morpeth had left for him. It merely explained the reason for their absence and begged him not to worry. He could expect them back in about a week's time.

Considering the notion that they might need assistance if the Earl of Stonington should discover their flight and follow them, as seemed likely, and with a strong suspicion that the three of them just might manage to make a muddle of the whole business, Sir William determined to follow them. In fairness, one might add that the thought of as much as another week away from Tina Morpeth also had some influence on his decision. Be that as it may, it was not much longer before he was reattired for traveling, repacked, recarriaged, and on his way north.

Sir William was quite right to worry about Heather's brother. Beauregard St. Vincent was in a rage. Ever since that terrible night when he'd learned that his hated half-sister, whom he had thought so safely immured in Cornwall, was at large and in London, he had not stopped searching for her. But he'd found not a trace. No one at the Flapping Crow had recognized her savior as Viscount Morpeth, and every line of inquiry he tried turned into a dead end.

He'd had hopes that the generous reward he'd offered

might do the trick. It had, in fact, resulted in so many false leads, entailing so much useless time and trouble that he soon bitterly regretted having posted it at all. Until, that is, the afternoon a certain Chimney-Sweep arrived at his door.

Now Jock, little Timmy's one-time master, was not a particularly bright fellow and had never been schooled in the higher forms of mathematics. He had been trying to add up two and two in his head for days, knowing that the right answer could add up to one hundred pounds. But for the longest time he kept getting three, or seven, or perhaps four and a half. It was only when he suddenly remembered a feisty girl in a yellow dress and parasol giving him a thundering scold over that scrubby lazy boy of his that the number FOUR seemed to flash in big red letters. And when he was able, from the foggy depths of memory, to attach the name Miss Braddock to the girl in the yellow dress, who was the same girl in the Flapping Crow, the Earl seemed satisfied with the answer. Bo St. Vincent remembered Miss Braddock, Tina Morpeth's goddaughter, very well indeed. Jock went off to Tothill Fields with a hundred quid in his shoe, and the Earl went off to Clarges Street with murder, or something very like, in his heart.

His stay there was of short duration—some ninety seconds perhaps—conversing with Bellows in the doorway. The formal statement that her ladyship and Miss Braddock had departed that morning for their estate in the north sent him scurrying off into a panic. Without so much as packing a nightshirt, he was into a chaise-and-four, racing north.

It may be assumed that Miss Honoria Stapleton was sojourning comfortably in Bath all this while, oblivious to the startling events taking place in London. And the assumption would not be far wrong, if one can describe as comfortable the shocking state of nerves that causes one to jump at every knock on the door and tremble at the sight of every tall, well-dressed gentleman one encounters. But such had been Miss Stapleton's lot recently, fearing as she did that her noble cousin would learn of her horrid crime in allowing her sister to escape. In the end, she'd been too much the coward to tell him.

Had she remained in Bath only one day longer, she would have encountered the very messenger she had been dreading, for the Earl had posted a fellow off after her on the very night of Heather's ill-fated appearance at the Flapping Crow. But by the time he reached Bath, Miss Stapleton was already on her way to London.

She had always kept up a voluminous correspondence with old school chums who possessed a better foothold in the ton than she, deriving great vicarious pleasure from the gossip her correspondents imparted. One of the most loyal, a Miss Choate, pleased her excessively with her barbed tongue and her incredible talent for nosing out any and every scandal. It was a letter from Miss Choate that sent Honoria hurrying off to town.

After reading some four pages, closely crossed, of the latest *on dits* and crim. con. stories, Honoria was giving something less than her full attention to the remainder of the letter, which inevitably drifted to an account of the newest Incomparable. Of course, for her part, Miss Choate could see nothing so very extraordinary about violet eyes, and she didn't know what the ton was coming to when young ladies of such decidedly *mysterious* antecedents were accepted at Almack's. But it was when Miss Choate mentioned the exceedingly beautiful and obviously valuable black pearls, which were by way of being a sort of trademark with Miss Braddock, that Honoria's eyes popped fully open and stared at the page.

She was on the Night Mail to London that very evening, arriving on the doorstep of her dear Miss Choate without so much as a by-your-leave. Early next morning saw her raising the knocker of the door in Clarges Street. The intelligence she gained there did not please her. With a quite pitiable groan, she took up her valise, left her dear Miss Choate without so much as a by-your-leave, and headed north once more.

Chapter Twenty-four

The trip from London to Morpeth cannot by any calculation be reckoned as short, being fully three hundred miles even in a sleek chaise with four fresh horses. Though blithely unaware of the veritable parade of interested parties following in their wake, those at the head of the line were very much aware that they were racing the clock, or at least the calendar. Heather's birthday was nearly upon them. They had to reach Scotland and get the wedding over with before it arrived.

And so they were making speed. They stopped only when absolutely necessary to change horses and refresh themselves. Even the closest of their pursuers, Sir William, was still some hours behind when they rolled into Newcastle and headed into the final lap of their journey.

By the time they reached Morpeth it was very late. They were greeted by a darkened house and a very astonished pair of elderly servants who were usually the sole inmates of Morpeth Hall.

A hastily prepared meal was downed by the weary travelers amid profuse apologies from the antique housekeeper of nothing better than a guinea fowl, a fishmeagre pie, and some Golden Pippins from the orchard. A message was sent off to the vicar at Huntford, the tiny village just across the Scottish border, to expect them around noon on the morrow, and they all dragged themselves off for a few hours of much-needed sleep.

Whatever fancies, dreams, or nightmares the three sleepers suffered that night, they were all down early next morning. Geoff had toyed with a slice of cold sirloin and worried a cup of tea, then set off on horseback for Huntford. He didn't know it was considered bad luck to see his bride before he met her at the church. He only knew he couldn't face Heather this morning, knowing how unhappy this forced marriage was making her. He went off before she could appear.

Lady Morpeth enjoyed a hearty breakfast of kippers and eggs, toast and tea, while Heather stared glumly out a window, her coffee growing cold.

"I oughtn't to go through with it, Godmama," she said finally. "It isn't fair to Geoff."

"Pooh, nonsense," said her godmama with a wave of the hand. "You neither of you know what is good for yourselves or each other. Come dear, we must hurry. I'll help you to dress."

Unbeknownst to Heather, her foresighted godmama had packed an ivory gown of satin and spider gauze into the trunks. She'd also put in a silver filigree comb and a beautiful Spanish mantilla of antique lace. Not even Heather could remain unmoved by the vision she presented thus attired. But the lovely bride staring back from the mirror was missing the glow of happiness that should have crowned her beauty, and two large tears rolled down her cheeks.

"Now, now, it won't do at all for the bride to cry, darling," said Lady Morpeth bracingly. She took Heather's hands. "You really must believe everything will work out all right, Heather. I promise you it will."

Mrs. Adleby, the old housekeeper, had picked a pretty posey of primroses, sweetpeas, and forget-me-nots from the garden. She handed it to Heather with a shy curtsy and a beaming smile as the bride and her soon-to-be mother-in-law stepped up into the carriage.

The Adlebys were definitely not used to so much excitement as they had had in the last dozen hours. No one ever came to Morpeth. Had they had any idea how many more people would be knocking at the door within the hour, they would have been amazed indeed. They were bubbling with the happy news of a wedding in the family, and since no one had thought to instruct them to keep that news to themselves, they had no reluctance in sharing it with each of the three travelers who soon appeared at Morpeth Hall.

Mr. Whistleton, the young vicar at Huntford, was new to his post. In fact, he had arrived only two days previ-

THE RELUCTANT SUITOR

ously and was still proudly arranging the books in the library of the vicarage that went with this, his very first position. He trembled with excitement when he learned that he was about to perform his first wedding, and for a viscount! He'd spent much of the night poring over the wedding service so as not to stumble over the words.

The arrival of the groom on his doorstep made him even more nervous, for not only was he a Peer of the Realm, he seemed a decidedly unhappy one. The vicar wondered if the wedding over which he was about to preside was an altogether proper one. One never knew in Scotland.

But the look that came over the Viscount's face when the beautiful bride stepped from her carriage in front of the little church banished any doubts he may have had. If ever two young people were in love, these two were.

"Well, well, I'm sure the happy couple is anxious to begin," he said brightly, breaking the odd look passing between the "happy couple." They entered the tiny, ancient chapel, glowing pink from the sunlight streaming through the stained-glass windows, and took up their positions. Lady Morpeth was happy to see that her son was to have a proper, respectable church wedding, even if it *was* in Scotland.

"And who is to give away the bride?" asked Mr. Whistleton, peering about the group.

The three others looked up with startled expressions. "Oh," began Lady Morpeth in dismay. "Oh, dear. I don't ... that is, we didn't ... what I mean is ..."

A voice from the doorway cut her off. "I believe I can be trusted with the chore," said Sir William Longchamps with a grin.

"William!" exclaimed Lady Morpeth. So taken aback was she at his unlooked-for appearance that she did not hear what he had said. Thoughts chased each other around in her brain in an effort to explain his arrival, the most notable being that he was obviously here to stop the wedding so he could marry Heather himself.

"How the devil ..." began Geoff.

"Sir William! Whatever are you doing in Scotland?" cried Heather.

"Now, now, all in good time, my dears. We are interrupting . . ."

Before he could get further, Lady Morpeth clutched his arm with a little "No!" and pulled him aside. "Please, William, I beg you not to interfere," she said in an undertone. "I know how you must feel, and indeed I'm terribly sorry for the pain this must be causing you. But these children are in love with each other. They may not know it yet, but they truly are. I beg you to let them be." The words rushed out as she stared unhappily at his third coat button.

"Well, of course, they love each other. I've suspected as much any time this past fortnight. And I assure you I have no intention of interfering, Tina." He put a hand under her chin and lifted her face to meet his. He gazed deeply into those magic green eyes and added softly, "Unless, that is, you consider it interference to make it a double wedding?"

"A double wedding? But William, I don't . . ."

She was stopped by the look in his handsome grizzled face, and he leaned down and planted the lightest of kisses on the tip of her nose. "Well, Tina? I know this seems an odd time and place for a proposal, at the very altar so to speak, but will you marry me? I warn you, I've been waiting twenty-five years to ask you, and I cannot guarantee my reaction should you refuse."

Questions raced through her mind and across her face, but all she said was, "Yes! Oh, yes, William. Yes!"

"Well, I say!" exclaimed Geoff as he saw the baronet kissing his mother again, rather more thoroughly this time.

"Oh, famous!" cried Heather, some of her own unhappiness forgotten.

"Here, here! What's all this? Highly irregular, you know. Highly irregular, indeed," blustered Mr. Whistleton, who was fast losing his nervousness at his first wedding to indignation at the impropriety of the proceedings.

The company did what it could to soothe his ruffled feelings, introductions were accomplished, and the wedding proceeded but now with a pair of couples for the hapless vicar to deal with.

Mr. Whistleton had gotten as far as "Do you, Geoffrey Curwen, take, umm, Margaret, is it . . . yes, Margaret St.

THE RELUCTANT SUITOR

Vincent to be your wedded wife?" when the door of the chapel flew open again. This time the gentleman standing there had no happy lover's grin on his face. It was contorted with a less happy emotion. The Earl of Stonington was definitely not at his best, and his anger was abetted by the sinking feeling that he had already lost the game.

"No he does not take her!" he blurted out. "I am this young lady's legal guardian, and I do *not* give my permission for this marriage."

"Ah, Stonington," said Sir William in a carefully casual voice. "I wondered how far behind us you were. Sad that it was just a bit *too* far, is it not? You do know that we are in Scotland, and you no longer have any say over who your sister marries. You've been playing a clever game, Stonington, but this is the last hand, and your cards are not very good, you know. You've lost the game for a bad bet."

The Earl, with very little to lose, made one last desperate attempt.

"Lady Margaret!" he spat out at his sister. "You will come with me. NOW! I shall take you home, before you ally yourself with someone interested only in your fortune." He glared at her, willing her to walk out of the chapel with him.

"Well, that's cool, I must say!" cried Geoff in indignation. "It's you, Stonington, who's only interested in Heather's money. Most likely you've had your sticky fingers in it for years. Well, I'll be damned if you'll get another penny. I'll see to it!"

"Do you know, Bo," said Lady Morpeth sweetly. "I really think you had best go. You would only be pained by sight of the wedding, I'm sure."

"You know, Stonington," said Sir William in his oddly pleasant voice, "I fancy the lady's right. I really wouldn't want to have to tell Bow Street even a part of what I've just learned from your sister's trustees about the sort of fiddling you've been up to. I think France, or the West Indies, would be a place you might find more beneficial to your health for the future."

The Earl seemed to grow smaller as the full realization of his collapse hit him. A picture of the enormous number of creditors he had promised to pay off next week rose in his mind, and he saw the irrefutable logic of Sir William's suggestion. Without another word, he turned toward the door, defeat visible in every feature, and left.

Heather let out a sigh of relief. The wedding party turned with expectant faces back to the harassed vicar. "Shall we proceed, Mr. Whistleton?" asked Sir William pleasantly.

"Well, I don't . . . highly irregular . . . girl's brother and all . . ." One look at the four determined faces decided him. "Well, let's see. Where were we?" He flipped over the pages of the service. "Yes, yes, here it is. Do you, umm, yes, Geoffrey, ah, Curwen . . ." He sputtered on in this fashion for some time, actually hoping that he might get through the thing after all. Until . . ."

"Stop!" shrilled yet another voice in the doorway as Honoria Stapleton threw it open with an ungenteel crash. "This wedding must stop!" The first person she encountered as she strode into the room was Sir William. "Humph! Morpeth, I presume," she blustered in an attempt to face him down.

"No," he replied calmly. "Who the devil are you?"

For one black moment Honoria had the sinking feeling that history was repeating itself and she had stumbled into the wrong wedding again. Then she saw Heather, clutching tightly to Geoffrey's hand. "Hah!" she exclaimed, pointing a long knarled finger. "Well, miss. What have you to say for yourself?"

Geoff turned to his bride. "Take it this is your Cousin Horrifica."

Heather couldn't help smiling. "Yes, it is," she acknowledged. "Hello, Cousin Honoria."

"Lady Margaret!" she began in her most authoritative tone, just as her noble cousin had done a short while before. "I am glad to see that I arrived in time to prevent this ridiculous marriage that you seem determined on. Come!" She reached for the girl's hand, and would have pulled her from the chapel. But Heather dug in her feet and refused to budge. When she spoke her voice was calm, kind even, but with more than a touch of steel.

"But I do not wish to go, Cousin Honoria. I am sorry you have been put to such inconvenience, but I have no wish to return to Cornwall, or to give up my fortune. You cannot make me go, you know."

Honoria stared at her cousin and knew her bluff had been called. Her old face seemed to crumple before their eyes, and she sank into a pew, muttering "What's to become of me?"

Heather started toward her, but Geoff placed a restraining hand on her arm. "Seems to me you didn't worry much about what was to become of Heather when you locked her away in that Godforsaken place."

"Nonsense!" she bristled defensively. "I had arranged a very advantageous marriage for her. She would have married Mr. Twitchit, a very proper sort of husband for her, I should think."

"A proper sort of husband!" echoed Lady Morpeth. "And I suppose my son is not?"

"Please, Godmama." Heather silenced her gently but firmly. "Cousin Honoria, you know you have not always treated me very kindly, but I don't believe you would have left me to starve. You were only tempted by the money Bo promised you, were you not? I know that you only wish to go and live with your sister and be comfortable. Geoff, do you not think. . . ?"

He glared at the old woman. "Planned to go to Bath, didn't you?" Honoria nodded. "Good! Can't stand the place. Bunch of silly old gossiping tabbies. Plan to stay there, do you?" She nodded again, and he made a decision. "Very well. Seems my wife"—he couldn't help smiling at the word—"don't want you to starve, though it beats me why she should care. So go to Bath. We'll see you have enough to keep you there comfortably. But on one condition!"

"Yes, my lord?" whispered Honoria.

"We neither of us have to see your hatchet-face again! Now get out of here, and let me enjoy my wedding. My agent will deal with you."

The old face wreathed with smiles. "Thank you, my lord! And may I say how happy I am to see my dear Margaret so happily settled."

"No, you may not! Out!" he yelled, chasing her out the door, one fist pounding the air.

"Well, Geoffrey!" said his mama, beaming. "That was

very well done. I begin to have very high hopes for you after all."

"If you ask me, Tina," said Sir William in an aside, "this marriage'll be the making of that boy."

"Thank you, Geoff." said Heather simply.

"D'you think we might get on with it?" asked the Viscount archly. "This getting married is turning out to be a deuced complicated business."

The vicar, somewhat against his better judgment, began his fourth and final attempt at wedding the parties before him. This time he was successful despite some stumbling over the words, fumbling for forgotten rings, and anxious glances at the door, wondering who would pop in next. But he did finally manage to say, "I now pronounce you both . . . *all* . . . husbands and wives!" and closed his book with a relieved snap.

Soon two lawfully wedded couples, in separate carriages, began the trip back to Morpeth Hall.

In Sir William Longchamps's carriage, the elder of the pair of newlyweds was glowing like happy children, with Christina, Lady Longchamps, snuggled cozily up in the crook of her new husband's arm. "And now, William, you will explain *everything* to me!" she demanded sweetly. And explain he did, in the short intervals when he wasn't too busy kissing her, or exclaiming over her beauty, or yelling joyfully out the window to a chance passerby that he was the happiest man in the world.

Things were not going so well in the other carriage. There was, as yet, no kissing, no shouting for joy, not even the smallest sign of a snuggle. Instead, the Viscount and his new Viscountess sat in opposite corners of the carriage, staring glumly at the passing fields.

This unhappy state of affairs went on for some time, each of them trying to build the courage to speak. Heather managed it first, and broke into the silence with a veritable flood of apology.

"Oh, Geoff, I'm sorry. So sorry. I've caused you nothing but problems ever since you first came to Cornwall and found me. And now I've forced you into a distasteful marriage just because of that odious money. But just as soon as the solicitors say I may do so, I'll agree to an annulment or a . . . a divorce." The voice that had begun so bravely petered out almost to a whisper.

"Don't want a divorce," answered the Viscount gruffly.

"But, Geoff, you shouldn't have to be saddled with me forever just because you were *forced* to marry me."

"Wasn't forced to," he said shortly, paused, then plunged on. "Wanted to!"

"Wanted to?" Two violet eyes, suddenly sparkling with hope, turned to two blue-grey ones sparkling with tenderness. "But, Geoff . . ." she began.

"Dash it all, Heather. Daresay you might not like it, but can't be helped. I love you. I should have realized it long since. Knew when you went away. I didn't know what to do. I . . . I didn't feel *whol*e anymore, like I'd lost a part of myself when I thought I'd lost you."

Yellow flecks of happiness danced in her eyes, like irises in spring. "Oh, Geoff. Didn't you see? I only went away because I couldn't even *think* about marrying someone else while you were there. It hurt too much, you see. Because I loved you," she finished quietly. "I always have."

"Heather." There was something in his voice that she recognized. She had heard it in the Temple of Pan when Robin spoke to Lady Susan. She had heard it in Court's voice when he spoke to Sophy. And her heart leaped with joy to hear it now, in Geoff's voice, speaking to *her!*

"Oh, Geoff." The space between them dissolved, and Heather, like her friends before her, gave herself up to the delicious pleasure of being crushingly kissed.

When she could speak again, she nestled cozily against his shoulder and said, "Are you sure you won't mind being married to me? It seems quite likely that you will always have to be pulling me out of some scrape."

"Very likely," he agreed, beaming down at his wife. "For y'know, Heather, you're the most unaccountable girl. Pig-headed, hoydenish, and altogether bothersome. And when that ridiculous vicar finally got around to saying you were really my wife, well, I knew I was the luckiest man alive."

"Your wife," she murmured happily.

He looked down at her, a strange mist seeming to cloud his vision, and almost whispered, like an incantation, "my wife." Then he kissed her again, to her very obvious delight.

This sort of nonsense continued for some time, with nothing of any import at all being said, and a great deal of kissing and giggling and sighing going on.

They were soon sweeping up the drive of Morpeth Hall. The carriage stopped; the door was opened; the steps were let down. But no happy couple emerged from the chaise.

Lord and Lady Longchamps, who stood waiting on the steps of the house, walked to the carriage and peered in to see what the trouble was.

"Oh," sighed the new Lady Longchamps when she saw that there was no trouble at all that her son wasn't handling very well indeed.

"That's all right then," she bubbled happily and led her new husband away.

About the Author

Megan Daniel, born and raised in Southern California, combines a background in theater and music with a passion for travel and a love of England and the English. After attending UCLA and California State University, Long Beach, where she earned a degree in theater, she lived for a time in London and elsewhere in Europe. She then settled in New York, working for six years as a theatrical costume designer for Broadway, off-Broadway, ballet, and regional theater.

Miss Daniel currently divides her time between her homes in New York and Amsterdam, together with her husband, Roy Sorrels, a successful free-lance writer. Her first novel, *Amelia,* is also available in a Signet edition.

More Regency Romances from SIGNET

- [ ] **MALLY** by Sandra Heath. (#E9342—$1.75)*
- [ ] **THE INNOCENT DECEIVER** by Vanessa Gray. (#E9463—$1.75)*
- [ ] **THE MASKED HEIRESS** by Vanessa Gray. (#E9331—$1.75)
- [ ] **THE DUTIFUL DAUGHTER** by Vanessa Gray. (#E9017—$1.75)*
- [ ] **THE LONELY EARL** by Vanessa Gray. (#J7922—$1.75)
- [ ] **THE WICKED GUARDIAN** by Vanessa Gray. (#E8390—$1.75)
- [ ] **THE WAYWARD GOVERNESS** by Vanessa Gray. (#E8696—$1.75)*
- [ ] **ALLEGRA** by Clare Darcy. (#J9611—$1.95)
- [ ] **CRESSIDA** by Clare Darcy. (#E8287—$1.75)*
- [ ] **ELYZA** by Clare Darcy. (#E7540—$1.75)
- [ ] **EUGENIA** by Clare Darcy. (#E8081—$1.75)
- [ ] **GWENDOLEN** by Clare Darcy. (#J8847—$1.95)*
- [ ] **LADY PAMELA** by Clare Darcy. (#W7282—$1.50)
- [ ] **LYDIA** by Clare Darcy. (#E8272—$1.75)
- [ ] **REGINA** by Clare Darcy. (#E7878—$1.75)
- [ ] **ROLANDE** by Clare Darcy. (#J8552—$1.95)
- [ ] **VICTOIRE** by Clare Darcy. (#E7845—$1.75)

*Price slightly higher in Canada

Buy them at your local bookstore or use this convenient coupon for ordering.

THE NEW AMERICAN LIBRARY, INC.,
P.O. Box 999, Bergenfield, New Jersey 07621

Please send me the SIGNET BOOKS I have checked above. I am enclosing
$_____ (please add 50¢ to this order to cover postage and handling).
Send check or money order—no cash or C.O.D.'s. Prices and numbers are subject to change without notice.

Name _____

Address _____

City_____ State_____ Zip Code_____

Allow 4-6 weeks for delivery.
This offer is subject to withdrawal without notice.

Big Bestsellers from SIGNET

- ☐ **LORD SIN** by Constance Gluyas. (#E9521—$2.75)*
- ☐ **THE PASSIONATE SAVAGE** by Constance Gluyas. (#E9195—$2.50)*
- ☐ **MADAM TUDOR** by Constance Gluyas. (#J9053—$1.95)*
- ☐ **THE HOUSE ON TWYFORD STREET** by Constance Gluyas. (#E8924—$2.25)*
- ☐ **FLAME OF THE SOUTH** by Constance Gluyas. (#E8648—$2.50)
- ☐ **WOMAN OF FURY** by Constance Gluyas. (#E8075—$2.25)*
- ☐ **ROGUE'S MISTRESS** by Constance Gluyas. (#E9695—$2.50)
- ☐ **SAVAGE EDEN** by Constance Gluyas. (#E9285—$2.50)
- ☐ **REAP THE BITTER WINDS** by June Lund Shiplett. (#E9517—$2.50)*
- ☐ **THE RAGING WINDS OF HEAVEN** by June Lund Shiplett. (#E9439—$2.50)
- ☐ **THE WILD STORMS OF HEAVEN** by June Lund Shiplett. (#E9063—$2.50)*
- ☐ **DEFY THE SAVAGE WINDS** by June Lund Shiplett. (#E9337—$2.50)*
- ☐ **ECSTASY'S EMPIRE** by Gimone Hall. (#E9242—$2.75)
- ☐ **FURY'S SUN, PASSION'S MOON** by Gimone Hall. (#E8748—$2.50)*
- ☐ **RAPTURE'S MISTRESS** by Gimone Hall. (#E8422—$2.25)*

*Price slightly higher in Canada

Buy them at your local bookstore or use coupon on next page for ordering.

More Bestsellers from SIGNET

- [ ] **ALEXA by Maggie Osborne.** (#E9244—$2.25)*
- [ ] **SALEM'S DAUGHTER by Maggie Osborne.** (#E9602—$2.75)*
- [ ] **ELISE by Sara Reavin.** (#E9483—$2.95)
- [ ] **THIS IS THE HOUSE by Deborah Hill.** (#E8877—$2.50)
- [ ] **THE HOUSE OF KINGSLEY MERRICK by Deborah Hill.** (#E8918—$2.50)*
- [ ] **THE WORLD FROM ROUGH STONES by Malcolm Macdonald.** (#E9639—$2.95)
- [ ] **THE RICH ARE WITH YOU ALWAYS by Malcolm Macdonald.** (#E7682—$2.25)
- [ ] **SONS OF FORTUNE by Malcolm Macdonald.** (#E8595—$2.75)*
- [ ] **ABIGAIL by Malcolm Macdonald.** (#E9404—$2.95)
- [ ] **HAGGARD by Christopher Nicole.** (#E9340—$2.50)
- [ ] **SUNSET by Christopher Nicole.** (#E8948—$2.25)*
- [ ] **BLACK DAWN by Christopher Nicole.** (#E8342—$2.25)*
- [ ] **CARIBEE by Christopher Nicole.** (#J7945—$1.95)
- [ ] **THE DEVIL'S OWN by Christopher Nicole.** (#J7256—$1.95)
- [ ] **MISTRESS OF DARKNESS by Christopher Nicole.** (#J7782—$1.95)

*Price slightly higher in Canada

Buy them at your local bookstore or use this convenient coupon for ordering.

THE NEW AMERICAN LIBRARY, INC.,
P.O. Box 999, Bergenfield, New Jersey 07621

Please send me the SIGNET BOOKS I have checked above. I am enclosing
$_____(please add 50¢ to this order to cover postage and handling). Send check or money order—no cash or C.O.D.'s. Prices and numbers are subject to change without notice.

Name _____

Address _____

City_____ State_____ Zip Code_____

Allow 4-6 weeks for delivery.
This offer is subject to withdrawal without notice.